MISTRESS OF MISHAP

Harry tucked Ellen's arm into the crook of his elbow. "You were enchanting this evening. There were no mishaps."

She forced a laugh. "I didn't step on your toes?"

"Not once!"

"Then I must consider the event to have been successful. Thank you for escorting me."

As she took his hand and stepped from the carriage, she caught her heel and tumbled into his arms. Involuntarily she clasped her hands around his neck.

Harry eased her to the ground, still holding her close against him.

Ellen moved away from his embrace and tried to laugh lightly. "No mishaps?"

He grinned. "I rather liked that one." Then he brought her slim hand to his lips. . . .

Other Regency Romances from Avon Books

MISTRESS OF MISHAP

CATHLEEN CLARE

AVON BOOKS  NEW YORK

MISTRESS OF MISHAP is an original publication of Avon Books. This work has never before appeared in book form. This work is a novel. Any similarity to actual persons or events is purely coincidental.

AVON BOOKS
A division of
The Hearst Corporation
1350 Avenue of the Americas
New York, New York 10019

Copyright © 1992 by Catherine Toothman
Published by arrangement with the author
Library of Congress Catalog Card Number: 91-92444
ISBN: 0-380-76815-1

First Avon Books Printing: July 1992

AVON TRADEMARK REG. U.S. PAT. OFF. AND IN OTHER COUNTRIES, MARCA REGISTRADA, HECHO EN U.S.A.

Printed in the U.S.A.

RA 10 9 8 7 6 5 4 3 2 1

For Robert,
Annie, and Robbie

1

The tall, honey-blonde, young woman put the last full-blown pink rose into the bouquet and stepped back to appraise her handiwork. A touch here and a touch there and it would be perfectly balanced. She accomplished this and smiled to herself. Whatever criticism anyone could aim in her direction, no one could dispute the fact that Ellen Trevayne grew beautiful flowers. Of course she had the assistance of a gardening staff, but the knowledge she had gained from her now-deceased neighbor, Miss Spencer of Shadybrook Manor, and the multitudes of cuttings and seeds the elderly lady had given her had all combined to make her gardens among the most admired in the county. Even Lady Adams, the squire's wife, had grudgingly admitted to it.

"Oh, how very pretty!" a voice exclaimed from the rear of the church.

Ellen turned, smiling at the vicar's wife. "Thank you, Mrs. Smythe. I do hope that Penny will be pleased."

"How could she help being anything but delighted! It was so kind of you, Ellen, to provide the flowers for the wedding. Penny couldn't have had them otherwise."

1

Ellen shrugged. "It was a pleasure. Every bride should have flowers. Not that she'll take great notice of them. She'll only have eyes for Jack!"

"They're a lovely young couple," Mrs. Smythe agreed. "Penny is fortunate. It's not every day that a blacksmith's daughter marries a well-to-do farmer. I do hope that she will be clothed to suit her new station."

"She will be. She's wearing one of my dresses! I helped her modify it into a bridal gown. But please don't tell anyone. She was embarrassed at accepting my offer."

"My goodness, Ellen! How kind you've been to the girl!" Mrs. Smythe hesitated. "I only wish it were your wedding we were celebrating tomorrow."

Ellen's smile faded. With a final glance at the huge bouquet on the altar and the smaller ones adorning the window recesses, she removed her apron and tossed it into her large wicker basket. "I doubt that day will come, Mrs. Smythe."

The vicar's wife flushed at her unwittingly cruel remark. "I must apologize, my dear. I didn't mean to be unkind. But I *do* wish it were your wedding! And one day it shall be, mark my words! It is simply taking you longer than most to find the right man."

"I am twenty-three years old, and you know my propensities for misfortune!" Ellen forced a light laugh. "Please don't be overset by what you said. I know you meant it in kindness. I'm glad you wish it were my wedding. I do too! But it isn't likely."

Mrs. Smythe gazed into the young woman's serious aquamarine eyes. "Someday a fortunate man will come along and he will recognize your sweetness and your prettiness."

"He had better be at least six feet tall." Ellen smiled ruefully. "And have an exceptional sense of humor. Most men do not search for awkward, over-tall wives.''

"There is nothing awkward about these bouquets!''

Ellen shook her head, then picked up her basket. "You of all people know how I am. I've cried on your shoulder often enough!''

Mrs. Smythe retrieved the two smaller baskets and followed Ellen from the church. "I have told you,'' she lectured in a motherly fashion, "that if you will forget your height and walk proudly, your awkwardness will disappear. You've outgrown much of it anyway. Pretend you have a coronet on your head!''

Ellen burst into laughter. "That thought would only double me up with giggles!'' She placed the basket into her phaeton and reached for the others. "Your idea of my balancing books on my head was much more realistic.''

"Then do it! Think it!'' Mrs. Smythe slipped her arm through the girl's. "Come now. I've had Maggie prepare tea for us. You mustn't turn me down.''

"Very well, especially if Maggie is serving those delicious macaroons! You must give me the recipe.''

"Of course I will,'' the older woman said, pleased. "I didn't know you liked them so well. They are Reverend Smythe's favorites too. Alas, he won't be able to join us today. He's visiting distant parishioners and Johnny has gone with him.''

The two women strolled to the vicarage and entered its cool hall. "How is Johnny?'' Ellen asked. "Have his studies gone well?''

"Indeed they have. He will make an excellent churchman, I believe. Johnny has always cared about people.''

"You must be very proud of him.''

"We are.'' Mrs. Smythe guided her guest into the small parlor. "I often wish that you and he had been of the same age. You would make a good clergyman's wife, Ellen. But of course, you must set your sights higher than that.''

As they sat down, plump, jolly-faced Maggie entered with the tea tray laden with tarts, tiny sandwiches, nut bread spread with cream cheese, and the favored macaroons.

Ellen greeted the maid and turned her attention to the small feast before her. ''I cannot imagine anyone being any happier than you and the reverend. No one could wish for more.''

''We *have* been happy.'' Mrs. Smythe poured the tea. ''I suppose that our only disappointment was in not having more children. Still, the church has provided us with a rewarding life and we have Johnny! I could not complain.''

''I shouldn't either. I envy you your cozy home. Perhaps I should seek a bachelor man of the cloth!''

Mrs. Smythe thought of Ellen's life since the death of her parents in the accident several years ago. She knew the girl must be lonely in that big house. To her, the vicarage must seem very warm and snug. But despite what she had said about Ellen making a good clergyman's wife, Mrs. Smythe doubted that she would long be satisfied with a small house, one servant instead of many, and a persistent lack of money. Ellen Trevayne was an heiress and had money of her own, but no honest man of the church would allow her to live in a more affluent manner than his parishioners expected. Her fortune would quickly go to the less fortunate and eventually she would become unhappy. No matter how caring and giving she was, Ellen was bred to be wealthy and to live a style of life that was above that which the church could provide.

''It is not,'' Mrs. Smythe said quietly, ''as comfortable as it seems. I was a vicar's daughter, so I was accustomed to the life. As I said, my dear, you must set your sights higher."

Ellen looked curiously at her older friend, wondering how the lady could consider her life to be anything but perfect. She had a well-respected and caring husband, a fine son, and a nice home. What woman could ask for more? Surely Mrs. Smythe realized that Ellen would be lucky if any man asked her to be his wife. No one had as yet, and she was rapidly becoming a fixture on the shelf. She was not in the position to pick and choose.

The vicar's wife smiled brightly. "If you will walk proudly. . . !"

"I shall entrap a duke!" Ellen laughed and nibbled a macaroon. "Is that setting my sights high enough? Or should I settle for a marquess? Or an earl? Dear me, what a tragedy it would be if I had to wed a viscount! Oh, there are so many men to choose from, I daresay I cannot make up my mind!"

"Do not joke about it! Your concern about your height is all out of proportion. Yes, you are taller than most women and, in a social gathering, it is ever present on your mind. *That* is what makes you awkward. When you forget about it, you are just as graceful as any attractive young lady. Carry yourself with dignity and don't think about it!"

Ellen sighed. "I shall try. I *have* been trying."

Mrs. Smythe nodded. "I know you have. I've noticed a difference of late."

"Mother was so graceful and so very poised. I must have been a great disappointment. And Papa had such high hopes . . ."

"You were not a disappointment. Ellen, you must not think thoughts like that. They both loved you very much."

Ellen gave a characteristic little shrug. "I know they did, but I wish I could have pleased them better."

"You shall! And they will know it. Of that I am firmly convinced!"

"I hope that you are right." Ellen smiled and set down her cup and plate. "I must be on my way," she said, standing. "I *will* try, for them and for you too. You are like a second mother to me."

"I am proud that you feel that way." Mrs. Smythe hugged her and kissed her cheek. "I know that good things will happen for you. You are too sweet a person for it to be otherwise. You will be at the wedding tomorrow?"

"Certainly!"

"Good! I have planned a small reception on the lawn afterwards. Will you assist me?"

"Of course I shall! Let me send food as well."

"It isn't necessary."

"Nevertheless, I insist. It will give me great pleasure."

"If people knew what you do for this parish . . ."

"I don't want people to know. It embarrasses me," Ellen said quickly.

Mrs. Smythe hugged her again. "If I had had a daughter, I would have wanted her to be just like you."

"With less height, please!" Ellen's eyes twinkled.

The vicar's wife shook her head. "*Just* like you!"

The nighttime rain had ended and a clear, fresh-scented summer morning dawned, enabling the Marquess of Singleton to continue his journey in his open curricle. After a satisfying breakfast in which the inn's staff outdid itself to please its noble guest, he set his team of matched dapple grays to the road. Despite the wet surface and occasional mud hole, he was able to maintain a spanking pace, soon outdistancing his large traveling coach which carried his valet and baggage, and his entourage of grooms leading several of his fine-blooded riding horses. If his luck held, he would reach Shadybrook in the early afternoon.

He was looking forward to this visit to his small estate in Kent. Shadybrook, though not as grand as Singleton Hall, his principal seat in Yorkshire, had its benefits. The previous fall, he had made a short stay there for the first time, and found it to be a modern, comfortable brick, pleasantly furnished in eighteenth-century Chippendale. It boasted a well-trained staff, friendly but somewhat self-conscious at serving a fashionable young lord instead of his elderly aunt, now deceased, whose home it had been. Best of all, it was located near Woodburn Hall, the home of one of his best friends, the Duke of Rackthall.

Harry Singleton hadn't seen Brandon or his duchess, Allesandra, since early last winter. Expecting a child, they hadn't returned to London after Christmas. Their son had been born in June. Harry had dispatched a multitude of gifts, and had received a note from Allesandra in return, begging him to visit them. Now he had finally gotten round to it.

He was anxious to see how Bran, former rake and fellow man-about-town, was responding to fatherhood. It seemed beyond belief that a man who had so thoroughly enjoyed London's myriad of pleasures could be content to bury himself in the country. Marriage certainly must have changed him.

Harry sighed. He didn't like to refine on thoughts of wedlock. At the age of thirty-two, it was past time that he himself should be setting up his nursery. The current heir to his title was his cousin, an insipid young man who dressed outlandishly, frittered away vast sums of money in London's most notorious gambling halls, and frequently drank himself into senselessness.

Returning home late at night last week, Harry had found young Markley passed out on his portico.

With the help of his disapproving butler, he'd managed to get the boy to the sofa in the library. By morning both Markley and two hundred pounds from Harry's desk drawer had disappeared. Overcome by the desire to turn the boy over his knee, he had searched all day for him and had finally located him in the filthiest house of ill repute Harry had ever seen. Snatching his cousin from the arms of a heavily painted prostitute, he had boxed his ears, taken him home, and lectured him soundly. It had been to no avail. The boy had merely laughed, reminded Harry of his own rakish ways, and informed him how little he cared for the opinion of others. No, George Markley was definitely not a suitable candidate to be the next Marquess of Singleton.

Harry felt he was being fair in making that assessment. He had sown his own share of wild oats, but he hadn't sunk to the level his cousin delighted in. What the marquess did, he did with style, be it womanizing, gambling, or drinking. He wouldn't be caught dead in the places frequented by young Markley. The boy's father might laugh at his offspring's behavior, but enough was enough. An only child, Harry was going to have to find a wife and find her soon, whether or not the thought of it made him want to cringe.

There were many young ladies who would give their eyeteeth to be the Marchioness of Singleton. Every Season, mamas threw their little beauties at him and set elaborate traps to catch him, but Harry had been smart enough to elude them all. He had certain requisites for his future wife and none of the offerings had possessed all of those qualities.

That was surprising for he thought that his requirements were really quite simple. The future marchioness would be of good family, virtuous, amiable of temperament, interesting enough to hold his attention, and well-graced in the social arts. She would be sensible enough to look the other way if her lord happened to stray, and, of course, she would be beautiful beyond belief. It shouldn't have been that difficult to find a young lady who met those standards.

But it was. Since he had begun looking in earnest, he had met dozens of eligible ladies. All of them seemed so young and immature that they had quickly bored him. He had to admit that it had been a mistake to wait as long as he had. The best choices were snapped up in the first year of their debut, leaving none to develop to the degree he desired. He was beginning to believe that his only choice must be to marry one of these impossibly childish girls.

Thrusting the thought from his mind, he turned his attention to his driving and passed the time appreciating the movement of his fine team of grays. At midday, he and his groom paused under a stand of oaks to let the horses have a breather and to enjoy the excellent repast packed for them by the innkeeper. From there, it would be an easy drive to Shadybrook.

At the point where they turned from the main road onto the country lane which ran past his gates, Harry noticed the lead horse bobble. The next stride proved him lame. The marquess quickly pulled up on the side of the road.

"Per'aps it's only a stone, m'lord," James suggested.

"Let us hope." Harry secured the reins and hopped down, the groom following. "At least it isn't all that far to the estate."

"No, sir." Taking his knife from his pocket the groom strode to the horse, picked up his near fore, and began cleaning the hoof. "This mud'd make it easy to wedge a stone."

Harry watched him dig carefully at the impacted

soil. He did indeed desire it to be nothing more. He was particularly fond of the grays, a recent and costly purchase.

"Aye, there it is. A sharp stone, m'lord."

"Thank God."

Before he could return to his seat, the beat of hooves caught Harry's attention. Around the turn came a one-horse phaeton at an amazing rate of speed. Passing perilously close to the curricle, its wheel struck a mud hole and sent a deluge of water over Harry, James, and the grays. Startling, the horses jumped and knocked the groom to the road.

"What the hell. . . !" Harry leaped to James' aid. "Are you hurt?"

The groom rose to his feet, shaking his head. "I'm all right, sir."

Relieved, the marquess turned his attention to the perpetrator of the deed. "What the hell do you think you're doing!" he shouted at the phaeton's driver, who had pulled up some distance ahead. He stalked forward. "A fine way to drive! You've covered us with mud and you've nearly injured my groom!"

The driver turned and peered over her shoulder, and only then did Harry look closely enough to realize that it was a woman.

"Oh, dear," she said, looking at him with horror. "Did I do that?"

"No!" he said hotly, glancing down at his drenched coat and breeches. "This is my normal country attire! You should see me in town, when I bedeck myself with gutter refuse!"

"I'm very sorry," she said, her blue eyes wide.

"Not nearly so much as I am!" Harry caught hold of his temper as he saw her distress. "I daresay," he said more kindly, "it was a runaway."

"It was not! I thought I handled that turn quite neatly! How was I to know that you would be there, blocking the road?"

"Blocking the road!" Harry cried. "If you will but look, you will see that my curricle is well to the side!"

She did as he suggested and again favored him with helpless aquamarine eyes. "It appears that I am at fault," she said stiffly. "I shall be happy to pay for any damages."

He watched her, wickedly enjoying her discomfort. "Who are you?" he asked at last.

"Sir, you are impertinent!"

"A thousand pardons," he said with a mock bow. "Permit me to introduce myself! I am the Marquess of Singleton, come to visit my estate of Shadybrook. Pray, madam, whom do I address? It will be impossible to forward my bill if I do not know who you are."

"The marquess! But . . ." Her face flushed pink. "Oh, dear." Clenching her jaw, she tilted her chin upwards. "I am Miss Ellen Trevayne, my lord. You may send your bill to Bridgeford Grange."

"To your father, I assume." He grinned lazily.

"To me. My father is deceased. I am the mistress of Bridgeford Grange. And now, if you will excuse me, I must be on my way." Her hands trembled on the reins. "Good day to you, my lord." Without waiting for a reply, she touched the whip to the horse's rump and sped away.

Despite his soaked and muddy clothes, Harry laughed. Both overbearing and overset at the same time, pretty Miss Ellen Trevayne was an enigma of opposites. It might be amusing to further their acquaintance. With the exception of Bran and Allesandra, he knew no one in the area. Miss Trevayne might prove diverting.

Ellen drove from the scene of the accident as quickly as possible without inviting further cause for a blistering critique by the marquess. How mortifying the whole affair had been! She had drenched him terribly with filthy, muddy water, probably ruining his exquisite attire. His once-fashionable cravat had streamed damply from his neck; his finely tailored blue coat was dripping wet and, when dry, would be splotched with brown; his buff breeches were thoroughly covered with mud. What could she have been thinking of when she flew around that turn so fast that her horse was nearly out of control?

She shrugged. When she left the vicarage she had been determined to avoid disaster, but here it was, another incident in a long line of mishaps that she couldn't seem to control. Now she had involved the marquess, a man whose property line marched with her own on one long side of Bridgeford Grange! It was beyond all the worst nightmares she had ever had. In spite of her tendency to bad luck, Ellen had always gotten along well with her neighbors. Now she had certainly started off on the wrong foot with this new one.

At least the weather was warm enough that he shouldn't be in danger of catching a chill. Even if his clothes were ruined, she had offered to make reparations. She had accepted the blame, apologized nicely enough, and, with the exception of that brief verbal sparring, had behaved with propriety. There was only one thing she hadn't done. There must have been a reason why he was stopped and out of his curricle. If he was having trouble, she had not offered him assistance.

Ellen checked her horse with brief thoughts of returning. But no, that wouldn't do at all. She would be awkward, as she always was in the presence of men she didn't know, and she would be especially nervous because of their previous encounter. She couldn't go back. Something horrible would be sure to happen. She set the horse to its previous pace.

Shadybrook was nearby. If the marquess had to walk, it wouldn't be very far.

Her thoughts returned to the appearance of the man. Before she had muddied him, he must have looked very dashing. His clothes must have been made by the finest tailor in London and they fitted his tall, slender frame to perfection, almost like a second skin. They were undoubtedly a creation of Weston, the most fastidious and fashionable craftsman of gentlemen's clothing, whose reputation was so exalted that even Ellen had heard of him. Just as certainly his boots must have been made by the famous Hoby and polished to a high gloss with champagne. It was his face, however, that was his most arresting feature. The Marquess of Singleton was the most handsome man that she had ever seen.

In the opinion of the ladies of the neighborhood, no man could be more handsome than Lord Brandon Rackthall. That was, Ellen decided, only because they had never seen Lord Singleton. His hair was very dark, almost black, with just a hint of soft wave. His eyes, too, were dark and "set in with a smutty finger," as her grandmother would have said. High cheekbones and a straight, finely chiseled nose proclaimed his aristocratic heritage. His lips were not full but they were sensuous nonetheless. She wondered what it would be like to be kissed by a man such as that. It could make a woman lose her heart.

The idea brought out goose bumps on Ellen's arms. She shook her head. Nothing like that would ever happen to her. A man like the devastating marquess was beyond her touch. Her father had been a simple baronet; her mother, the daughter of a London businessman. Such a man would never look twice at the offspring of such a match, especially a girl as clumsy as she!

Sir Anthony Trevayne had been a member of the *ton*, even though he perpetually lacked the money to fly with the highest. To set his finances straight he had married Ellen's mother and her dowry had made him well-to-do. Despite its being a marriage by contract, the couple had been happy together, but Sir Anthony had never again regained his status in society. Ellen had her Season, but it had been a failure. After that, the Trevaynes had retired to the country, seldom going to London and never attempting to participate in the city's social activities. The trips to town had been only to buy clothing and trifles, and to visit her wealthy grandfather. She loved the old gentleman dearly, but many of his ways and ideas were not her own so she was always happy to return to Bridgeford.

To be fair, Ellen couldn't blame her unsuccessful social debut entirely on her maternal background. She saw herself as undesirable. At five feet eleven inches tall, she towered over many of the gentlemen and it was true that her height made her awkward. Furthermore, she was nervous around unmarried men, feeling like a horse on display at an auction and half-expecting someone to examine her teeth. She wasn't in the least capable of the coy, flirtatious behavior that seemed to be expected of a sixteen-year-old young lady. The Season had been an agony of sitting on the sidelines at balls. It was no wonder that the family had removed permanently to Bridgeford Grange.

But all of that was past now. When her parents died, she had inherited the unentailed estate and a comfortable sum of money from her father. From her mother, she had received a large fortune and a fine collection of jewelry. At twenty-three, she was the independently wealthy mistress of a notable property. She had tried to make herself believe that was enough.

Mrs. Smythe had always maintained that every woman should have a husband, but Ellen hadn't agreed with her. She liked her life at Bridgeford. The local gentry treated her as an older woman, allowing her the freedom to do much as she pleased. Her servants doted on her and, although they sometimes disapproved of her independence, they loved her too well to let it make any difference in their treatment of her. She had her beloved horses, her two well-matched and fiercely loyal Saint Bernard dogs, her beautiful gardens, a good friend in Mrs. Smythe, and a very close confidante in Allesandra, Duchess of Rackthall, who lived only a few miles away. She should be satisfied, but of late, she was not.

She had begun to feel that way after the birth of Allesandra's baby. He was such a sweet child, so good and so cuddly. When Ellen held him, she couldn't help wishing that he were hers. No foal or puppy could hold a candle to little Brannie's charm. But having a baby required having a husband first.

Her grandfather had been pleading in every letter for her to come up to London to meet the sons of some of his business associates. He had blatantly told her that she must wed and that she had better get about it before she was much older. In fact, he had stated in no uncertain terms that if she came to town, he would *buy* her a husband.

The idea was mortifying, but Ellen had to admit that his was probably the only way. No one would fall in love with her. She would never have anyone look at her the way the duke looked at Allesandra. Money was her only asset.

It was all well and good that she take Mrs. Smythe's advice and try to forget her physical shortcomings, but she doubted that it would solve the problem. It would, perhaps, eliminate her social awkwardness, but it would not erase any inches. The majority of men simply were not attracted to women taller than they. It seemed as though most of them were interested in petite, fragile ladies towards whom they could feel protective. That certainly wasn't Ellen Trevayne! No, if she were ever to have a family, she would have to agree to her grandfather's scheme.

With a small sigh, she turned through the gates of Bridgeford Grange. Perhaps in the fall after the harvest, she would visit him. At least his circle of friends could not be as intimidating as the members of the *ton* had been.

2

The day after Penny's wedding, Ellen dressed neatly in her trim blue summer-weight riding habit and plumed hat and rode out after breakfast, her destination Woodburn Hall, the home of the Duke and Duchess of Rackthall. The morning was cool and slightly misty, but she didn't mind the dew on her face. After the unusually hot steaminess of the days before, it seemed refreshing.

The journey could be accomplished in an hour at a steady trot, but she took her time, walking and trotting, with an occasional canter. While she rode, she reviewed the decision she had made about following her grandfather's suggestions. Before she asked Allesandra for her opinion, she wanted it all to be clear in her own mind.

It was nice to have a friend like Allesandra, a person to whom one could open one's heart. Mrs. Smythe had always been a valuable confidante, but there were certain subjects that were easier to discuss with a friend of one's own age. Ellen had several girlhood friends, but they had drifted away when they became young ladies and she had never achieved the closeness with them that she had with the duchess. No one, it seemed, wanted a friend of Ellen's height and awkwardness, nor one with such

17

a propensity for getting into muddles. Allesandra didn't seem to care, and even the handsome, sophisticated duke appeared to enjoy her company. As a result Ellen was comfortable in their presence and less inclined to mishap.

It had not always been so. On her first visit to Woodburn Hall, after meeting Allesandra at church, Ellen had almost knocked over a priceless vase. Horrified, she had poured out her misery at being so awkward and so tall. Instead of passing it off with a mere phrase of sympathy, the young duchess had listened understandingly and had soothed her fears. Allesandra had even admitted that she too had feelings of inadequacy from time to time. From that moment, the two had become fast friends.

Ellen hadn't yet told the duchess of her grandfather's scheme. When he had first started his campaign, she had been so opposed to the idea that there had been no need to discuss it. After several months, though, and after seeing Allesandra's perfect happiness with her husband and new baby, she had seen the wisdom of it. Now she only needed to hear and contemplate her friend's thoughts on the subject before entirely making up her mind and informing her grandfather of her decision.

She turned her horse through the gates of Woodburn and trotted down the long avenue of ancient oaks. She hoped the duchess would be at home and available for chatting. It had been some time since they had had a comfortable coze.

Allesandra greeted her as the butler opened the door. "I saw you from the upstairs window. I'm so glad you've come!" she said happily. "Brandon is busy with his paperwork and Brannie is napping, so I had nothing to do! Come in, Ellen, and tell me all your news!"

"There isn't much." Pulling off her gloves, Ellen

followed her into the salon. "I helped Mrs. Smythe at Penny's and Jack's wedding yesterday."

"Oh, dear. I should have attended, shouldn't I? But Brannie was out of sorts and I didn't want to leave him. Was I missed?"

"What a question! Of course you were!"

"I tried to enlist Brandon to go, but he refused. Men don't like that sort of event. Have you been doing nothing else?"

"There was one thing." Ellen flushed. "You wouldn't believe what happened to me the day before!"

Allesandra sat down, her green eyes alight with mischief. "Who was your victim this time?"

"It was perfectly awful." Ellen took off her hat and set it beside her on the love seat. "Are you acquainted with the Marquess of Singleton?"

"Handsome Harry," the duchess replied drolly. "Of course I know him. He's one of Brandon's best friends."

"Oh, dear!" Ellen wailed.

Allesandra laughed. "What have you done to poor Harry?"

"I was driving from the village and came across him along the side of the road, apparently having trouble with one of his horses. I was going rather quickly but not recklessly, of course!"

Her friend raised a dark eyebrow. "Of course!"

Ellen flashed her a guilty smile. "Unfortunately there was a great mud hole beside him. Now really, Allesandra, who in their right mind would stop beside a huge puddle of water?"

"Obviously," said Allesandra, "Harry did."

"I couldn't help it!" She shook her head. "There was a turn before, you see. By the time I had straightened out from it and noticed him there, it was too late. Muddy water flew over the marquess, his groom, and his horses."

Allesandra broke into giggles. "I wish I had seen Harry! He is so fastidious in his dress."

"He was rather angry," Ellen admitted. "I did the right thing, though. I offered to pay for any damages."

"Oh, don't bother with it!" the duchess cried mirthfully, tossing her black curls. "He can afford it many times over!"

"Still, it was proper of me to do so, wasn't it?"

"Yes, it was!" she assured her. "So Harry is visiting in the county. That should prove interesting. He is a very eligible bachelor, you know. I wonder when we shall see him."

"Not while I am here! If he appears, I shall run out the side door! And I am sure he has no desire to see me either but—oh, Allesandra, isn't he the most handsome man you have ever seen?"

"Well . . . no . . ."

Ellen laughed. "Of course you think that Brandon is, but really, don't you agree that Lord Singleton is handsome?"

"Very." Allesandra looked closely at her friend. "And since you think so too, perhaps you had better be here when he comes to call!"

"Oh, no! Something dreadful would be sure to happen! Don't tease me, Allesandra. I am not of his rank, not by family, or looks, or . . . or anything!"

"Once I remember saying that I was not of Brandon's."

"What? Why, your father was a peer, you are a darling, and you are perfectly beautiful!"

Allesandra shook her head. "Nothing mattered. He intimidated me. But in the end, things turned out so wonderfully!"

"Indeed! But fairy tales only happen to a few. Never to me! Be that as it may, I really did come here to discuss something along the same lines." Briefly she told of her grandfather's plans and added, "If we will be honest, it is the only way I will ever have my own family. I had thought that what I had was enough, but it isn't," she murmured wistfully. "Particularly after seeing you with Brannie. I want that too."

"My own marriage was arranged by my aunt," Allesandra said slowly, "but happily, we fell in love."

Ellen sighed. "I wonder if it is really necessary to be in love to be happy?"

"I don't know . . . I was very miserable when I found that I loved Brandon and thought he didn't love me. But a great many marriages are arranged and they seem to go along well enough. I would wish more for you, though. Loving, and being loved, is something very special."

"That isn't going to happen to me. No gentleman is going to choose me unless he does so for the money. Allesandra, you shall not hurt my feelings with your honesty."

"I am not at all convinced that no one will choose you for yourself! Ellen, we are going to London in the fall. You may travel with us," the duchess said briskly. "Let your grandfather introduce you to the sons of his associates, but let Brandon and me take you round as well. I cannot see letting yourself go to the highest bidder."

"I had a Season in London," Ellen said sadly. "It came to nothing."

"This time will be different. You are older now."

"And just as awkward and ill at ease. You know it will be of no use!"

"I intend to help you. First we shall shop. You are quite pretty, Ellen, and when dressed in the latest fashion, you shall be stunning."

"Until I stumble on the stairs or tip over the first vase . . ."

"That is not going to happen!"

A knock sounded at the door and a servant brought in a tray of light refreshments, setting it down on a low table between them. Allesandra poured the tea and handed her a cup. "Do you dance well?"

Ellen laughed. "Need you ask? I was taught, of course, but I am just as awkward at that as I am at anything else. Oh, yes, I cut quite a caper on my partners' toes!"

"How long has it been since you tried?"

"Not since my Season. Allesandra, it is no use! I will never . . ."

"Perhaps Brandon could assist you," she interrupted.

"He will murder you, Allesandra!"

"Who will murder her?" The tall blond-haired duke entered the room, and, lifting his wife's palm, he kissed it sweetly. "Do I detect some sort of scheme?"

"Ellen is going to London in the fall, darling. I have volunteered you to assist her with her dancing."

He turned to their guest. "It shall be a pleasure." Taking her hand, he brought it to his lips, his blue eyes sparkling.

Ellen smiled, feeling a shiver course through her body. No matter that he was her friend's husband, he could never fail to make a woman feel that she was very special indeed. "Please be sure, sir, that you wear very stiff boots."

"Ah, but you shall be waltzing on air," he said gallantly.

She laughed. "More like I shall be waltzing on your toes!"

Brandon Rackthall grinned, sitting down beside Allesandra and accepting the cup of tea she had poured for him. "So we shall all be in London at the same time. I'll have two pretty ladies to escort."

"Not often I fear, Your Grace." Ellen flashed her eyes at him. With the duke, she was able to display some of the liveliness expected of a charming young lady. "My grandfather does not move in the same circles. I must meet with his friends."

"But you shall allow us a goodly sum of your company?"

"Enough for you to find diverting, I'm sure."

"Excellent! There is never a dull moment when you are around."

"Enough, you two!" Allesandra interrupted. "Brandon, guess what news Ellen has brought? Harry Singleton is visiting at Shadybrook."

"Indeed? I shall have to post a guard for you, my dear. Harry has always appreciated you entirely too much for my comfort!"

The young duchess blushed prettily. "I wonder when we will hear from him?"

"I believe he is only just arrived," Ellen said. "According to the servants' grapevine, Lord Singleton got here the day before yesterday."

"And Ellen gave him a warm welcome!" Giggling, Allesandra told her husband of her friend's adventure on the road.

The duke laughed long and hard. "I would give anything to have seen him! He always thinks so well of himself and dresses so impeccably! To see him in such a state would be priceless. Would you care to repeat the incident, Ellen?"

"I would not! I was absolutely mortified! I never want to see him again."

"That will be impossible," Brandon replied. "We must have entertainment for him and we will depend upon you to attend."

"If that is the case, sir," she said wryly, "I will be the entertainment, as you well know!"

"What could happen at a simple dinner party?"

"A great deal, if I am concerned in it!"

"Brandon is right," Allesandra seconded. "It will give you practice for London. After all, we'll only invite neighbors."

"And Lord Singleton!" Ellen groaned.

"A little at a time," Lord Rackthall reassured her.

"You must promise us," his wife begged. "Really, Ellen, it would look odd if you did not attend."

"Oh, very well." Ellen looked doubtfully from one to the other. "You know I cannot refuse you! Just do not say that I didn't warn you when something perfectly awful happens."

Ellen stayed for luncheon at Woodburn Hall and, in mid-afternoon, returned home. She had planned to spend time on the estate accounts, but it was too lovely outside to waste the rest of the day in her office. Changing into a well-worn dress, she summoned her two Saint Bernards for a walk.

Friendly and Taffy ambled beside her and playfully bumped her legs for a short while, then ranged ahead in search of further amusement. They soon disappeared from sight into a copse of woods, but she was not concerned about their whereabouts. After searching the little grove for rabbits and other prey, they always ended up at the stream on the other side, just over the boundary between Bridgeford and Shadybrook.

Ellen followed leisurely, enjoying the breeze on her face. Hearing them far ahead, she passed through the woodland and crossed over a stile onto the neighboring property where the ground began to descend to the brook. Climbing down the bank, she walked along the narrow shoreline. The stream was swollen and muddy from the recent rains, deeper in fact than she had ever remembered it being, and the path along it was slick. She began to regret her decision to walk beside it. Ahead was a wider spot, a place where she had often picnicked as a child. The incline was less steep there; she could climb back up with ease.

Reaching it, she paused, listening for the dogs. They were out of earshot now, but she knew they would soon return to search for her. She started up the bank, but as she did, the breeze picked up, catching her straw hat and lifting it from her head.

"Fustian!" Ellen watched it sail through the air and attach itself to a branch overhanging the water. "Now what shall I do?"

She made her way back to the water's edge and stared at the offensive headgear, with its jauntily waving ribbons. If she could get a long enough stick, she might be able to reach it. She must be very careful not to fall in, for swimming was one outdoor pursuit that she had never attempted.

"What, may I ask, are you doing?" a male voice inquired.

She started, then whirled around and looked up the bank at the horseman sitting gracefully on his shining chestnut stallion. Her eyes were drawn first to the horse. He was a finely bred animal of light-golden brown with a creamy, silken mane and tail. His forehead was emblazoned with a perfect white star, but there was not another touch of white on him. Tall enough to be proportionate to a rider of the greatest height, he was the living picture of what Ellen desired in a thoroughbred.

"Again I ask, what are you doing?" His voice wasn't particularly arrogant, but it contained the demanding note of a man who was accustomed to being listened to and obeyed.

Reluctantly she concluded her study of the horse and lifted her gaze to his rider. She needed only a brief view of his dark good looks to recognize the marquess.

"Miss, I believe you are on my property. Does

that not entitle me to an explanation of your activity?''

"You are Lord Singleton," she said inanely.

He inclined his head in an aristocratic nod.

"Oh, dear. I . . . I often go walking by your brook. I hope you don't mind?'' Perhaps he didn't recognize her. Their previous encounter had been so brief and she had been well-attired. Today, in this shabby dress, her hair certainly mussed, she would present an entirely different appearance.

"I don't mind at all, but who . . . ah, Miss Trevayne! I didn't recognize you at first.''

Her heart sank. "My estate marches with yours on this side, my lord. I was walking my dogs when my hat blew off. I shall retrieve it, and the dogs, and be on my way.''

His fine gray eyes looked past her to the straw hat snagged on the tree limb. "I shall come to your assistance, although I might have wished the same consideration from you after the unfortunate occurrence on the road the other day.''

Ellen flushed scarlet. "It isn't necessary. Really it isn't! I can take a stick and . . . Oh, I don't care about that old hat anyway!''

Lord Singleton ignored her, riding down the bank, his horse sliding in the soft mud. Drawing up beside her, he dismounted with languid elegance. "If you will hold my horse, Miss Trevayne? He won't cause you any trouble.''

She took the reins, discovering, as she stood beside him, that the marquess was one of the few people tall enough to cause her to tilt her chin upwards to look into his eyes.

He stepped to the edge of the stream, held on to the tree with one hand, and leaned out.

"Do be careful!'' Ellen cried. "It's very slippery!'' Hastily she tied the horse to a low branch. "Wait! I shall help you balance!''

"It's quite all right."

"Here." She reached for his coattails. "I shall hold on . . ." Her foot slipped, pitching her forward against his back. His precarious balance lost, Lord Singleton fell headlong into the brook, herself on top of him.

Water closed over Ellen's head. Arms flailing, she brought herself to the surface. "Help!" she screamed. "I can't swim!"

An arm circled her as she started down again. "Help me!" She kicked frantically.

"Shut up!" cried the marquess. "And quit fighting me!"

She clutched at him desperately. "Please!"

He swam one powerful stroke and stood her on her feet in the shallows. "You're all right now."

Coughing wildly, Ellen gasped for breath. "Oh, dear," she moaned, moving away from him and splashing up onto the shore. "I am absolutely mortified!" She looked at him with horror. "Look at your clothes! Your fine cravat!"

He followed her, dripping, onto dry land, water squishing in his once-shining boots. "My cravat?" he said sarcastically. "Interestingly enough, I tied it in a Waterfall this morning. That was no doubt a harbinger of my fate."

Ellen squared her shoulders. "It is, of course, my fault." She tried to make her voice steady, but her words came out in a tremble. "I shall pay for any damages. If you will send your bill . . . oh, dear, you are hurt! Your hand is cut, Lord Singleton!"

But he wasn't looking at her, or at it. He was gazing past her to the place where his horse had stood.

She turned to see a set of broken reins dangling from the tree branch. "Oh, my!"

The Marquess of Singleton took several deep breaths. "So much for my offer to take you home, Miss Trevayne. It appears that we both must walk."

"It isn't so very far," she said timorously.

"No! Only upwards of a mile, I should think! This unlucky place is quite on the backside of my property!"

"I am sorry, sir."

"For what happened today?" the marquess said hotly. "Or for the other day as well, when you dashed me with mud and left me by the roadside?"

"I am sorry for everything," Ellen said miserably. "My home is much closer than Shadybrook Manor. If you would care to come there, you may go home in my carriage."

"No, thank you, Miss Trevayne. I have had quite as much of your company as I can stand for one day!"

Her temper flared. "Well, that was certainly uncalled for! It was an accident. Furthermore, I did not ask for your help!"

"If you had done as I instructed," he railed, "we would both be dry, I would still have my horse, and you would have your silly hat on your head! Any ninnyhammer knows not to tie up a horse by the reins!"

"Go to hell," Ellen said in a most unladylike fashion, and started up the incline.

"Hades would be preferable to the company of some women!" he shouted after her.

Gaining the top, she stiffened her back and strode purposefully towards her own property with his laughter ringing out behind her. If Brandon and Allesandra expected her to come to an entertainment which included the marquess, they would be disappointed. She would never agree to lay eyes on that odious man again.

Once again, Harry presented himself at Shadybrook Manor in an entirely disreputable condition. It had been bad enough on his arrival when he had been forced to greet his entire staff in clothes befitting a well-digger. To have it happen again, just two days later, would surely cast doubt on his lordship's personal habits of cleanliness.

"I met up again with Miss Trevayne," he said in reply to his butler's wide-eyed, unasked question. "Did my horse make it home?"

"Yes, my lord," Hopkins replied worriedly. "We sent out searchers."

"Evidently they didn't search in the right direction," he snapped, entering the salon and pouring himself a glass of brandy. "Hopkins?"

"Sir?"

"What sort of a woman *is* she?"

The older man wrung his hands. "I don't understand, sir."

"What sort of woman is Miss Trevayne? Apparently she lives alone and has a penchant for drenching any man unfortunate enough to come her way."

"I'm sure it was . . . they were . . . accidents, my lord. Miss Ellen wouldn't do such things on purpose!"

Harry snorted. "Has she no relatives? Or should I say, no keeper?"

"There is a grandfather in London, her mother's father. I understand that he is quite wealthy."

Harry swirled the liquor in his glass. "Strange that she does not choose to live with him."

"It would not seem so, my lord, if you knew Miss Ellen!"

"An independent lady, I assume."

"I suppose that one might call her so," Hopkins said cautiously, stiffening his shoulders, "but a *lady* nonetheless."

The marquess caught the warning in his butler's voice and burst into laughter. "Good God, Hopkins! Do you think I am planning to seduce her? Far be it from me!"

"No, sir. Certainly not, sir! It's just that Miss Ellen's situation might invite . . . er . . . give the impression that one might . . . er . . . a man of your nature . . ." He broke off in confusion.

"Indeed? What rumor have you heard of me?" Harry demanded.

"Nothing at all, my lord!" Hopkins' guilty expression belied his words.

"You are withholding the truth."

The man stared at his toes in misery. " 'Tis nothing but gossip. No one really pays heed to gossip, my lord, and there is little good served by repeating it."

"Still, it is sometimes amusing to hear what is being said of one." Harry held out his glass for a refill. "Repeat the gossip, Hopkins. I wish to hear it."

"Oh, Lord Singleton," the butler wailed, topping off the glass, "I scarce paid attention to it! It merely concerned your . . . er . . . enjoyment of women."

"Indeed." Harry grinned. "That's true. I do enjoy women. Doesn't any man?"

"Opera dancers," Hopkins stammered, "and women of a certain reputation. Mistresses, my lord!"

"I see. Well, I have none at present. Have no fears! I wouldn't bring any of my ladybirds here, nor do I intend to make Miss Trevayne one of them. Damme, do you think me mad? The further away I can stay from that female, the better!"

The butler drew a breath of relief. "She is innocent, sir, even if she has reached a certain age."

"It is of little interest to me." He set the glass aside. "Now if you will arrange a bath for me."

"Yes, sir. My lord?"

"Yes?" Harry stopped his progress towards the door.

"You received a message from the Duke of Rackthall." Hopkins handed him the envelope.

"Good! I am glad to be reminded that there is one sane person in this county!" Leaving the room and mounting the stairs, he entered his big front bed-room. "Daniel, are you there?"

"Yes, my lord." The valet walked from the dress-ing room and stared at his gentleman. "Oh, my God!"

"Indeed."

"What happened, my lord?"

"Miss Trevayne shoved me into the stream."

Daniel began to remove his master's sodden clothes. "What kind of lady would . . ."

"I don't know and I don't intend to investigate further. She must be in the employ of Weston! Hop-kins is sending up a warm bath, Daniel. That breeze made me chilly. And pour me some brandy." He finished undressing himself and slipped into a silver brocade dressing robe. Settling into a comfortable chair he opened Brandon's letter.

It was a short missive, in reply to the one he had sent earlier, and it requested that Harry call on the duke and duchess as soon as possible. Tomorrow he would do it. It was too late today and, besides, he had had his fill of the outdoors.

Leaning back, he sipped his brandy and thought of Miss Ellen Trevayne. Despite his irritation with her, he couldn't keep from grinning. She had run through a range of emotions, from embarrassment to fear to misery to rancor, in the shortest amount of time. One minute she had been apologizing, the next minute she was telling him to go to hell. No woman had ever said *that* to him. Whoever she was and whatever misfortune befell those around her, she was not boring.

It must have come from her city-bred mother. No gently born lady would behave like that, especially in the presence of a marquess. Perhaps her indepen-dence had an effect on her as well. She was probably well-to-do and used to getting her own way. Her grandfather had apparently not cared about looking after her or, if he had, she had ridden roughshod over him. He couldn't blame the man for leaving well enough alone. Whoever rose to take responsibility for Ellen Trevayne was taking on a terrible challenge.

Harry sneezed. With any luck at all, he would not cross her path again. And if he did, he would take care to stay out of her way.

3

In the morning, Harry awoke with a dull headache, a raw throat, and a dripping nose. Painfully ringing the bellpull, he drew up the bedspread
and fell back onto the pillows, shivering. His whole
body, from head to toe, seemed to hurt.

"Good morning, my lord," his valet said brightly
as he entered and threw back the draperies, flooding
the room with sunshine.

"I'm miserable," the marquess croaked.

"Sir, are you ill?"

"I'm freezing to death, I ache all over, and my
throat feels as though someone took a knife to it."
He sneezed.

Daniel quickly procured a handkerchief. "You
must have caught a chill yesterday."

"Get me some blankets. My God, I have not been
sick in years!"

"No, sir. Never since I have been in your employ." The valet carefully covered his master with
two thick comforters. "What shall I do, my lord? Do
you wish your breakfast?"

"No. Only some coffee. The heat will feel good
on my throat." Shivering, Harry bundled the blankets around him. "But if I am asleep upon your return, just leave me lie."

"Yes, my lord." The valet walked softly from the room.

Harry closed his eyes and drifted off to sleep, only to be awakened by a cool hand to his forehead.

"Feverish," proclaimed his housekeeper, Mrs. Hopkins. "What a fool you are to cover him so. He needs to be bathed in tepid water."

Harry looked up into her frowning face. "Leave me alone," he protested weakly.

"I know what needs to be done, young man. You," she addressed Daniel, "bring me a basin of tepid water and a cloth."

"Mrs. Hopkins," the marquess remonstrated, watching her roll up her sleeves, "my valet can do whatever is necessary. I have no clothes on under here!"

"So much the better."

"Please!" Harry's exclamation came out as a throaty squawk. "Just tell Daniel what to do. If you persist in this course, you are going to have trouble."

She stood over him, hands on her hips. "I took very good care of your aunt until the poor lady's dying day!"

"I'm sure you did, Mrs. Hopkins, but this is different. In the first place, I am a man; in the second, I have no intention of dying." Harry paused to sneeze. "My valet can handle the situation. Please leave now. I must get up for a moment."

"Well . . . I shall see to your breakfast."

"Just coffee, please, Mrs. Hopkins."

"You must keep up your strength," she admonished.

"Yes," he agreed hastily, hoping that she would go away more quickly. "I'm sure you know best, having taken care of an invalid."

"Well, I do." She slowly backed from the room. "I will instruct that valet, and I will return with something nourishing for you. You'll feel better in no time, my lord.''

"I'm sure I will.'' Even if he didn't feel better, he could certainly pretend.

He was beginning to think that Shadybrook Manor wasn't such a nice place after all. First he had been treated like a lecherous seducer of innocent ladies, now like a combination of little boy and invalid old woman. To say nothing of what he had suffered at the hands of Ellen Trevayne! Perhaps he should have gone to Yorkshire. He would have had to endure his mother's complaints and criticisms, but life would have been infinitely more simple. He probably wouldn't have gotten ill either.

After enduring Daniel's ministrations with the tepid water, Harry was confronted with a breakfast that Mrs. Hopkins deemed suitable for a sick person. The valet dressed his lord in a soft linen nightshirt, plumped up the pillows behind him, and set down the bed tray. Standing back, he rolled his eyes towards the ceiling.

"What is this?'' Harry cried, looking at the large bowlful of milky, soggy substance before him.

"I think, my lord, that it is milk toast.''

"Dear God in heaven,'' the marquess groaned. "What have I done to deserve this?''

"It does look rather terrible,'' Daniel ventured.

"Can you eat it?''

"Oh, my lord!''

"That is asking too much, isn't it? Throw it out the window, give it to a dog. Do something with it, Daniel, but don't send it back to the kitchen. Mrs. Hopkins will come in person to shove it down my throat!''

"Yes, my lord.'' Daniel removed the offensive offering and left the marquess to his coffee.

By now Harry felt worse than he had upon wak-

ening. He downed his coffee and lay back on the
pillows, once again trying to sleep.

"My lord?" The now-familiar high-pitched voice
pounded his brain, and he wrenched himself out of
his peaceful doze. "Mrs. Hopkins," he said feebly.

"Drink this."

Harry could see Daniel standing behind her ample
form and shrugging his shoulders. "What is it?" he
asked.

"It will make you feel better."

"Will it make me sleep?"

"Yes, my lord, it will do that too."

"Thank God." He sniffed at the non-odorous liq-
uid and took a tentative sip.

"Drink all of it, young man," Mrs. Hopkins said
firmly.

Harry gulped it down. "There! Now if I can have
some peace and quiet, I'm sure I can sleep and will
feel much better."

"I'm sure you will." With satisfaction, she took
back the glass and bustled out of the room.

"Lock the door, Daniel!" the marquess cried.
"Stay either inside or out, but leave me alone and
see that others do so as well!"

"I'm to bathe you again, my lord, with tepid water."

"Like hell you will! If you so much as touch me,
I'll turn you off without a character! And that goes
for every servant in this house!" he shouted. "I have
had enough, Daniel! Enough!" Jerking the covers
over his head, he engaged in a fit of sneezing and
had to resurface to accept a clean handkerchief from
his valet. "This is all Miss Trevayne's doing! I hope
she is as ill as I am!"

Ellen was among the first of ten guests to arrive
for the Duke and Duchess of Rackthall's dinner
party. She had come only under duress and after

the pleadings of Allesandra. She was not looking forward to meeting again with the Marquess of Singleton, who had been ill for three days as a direct result, Ellen knew, of the dunking in the stream. However, Allesandra was her dear friend and she couldn't bear to disappoint her.

She did look well this evening. Her aquamarine silk gown matched her eyes to perfection and brought out their vivid color. Her maid had done up her honey-blonde hair into a new style, a casual knot on the top of her head, with cascades of tendrils becomingly escaping it. For accent she wore her best pearl necklace and teardrop earrings. Next to Allesandra's classic beauty and the girlish prettiness of the squire's daughter she knew she was eclipsed; nonetheless, she felt she was at her best.

She entered the drawing room and greeted her host and hostess, then smiled at the vicar, his wife, and their nineteen-year-old son.

"Ellen!" Mrs. Smythe said warmly. "How pretty you look!"

"Thank you," she murmured gratefully, and nodded at the squire and his family, who were sitting some distance apart. "I do hope that nothing horrible happens."

Reverend Smythe laughed. "You are among friends, my dear. Nothing at all will happen."

"Come and sit with me." His wife patted the chair beside her. "I want to compliment you again on the flowers you brought to church. They were so very pretty! And I did appreciate your help. Thanks to you, Penny had a lovely wedding."

"And because of you too!" Ellen sat down nervously on the edge of her chair. Chatting of parish affairs, she smiled pleasantly at other guests who entered, until she noticed the discontented expression on the squire's daughter's face turn to one of delight. Looking towards the door, she saw the marquess greeting the duke and duchess. "Oh, dear," she murmured.

His attire, like that of the duke, stood out among that of the local gentry and boasted of the skill of London tailoring. He was dressed conservatively in dove-gray, his intricate cravat enhanced by a brilliant sapphire stickpin. His waistcoat was of shimmering dark-blue silk.

He looked around the room, his gaze alighting on Ellen. With a faint smile, he inclined his head. "Miss Trevayne."

"My lord," she acknowledged, just as coolly.

Then the company surrounded him and Ellen was able to take a deep breath of relief. With all the others, particularly Squire Adams, his wife, and the insipid Patsy, doting on his every word, she should be successful in avoiding any further contact with him. She stayed where she was, conversing only with the Smythes until dinner was announced and Allesandra extended her arm pointedly towards her.

"Harry, you will escort Miss Trevayne, please?" The duchess smiled sweetly.

For the first time in their friendship, Ellen felt that she could have strangled Allesandra. Woodenly she watched the marquess politely acquiesce. With a none-too-pleased expression on his face he came forward, bowed to her, and offered his arm.

"Miss Trevayne?"

"Thank you, my lord." She stood stiffly and slipped her hand into the crook of his elbow.

"Can you not smile?" Lord Singleton said softly into her ear. "We should be quite safe. There is no water close by."

Ellen looked at him helplessly.

"You are quite lucky, you know," he whispered. "Miss Patsy Adams would kill for this honor."

"You odious man," she said tightly.

"I thought that would bring about a rise."

"If you think I am enjoying this, you are sadly mistaken." Ellen tripped on the division between hall and dining room and briefly clung to him. Behind her, she heard a trill of laughter.

"Are you all right?" the marquess asked more kindly.

"Perfectly."

They entered the dining room and she found to her dismay that she was seated next to him. At least Patsy Adams was nearby so there would be no lack of conversation, and Allesandra, of course, was at the foot of the table on Lord Singleton's other side. Hopefully Ellen could fade quietly into the background, which was exactly what she intended to do.

She picked at her dinner while the talk flowed over and around her. After a few attempts at drawing her out, Allesandra gave up and left her at peace. The marquess largely ignored her, directing his conversation towards his hostess, Patsy, and the squire. He seemed to be quite interested in agricultural improvement and appeared to be trying out the new methods of farming at Shadybrook and at his other properties. He found a kindred soul in the squire who had set into operation many innovations at his own estate. Patsy was clearly bored but pretended to be otherwise while Ellen, though interested, remained silent. Even though she was knowledgeable on the subject she knew that her fluttering nerves would cause her to say something ridiculous.

By the beginning of the dessert course, she began to feel more at ease. The ordeal was nearly accomplished, no mishaps had occurred, and she could soon retire to a corner of the drawing room. No doubt Patsy would entertain them on the pianoforte and she could remain unnoticed for the rest of the evening.

"You are very quiet tonight," Lord Singleton said to her.

Jolted from her reverie, Ellen looked into his un-fathomable dark eyes. "I have nothing to say, my lord," she answered stiffly.

Across the table Patsy Adams audibly smothered a giggle behind her dainty hand. "Miss Trevayne is usually silent, sir. I believe that she despises any gathering that does not include her horses or her dogs."

"Or water?" he asked softly.

Patsy overheard. "Water? What about water?"

Ellen blushed scarlet. How could he have men-tioned that? Now everyone would hear the tale! Once the squire's daughter was intrigued by a sub-ject, particularly one that was detrimental to others, she would pursue it ruthlessly. Ellen bit her lip and lowered her head, clenching her hands together to still their trembling.

"Come now, my lord," Mrs. Adams said, smiling amusedly, "it is naughty to refer to something with-out further explanation!"

Furious, Ellen heard him begin to relate the awful events of her encounters with him. It was beyond belief that he could set out to mortify her so! She flashed a helpless glance at Allesandra and saw that her friend's mouth was pursed angrily.

"I believe," the duchess interrupted coldly, "that we shall leave the gentlemen to their port." She fa-vored Lord Singleton with a haughty glare and rose, leaving the ladies with no choice but to follow her to the salon.

Happily the rest of the evening passed without further incident. With the exception of Patsy, the company was pleasant, but Ellen left as soon as she could do so without being considered impolite.

At the door Allesandra kissed her cheek. "Harry should be ashamed of himself!" she hissed. "His manners are always impeccable. If I had ever dreamed that he would behave in this fashion I would never have subjected you to this evening!''

Ellen shrugged. ''It doesn't matter. I suppose people might find those tales amusing. We ourselves laughed when I told you about them, didn't we?''

''It's those deplorable Adamses!''

''They are not among my favorite people, nor is Lord Singleton.''

''I agree! And if I ever find him beside a pool of water, I shall push him in myself!''

Harry morosely spent the next morning regretting the incident of the evening before. He had behaved badly in telling the story of his misadventures with Miss Trevayne. He had never before been unkind to a female, not until Ellen Trevayne had splashed her way into his life.

Bran had been surprised at his conduct, but he had shrugged it off. Allesandra, on the other hand, though outwardly remaining the perfect hostess, had been angry with him. That Ellen Trevayne was her special friend was plain to see. Harry had apologized, but he had the feeling that it wasn't enough.

The other guests had been dismayed as well, with the exception of the squire's wife and their insipid daughter. Miss Patsy Adams had made a nuisance of herself, fawning over his every word and batting her pale eyelashes at him. She was the type of female who enjoyed seeing another member of her sex in distress. It was probably just as well that Miss Trevayne had left early. Otherwise, Miss Adams would undoubtedly have made her evening miserable with sly jokes and innuendoes.

His own servants, too, seemed less than pleased with him. No doubt they had heard the story through the vast and effective servants' grapevine and had decided to side with Miss Trevayne. All morning they had been unusually quiet and had treated him with a cool reserve.

After a luncheon that was scarcely adequate and served with near-sullenness, Harry made up his mind to try to rectify the situation. No matter what she had done, he owed Miss Trevayne an apology—for the sake of his own conscience, if not for her peace of mind. Calling for his horse, he mounted and trotted out in the direction of Bridgeford. This mission should appease everyone.

It was with trepidation that he passed through the gates of the park. He wondered suddenly if he should have worn old clothes, instead of the fashionable skintight buff breeches and brown linen coat. There was no knowing what sort of disaster awaited him at the hands of this mistress of mishap. No matter what, he must stay away from all bodies of water.

He was vaguely surprised at the appearance of Bridgeford Grange. He had somehow pictured a shambles of a place with overgrown grounds, tumbledown house, and a pack of dogs running wild. It wasn't that way at all.

The house was a very old stone mansion, and somewhat rambling, but it was neat and attractive with the sun glinting from its diamond-shaped panes. The gardens were as extensive and as well-kept as those at Shadybrook, and were blooming just as riotously. When he drew up in front, a uniformed footman immediately appeared to take his horse and the door was opened by a formidable butler before he reached the top step.

"Sir." The man bowed formally.

"I am the Marquess of Singleton," Harry said. "I have come to see Miss Ellen Trevayne."

The servant bowed him into the hall. "Wait here, my lord. I shall see if she is available."

Available? She had better be available, after he had

swallowed his pride in coming here. No woman was "unavailable" to Lord Singleton.

He fidgeted, glancing around the hall. The inside of Bridgeford Grange was as much of a surprise as the outside. It was tastefully furnished with very old and valuable antiques. On the floor was a thick, richly colored Oriental carpet. In the center of the room a mammoth bouquet of flowers graced a Tudor oak trestle table. Harry wondered how the arrangement had survived Miss Trevayne's penchant for disaster.

After what seemed like an interminable wait, the butler reappeared. "She will see you, sir," he intoned in a voice that intimated that the marquess was lucky indeed. "If you will wait in here, my lord?"

Harry followed him into a large drawing room, similarly furnished with fine, well-cared-for antiques. He stood, thinking of how little Miss Trevayne resembled her environment. It certainly didn't seem the type of place for an accident-prone woman. There was too much gentility here.

The door opened and she made a slightly flustered entrance. "My lord." Cheeks pink, she curtsied.

"Miss Trevayne." He bowed gracefully.

"Won't you sit down?" she said, taking a chair next to the fireplace. "I have ordered tea, but you may prefer brandy. My grandfather does. I keep it on hand for his visits."

"Thank you. Brandy would be fine."

She tugged the bellpull and the butler instantly entered. "Brandy for my lord, if you please, Gore." She clasped her hands together in her lap, but Harry could see their trembling.

"You have a very lovely home, Miss Trevayne." He accepted the glass from the servant and took a sip of the excellent brandy.

"Thank you, sir." She forced a smile. "But you did not come here to discuss the merits of my furnishings."

"No." He swirled the liquor in his glass. So she would have him come right to the point. There was no beating around the bush with her. "I came to apologize, Miss Trevayne. My conduct last night was beyond all sense of decency. I can only beg your forgiveness."

She lowered her head, her hands clenching even tighter.

"I was very rude and I am—"

"No," she said softly, "do not continue to blame yourself. What you told was true." She raised her eyes and Harry saw what a clear aquamarine they were.

"Nevertheless I am sorry." He couldn't take his eyes from hers. He wondered why, in their previous encounters, he had never noticed how very prettily they sparkled.

"Then let us forget the matter." The tea tray arrived, the servant setting it between them on a low table. As if she feared disaster, Ellen avoided it. "Please serve yourself, my lord. The cakes and the sandwiches are very good, I believe."

Though he wasn't hungry so soon after luncheon, Harry helped himself to a small sandwich, just to be polite. "Do you often go to Woodburn?"

"Oh, yes. The duchess is my very best of friends!" She hesitated. "But do not deprive yourself of their society. I know that you and Lord Rackthall have been friends for a long time. I promise that I shall not go there while you are in the neighborhood!" she said quickly.

"Madam, that is not my wish at all!" he protested.

"Let us be honest," she said. "I am terribly prone to mishaps, especially, it seems, where you are con-

cerned. I wish to avoid any other accidents! I shall
even refrain from going to church if you are like to."

"I don't go to church."

"You don't?" she asked with some surprise.

"No. I don't like it."

She burst into laughter. "My lord, I have never
heard anyone make such an admission! People who
do not attend usually make some sort of acceptable
excuse. Whyever don't you like it?"

"I find it boring." Harry grinned. When Ellen Trevayne laughed, she was entrancing, as indeed she
was when she expressed her anger. Venting emo-
tion caused her to lose her stiffness.

"Reverend Smythe wouldn't like that! He will be
very disappointed not to see you in the congregation
tomorrow morning."

"I'm sure he would prefer your presence to mine,
and I shall not prevent you from attending."

"You should go, my lord, being new in the neighborhood. It is a friendly church and Reverend
Smythe is a good vicar. Perhaps you will not be
bored too greatly."

"I will go only if you accompany me," Harry
heard himself say. My God, what was he getting
himself into? What sort of disaster would befall him?
And in church no less!

The laughter disappeared from her face. "Oh, my
lord, I could not!"

"Coward!"

She set her jaw. "I am not a coward. I hope that
I am using reasonably good sense. No, my lord, it
is out of the question!"

"Then you will prevent me from attending," the
marquess said just as stubbornly. No young lady had
ever turned down an invitation from him and he
wasn't going to let it happen now, even if it was
Miss Ellen Trevayne. "I shall tell Reverend
Smythe."

"And I shall tell him that you didn't want to come anyway! You are looking for an excuse, my lord, and it shall not be me!"

"Oh, but it is, and you know it!"

She favored him with a fiery glare.

Harry finished his brandy and stood. "I shall call for you tomorrow morning."

"I'll not be ready!" She sprang to her feet. "I won't go!"

"Then I suppose I must dress you myself and drag you out of here," he said smoothly.

"You wouldn't dare!"

"No?" Grinning mischievously, he took her hand and brought it to his lips. "Until tomorrow, Miss Trevayne."

"Lord Singleton," she said pleadingly, "who knows what accident might occur? Surely you must not insist! Not after all that has gone before!"

"Perhaps it will be interesting." Wondering why he had gotten himself into this situation, Harry took his leave of Bridgeford Grange. He had come only to apologize; now he involved himself in an outing in which he would very likely become the victim of some unknown disaster. Ellen Trevayne had completely scrambled his better judgment.

4

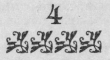

Although Ellen wondered if the marquess would indeed make good his ultimatum of escorting her to church, she dressed and readied herself just in case he did. Clad in a pink silk dress and matching hat, she descended the stairs and entered the drawing room to wait. Seating herself by the window, she watched the gravel lane, hoping that the approach to Bridgeford Grange would remain empty.

If he did appear, she knew she should be ecstatic. Any other young lady in the county would give her eyeteeth for an invitation from Lord Singleton. Even if he were not so handsome, he need only crook his finger, particularly the one which bore his signet ring, to bring them flocking to him. Ellen wished she could be happy like the others would be if he showed an interest in them. Instead she was painfully nervous.

The marquess must have had an ulterior motive in mind when he requested her company. She had thought long and hard about it the night before and decided that he must desire to be seen with her in public to prove that apologies had been made and that no hard feelings existed between them. It wouldn't do for neighbors to feud, nor would it be comfortable for Allesandra and Brandon if their friends detested each other.

A sleek black carriage, trimmed in red and pulled by a fine team of blacks, came trotting smartly into view. Ellen's heart leaped to her mouth as she saw the crest on the door. So he had come. Standing, she began to pace the floor, valiantly trying to control her overwrought nerves. What would happen now? Somehow she must contrive to avoid an incident.

Gore opened the door to the drawing room, the marquess hard on his heel. "Lord Singleton," he announced gravely.

His lordship swept her a beautiful bow. "You are ready, Miss Trevayne?"

"Y-yes," she stammered.

"Then shall we?" He offered his arm.

"My lord, are you sure you wish to go through with this?" Ellen asked quickly.

He nodded pleasantly. "I'd prefer to be escorting you somewhere else, but church it shall be!"

She drew back. "This is not a good idea."

He followed her and tucked her arm into his elbow. "Shall I drag you then?" he said softly, as if he intended to follow through on his threat.

"No, my lord." Ellen lifted her chin. "But I warn you, whatever happens will be on your head."

"I'm sure it will," he replied teasingly and led her from the house, handing her into his carriage.

She centered herself on the luxurious seat, hoping that he would sit across from her. The marquess entered and, without a comment, sat down beside her, wedging himself between Ellen and the side of the vehicle. Her cheeks warmed as she felt the hard lines of his body against hers. She moved over.

He laughed lightly. "Perhaps I should have sat opposite you, Miss Trevayne. I could have enjoyed your beauty much more easily."

Ellen's cheeks grew warmer still. "Please, sir, the situation is impossible enough without your jesting."

Turning towards her, he studied her intently. "I am not jesting."

Dismayed, she looked into his gray eyes, realizing that she was fast falling victim to Lord Harry Singleton's famous charm. She hated him for it. He was making a fool of her and she was allowing him to do so.

"Has no one ever told you how beautiful your eyes are?"

She wrenched her gaze away. "Stop it! I shall not listen to this false flattery. My lord, if you wish to continue this charade, you will confine yourself to proper topics, such as the weather or the scenery."

"Very well." He sighed, leaning back against the squabs. "It is a nice morning, is it not?"

"Yes, it is very decent."

"Do you think it will rain?"

"No, my lord."

"I am not so sure. There is a very small dark cloud over there that may cause some problems. I hope it doesn't ruin our picnic."

"Our what!" Ellen cried.

"Our picnic. My cook has prepared a hamper of the most delicious food. We'll picnic on the way home."

"Oh, no, we shall not! It isn't proper!"

"Whyever not?"

"We have no chaperone!"

"Nor have we one now," he pointed out. "I didn't think it was a matter of concern for such an independent young lady as yourself."

"This is different."

"Ellen Trevayne, we are neighbors and I hope that we will become friends as well. We started off on the wrong foot and I am trying to make amends. Won't you meet me halfway?''

She felt ashamed of herself. He was going out of his way to be nice to her and she was not making it easy for him. There were other young women, such as the very feminine Patsy Adams, whose company he would prefer. Yet he had chosen to take her to church and to arrange a picnic to forge neighborly bonds.

''Very well,'' she said as they stopped in front of the ivy-hung brick church.

''Good.'' He stepped from the carriage and helped her down.

Ellen slipped her arm through his and started forward. ''Are you sure you wish to go through with this?'' she asked him again.

''Why should I deny myself the company of a lovely young woman?''

''You may live to regret it,'' she threatened, laughing.

''Just so long as I do live, Miss Trevayne.'' He grinned down at her and opened the door.

They entered the cool, slightly musty interior. Most of the worshippers were in their usual seats by now and the organ was playing. Ellen quietly led the marquess to her pew, made her genuflection, and slipped into the velvet-cushioned seat. Setting aside her reticule, she dropped to the kneeling bench.

Prayers refused to come. She was too conscious of the dark, handsome man beside her and of the unintelligible whispers that reached her ears. When the marquess sat back in the seat, she joined him.

From across the church she caught Allesandra's surprised expression and Brandon's irreverent grin. Other parishioners were not so pleased. Patsy Adams looked sullen and her mother's face was absolutely thunderous. Ellen wondered if Lord Singleton had noticed and decided that he probably had. He seemed to be a man who missed nothing.

It was hard to concentrate on the beautiful Anglican ritual. She stood, knelt, and sat when she should, hoping that nothing terrible would happen, and, in the end, nothing did. The service concluded, the marquess escorted her up the aisle, his eyes on no other lady but her. It was flattering and it gave her a very unchristian feeling of satisfaction to be stealing a march on her prime antagonists.

The Reverend Smythe stood on the porch shaking hands with his flock. "Lord Singleton, I am so glad that you have joined us this morning. And Ellen." He beamed at her. "Won't you join Mrs. Smythe and me for a cup of tea in the vicarage?"

"I am sorry," Lord Singleton drawled politely, "but we have a pressing engagement elsewhere. Another time, perhaps?"

"Anytime, my lord!"

Nodding pleasantly to those around, the marquess drew her down the stairs to where the Duke and Duchess of Rackthall were awaiting them.

"Well, Harry," Brandon teased, "I didn't know you were a churchgoer."

"I didn't know you were either."

The duke raised an eyebrow and glanced at his wife. "Things change."

Allesandra drew Ellen aside. "What is happening?"

"He came to apologize," she whispered, "and here we are. I shall tell you the full story another time, but don't get the wrong impression. He is merely trying to be a good neighbor."

"Are you sure?"

"I'm positive."

"Join me for tea tomorrow."

Brandon caught her words. "I have just invited Harry as well, love."

"I am truly sorry," Ellen said firmly. "I will be very busy tomorrow. I cannot possibly attend."

The marquess looked at her quizzically. She was afraid that he would begin a discussion on the subject, but he let her statement go unchallenged. "I shall be happy to accept," he said.

Ellen felt a slight disappointment. Secretly, she supposed, she had wished him to desire her company, but it was too much to be hoped for. He was too far above her in sophistication, polish, and, most of all, rank. Yet if all went well, perhaps he could become her friend.

Harry's footman spread a large run on a grassy rise under a large oak and set down the hamper, returning to the carriage to have his own box lunch with the coachman. Ellen sat down, carefully arranging her skirts to hide her slender ankles. The marquess knelt across from her, setting out the contents of the wicker basket.

His cook had indeed prepared a sumptuous repast. There were two whole roast chickens, potato salad, stuffed eggs, muffins, fresh fruit, and a large lemon cake. All of this was to be washed down with two chilled bottles of champagne.

Ellen surveyed the feast eagerly. She hadn't had much appetite for breakfast and now that the day was going so well, she found that her stomach was growling in protest. "It all looks so good, but I mustn't drink much of that champagne," she said smiling. "Drinking spirits is definitely not a good idea for someone like me!"

She felt better about her propensity for mishap since she had joked about it on the church steps. Laughing about it somehow made it easier. It even made her less nervous in his presence. She filled her plate with the delicious food, but when he handed her a crystal glass of champagne, she set it far to the side. "I shan't take a chance on spilling that."

Harry grinned, noticing her stiffness disappear. "It should be reasonably safe over there."

"Don't count on it, my lord."

"Nothing is going to happen," he said with confidence. "Our previous difficulties were simply a matter of chance."

"I wish I could say that, but it is not the case." She sighed. "Those things happen to me all the time. Lately it has been worse. I fear I am prone to accidents."

"Why?"

"If I knew that, I would do something about it!" She shook her head and nibbled on a chicken wing. "My life would have been a great deal different if I hadn't been so tall, so gawky, and so clumsy!"

"Aren't you being a little hard on yourself?" he asked quietly.

"Wouldn't you be?"

"I suppose so. At Eton I shot up taller than the other boys my age and it made me awkward. They made fun of me, of course, and that made it worse."

"But you grew out of it, and you are not unusually tall. You are not so much taller than Brandon. In a man it is attractive; in a woman," she said soberly, "it's a death knell."

"Oh, come now. It can't be that bad."

Ellen ate for a few moments in silence, then took a sip of her champagne. "Tell me, my lord, would you ask a woman to dance with you if she towered above you?"

He smiled. "I have never been faced with that decision."

"But if you were?"

He nodded. "You have made your point. But Miss Trevayne, there are a great many men who are as tall or taller than you."

"Then we must acknowledge my awkwardness and my propensity for disaster!"

"Which probably come about from your being self-conscious."

"Perhaps."

The subject was continuing on too long and it was too personal. Ellen couldn't believe how she could tell him things that she had related to only a very few people in her entire life. Lord Singleton was easy to talk to. This was like what she'd always imagined if she'd had an older brother. Almost regretfully, she changed the subject.

"Lord Singleton, do you have a sister?"

"No, nor a brother."

"I always wished for brothers and sisters."

'I don't think I particularly cared." He grinned. "I enjoyed being spoiled."

Ellen laughed. "I suppose I must admit to that too. Who is your heir?"

"A cousin." A look of distaste crossed his handsome features. "A young profligate wastrel. If rumor names me a rake, a word has not been invented which can describe him. He shocks even me!"

"You? A rake? I do not believe it! No more than I believed it about Brandon."

He smiled at her naiveté, thinking of his chain of mistresses, the countless card games, wagers, and late nights.

"Still," she said candidly, "you must take measures to ensure that your cousin does not inherit."

"I assure you, Miss Trevayne," the marquess replied with mock seriousness, "the matter has been on my mind of late."

With horror Ellen suddenly realized that she had, in so many words, told him to get married and have children. Her cheeks flamed with color. "Oh, dear. You must tell me to mind my own affairs! You see?

I cannot go along for half an hour without saying or doing something dreadful!''

"Some would call it honesty. I find your frankness quite refreshing.''

"You are too kind.'' Avoiding further conversation she finished her meal, drawing out the time it took to consume the last bit of cake.

The marquess refilled her glass. "If you change your mind about going to Woodburn tomorrow, I shall be happy to accompany you.''

"Thank you, but I am truly busy. I must supervise the kitchen work tomorrow.''

"Nevertheless, if you find yourself able to go, just send a note round.''

"Very well,'' she said somewhat stiffly.

"Miss Trevayne,'' Lord Singleton stretched out on the rug, crossing his long legs and gazing up into the sky. "You have become tense again because you feel you have made a faux pas. It is not worth it.''

She twisted her serviette in her hands. "I wish us to be friends. I like to be in harmony with my neighbors.''

"Friends are honest with each other, are they not?''

"Yes, my lord.''

"Well then. You were right in what you said, and there's an end to it! Agreed?''

"Agreed.'' She began to tidy up the leftovers. "My lord?''

"Yes?''

"We are friends, aren't we?''

"I feel as though we are.''

"I have never had a man for a friend. With the exception of Brandon, of course, and Allesandra is really my friend there. I've never been able to talk with a man as I have with you. It is very pleasant.''

He turned on his side and leaned on his elbow. "I'm glad.''

"It is like having a brother. You don't mind, do you?"

"No, of course not," he said with some surprise.

"Good! Now, I really think we should be going. We mustn't be gone long enough to cause comment."

"As you wish." He got up and reached for her hands, lifting her to her feet.

"I'm glad you insisted on this outing." Ellen smiled into his dark eyes.

"Would you like to do it again?"

"Oh, yes!" she said breathlessly. The enthusiastic words slipped out before she even thought about it. Her cheeks colored. Had it sounded as though she were fishing for an invitation? No, it couldn't. After all, she had turned him down on the visit to Woodburn. She almost wished that she hadn't, but it really was for the best. Becoming too close to Lord Singleton would be a greater disaster than anything she could imagine.

She was silent on the return drive to Bridgeford and he did not prod her to converse. As they drew up in front of the house, he repeated the invitation for the following day. She couldn't help wavering for a moment before she turned him down once more, agreeing to send him a note if she changed her mind.

"Very well." He stepped down and reached up to assist her.

As they strolled towards the door, Ellen caught a movement from the corner of her eye. Glancing at the park she saw Taffy and Friendly romping in the pond, having evidently escaped the kennel. At that same instant the burly Saint Bernards spotted their mistress. With expressions of pure delight they galloped towards her.

"Oh, no!" Ellen shrieked. "My lord, get back into the carriage!"

"What?" He turned quizzically.

"Hurry!" She gave him a push.

It was too late. The animals were upon them, leaping and wagging their tails, sending sprays of muddy water in all directions. Friendly stood on his hind legs and planted his huge paws on the marquess' chest. Caught off balance, Harry stumbled backwards and fell onto his posterior. Taffy licked his face.

Ellen, joined by servants, managed to drag the dogs away. She stood over him, wringing her hands. "Oh my! Are you all right, my lord?" she asked tremulously.

Harry took a deep breath and got up without a word.

"I am so sorry." She retrieved his hat and looked at it unhappily. It was damaged beyond repair and there was a great paw print right in the middle.

He jerked it from her hands and sailed it towards his coach. "Miss Trevayne, have you ever heard of Weston?"

"Y-yes."

"Are you, by chance, an investor in that concern?"

"I don't think so." She recognized his drift. "Oh."

"You should check into it. I am certain that your returns would be astonishing. Good day." He lifted his hand to touch the brim of a nonexistent hat, turned it into a salute, and stalked towards his carriage.

"Good day, my lord." She stood forlornly and watched him drive away. The beautiful day had been ruined. Now she would absolutely never see him again. Lifting her mud-splattered skirts, she ran weeping to the house.

When he received no note from Ellen Trevayne agreeing to accompany him, Harry set out alone for

Woodburn Hall. He wasn't surprised. After the incident with the dogs, she was probably perfectly mortified.

Up until he made the acquaintance of Taffy and Friendly, he had to admit that he'd enjoyed himself the day before. Miss Trevayne had relaxed in his company and had proved an interesting companion. He doubted that she had ever talked about her problems with more than a few very close friends. For the greater part of the picnic that was how she had treated him. Like a brother, she had said.

Harry laughed to himself. He had never had a woman wish that he was her brother, and yet that thought seemed to give Miss Trevayne the most pleasure. She was a very unusual young lady. In retrospect, even the canine episode didn't seem so bad. It truly wasn't her fault and she *had* tried to warn him. He just hadn't reacted in time. Poor Miss Trevayne. Trouble did seem to follow her.

He supposed that she had suffered greatly at the hands of both men and women. No female as tall as she could escape ridicule by those who enjoyed that type of sport. That most certainly would have contributed to her awkwardness. He remembered Patsy Adams giggling at Ellen. That type of thing had probably happened to her many times.

Women could be very cruel to each other. He had seen it so many times in London. Cutting remarks, set-downs, the deliberate spread of scandal were a major part of social intercourse among many of the ladies and, to be honest, among some of the gentlemen as well. Men, however, had a more direct recourse on the field of honor. Harry wished society had permitted Miss Trevayne to box Patsy Adams' ears.

If she had done that, though, she could have boxed his as well. He deserved it more than Miss Adams. Since he had grown to know Miss Trevayne better, he was even more ashamed of his behavior, both yesterday and before. After the dog incident he should have laughed and made light of the misfortune. Well, he would make atonement for all the ill will he had exhibited.

There would be social affairs during his visit to the neighborhood. At them, he would show Miss Trevayne his particular attention. The notice of the Marquess of Singleton, one of the most sought-after prizes on the Marriage Mart, would give her great cachet among the locals. Since she considered him to be like a brother, it would be all the easier because she wouldn't fall in love with him. And to put the icing on the cake, he would never ask Miss Patsy Adams for a dance unless it was an absolute social necessity. That unparalleled set-down might do that young lady some good.

Feeling pleased with his plan, Harry urged his stallion into a gallop and covered the distance to Woodburn Hall in record time. Arriving early, he found the duke and duchess in the library with their new son.

"Oh, Harry, I'm so glad you're here!" Allesandra exclaimed. "You've not seen Brannie awake."

The marquess glanced at the baby's big, wide-open blue eyes. "He's very pretty, my dear."

"Would you like to hold him?"

"No, thank you."

"Come, Harry, don't be shy!" The duchess smiled. "He won't break, you know."

"I'd rather not." He sat down and accepted a glass of brandy from the duke.

"He really doesn't do much yet," Brandon said. "Eats, sleeps, cries, wets himself."

"He smiles!" Allesandra gave the baby a little shake and the plump cheeks spread wide into a toothless grin. "Look at his dimples."

"Yes, darling, I'm sure he leads a very fulfilling life."

"You're making fun of us," she said hotly. "You know you like to hold him and make him laugh. Don't let him tell you otherwise, Harry!"

His lordship couldn't keep from chuckling. Try as he might he couldn't picture his friend holding a baby and enjoying it. Bran couldn't possibly have changed that much.

"You see? He doesn't believe it." She deposited young Brandon in his father's lap and moved to the desk to pour herself a drink of ratafia.

The baby began to cry. "Hush now. You're making your mother a liar." With a practiced gesture, Brandon smoothly moved his son to his shoulder to comfort him.

My God, Harry thought, astonished, *is that the way it's going to be? Is that what marriage does to a man?*

The duke caught his expression. "Just wait, old boy," he said, grinning.

"I shall," Harry replied emphatically. But, in all honestly, he couldn't wait much longer. His Grace was lucky to have a wife like Allesandra. If Harry was going to have to live like this, he would have to choose someone very special.

"I was surprised to see you with Ellen yesterday," Allesandra remarked coyly.

"It was the least I could do to make amends. She is my neighbor here."

"Ellen is a lovely person," the duchess continued.

"Yes, she is," Brandon interrupted, rising to return little Brannie to his mother. "Now if you would excuse us, my dear, I would like to show off my stables. Bring your glass, Harry."

His wife was not about to let them escape so easily. "Ellen will be going up to London with us this fall. Of course she will be staying with her grandfather, but I'm sure we shall frequently enjoy her company. May we depend upon your kindness to her, Harry?''

Harry nodded. Unless he mistook his judgment, the duchess was intent on making a match for her friend, and he was the quarry. Well, that would not happen. He led too ordered a life to have room for a scattershambles of a wife. Besides, Miss Trevayne looked upon him as the brother she had never had.

''Come along, Harry,'' the duke urged.

The marquess was all too willing to follow. Standing, he bowed to Allesandra. ''Thank you for inviting me.''

She inclined her head. ''Come anytime. You are always welcome.''

He followed Brandon from the room and told him, ''You both must come for supper at Shadybrook.''

''I'd like that. I've never seen the estate.'' The duke paused. ''Harry, you mustn't let Allesandra talk you into anything you'd rather not do. She's very good at it.''

''I won't.'' He grinned, realizing that Bran's thoughts echoed his own.

''I'm going to speak with her about it.''

''Truly, it isn't necessary.''

They walked down the hall and towards the side door. ''I like Ellen very much,'' Brandon went on, ''but she isn't your type.''

''Who is? I'm beginning to wonder that myself.''

''Someone cool and sophisticated and able to handle herself at all times.''

''That person sounds like a dead bore.''

Bran shrugged. ''You asked what I thought. You've always struck me as the type of man who wants perfection.''

''I don't know about that,'' Harry protested.

''You're fastidious.''

''I am?'' he said incredulously, remembering a few

escapades he and the duke had shared that had been anything but fastidious.

"Even your ladybirds have been the perfect mistresses. You are a perfectionist at managing your estates. You play cards perfectly. Even when you become foxed, you do it perfectly!" Brandon chuckled.

"Now *I* sound like a dead bore."

"Never, Harry. You've always had style! Damme, let's leave this subject. You know what you want, if and when you decide to marry, and I hope you find it. I'm having a smashing good time with Allesandra!"

"You're very lucky."

"Yes, I am." Brandon turned the topic to horses, stabling, and pasturage, and began showing Harry the additions and improvements he had made to Woodburn's facilities.

5

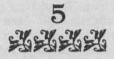

When Harry left Woodburn, he was ill at ease. Bran had changed so much that he sometimes seemed beyond all recognition. Marriage to Allesandra had settled him thoroughly.

The duke had never enjoyed rusticating in the country, preferring the sparkle of London and Brighton. When he did ruralize, it was to attend the marvelous entertainments given by the sporting members of the *ton* who filled each hour with a full spectrum of activities and diversions. Now he seemed as contented as a country gentleman, overseeing his lands and livestock with interest and concern. He could discuss plows, crops, and tillage like an expert, and he seemed in no hurry to return to London.

But what amazed Harry the most was the man's behavior with his small son. The duke handled the child with such confidence and he obviously enjoyed doing it. That certainly wasn't like the friend he remembered.

Harry didn't like babies. They were messy, loud, and sometimes smelly. When he had children of his own he would keep them at arm's length until they were old enough to behave like proper human beings. *If* he had children.

He sighed. There it was again, hitting him in the face and nagging at his conscience. He had to find a wife.

Harry wondered if any of his bachelor friends were wrestling with the same thoughts. The subject had never been broached among them. He was slightly older than they were, so it was possible that it hadn't occurred to them yet. They'd all been shocked by Bran's marriage for he and Harry had been the greatest rakes of the group. Perhaps they gave little thought to seeing themselves in the same situation.

It was not so with him. Bran's example, together with Markley's depravity, had convinced him to take action. He would marry someone before the Season was over. He had to. It was his responsibility. How many times had he been been over it all in his mind?

There seemed to be two types of marriage among the *ton*. By far the most common was the marriage of convenience, a most businesslike affair. In one form it existed between persons of equal social standing and was enacted for the sole purpose of getting heirs and bowing to a society that dictated that no man or woman remain single. In its other guise the participants were not particularly equal in status, but one sought to repair a fortune or settle large debts at the expense of the other.

Frequently in the arranged marriage the principals became estranged or merely tolerant, each going in his or her own direction. The husbands found their way into other women's beds while the wives entertained other men in theirs. Harry didn't think he'd like his wife sharing her favors with others. He'd laughed too often at cuckholded husbands.

There was always the possibility, though, that husband and wife in a marriage of convenience would grow fond of each other and maybe even fall in love. Then it would become the other kind of marriage, the marriage of love.

Brandon and Allesandra had that type of marriage. Anyone could see that they were entranced with each other. Nothing short of a deep love could have changed the duke so completely. Harry had fancied himself in love, particularly during his youth, but he'd never experienced that sort of overwhelming passion. As a man of the world, he'd laughed about it. It was the stuff of foolish novels that women read. Now he had seen that it did exist, but he imagined that it happened to only a few.

No, his must most likely be a marriage of convenience, hopefully with a lady he could be fond of and who could be fond of him. Again he mentally reviewed his requirements. She must be well-born, amiable, virtuous, interesting, and beautiful. Was it asking too much? Perhaps he could settle for slightly less.

Ellen looked over the rows of bottled peaches and felt the pleasure of accomplishment. It had been hard work for everyone involved, including herself, and had consumed a full day and a half, but the effort had been well worth it. Bridgeford's larders were more than satisfactorily stocked, even considering the sizable offering she had set aside for Reverend and Mrs. Smythe.

Stretching, she massaged the tired muscles in the small of her back. It wasn't necessary or even proper for a woman of her fortune to engage in kitchen work, but she enjoyed it nonetheless. It was her hobby. Living alone as she did, her servants were friends as well as employees. Many of them had known her from her birth; others had been her playmates as a child. They looked out for her, as she did for them, and if she liked the camaraderie of the kitchen, who was there to find fault? It did ease the loneliness.

It was Gore, the butler, who found her daydreaming in the cellar. "Miss Ellen, my Lord Singleton has come to call."

"Oh, dear!" Ellen wiped her hands on her soiled apron and looked down at her sweaty, stained attire. "It is impossible! Please make my apologies."

"Miss Ellen!" her housekeeper protested, overhearing and darting into the room. "His lordship is such a nice young man! You can freshen up in a jiffy! We've still hot water from the bottling."

"I fear it would take longer than he would desire to wait. No, I shall not see him."

"You must make an effort. Get along now! Mr. Gore can inform my lord that it will take you a while to freshen yourself. Serve him tea or a glass of brandy, Mr. Gore, and whatever refreshment will occupy him." She pushed Ellen from the room. "Make haste! We can't let him get away."

"Mrs. Everett!" Ellen cried, accustomed to her motherly interference, but shocked at this revelation. "Don't expect to find me set in that direction! He is much too fine for me!"

"He is not," the housekeeper firmly declared, prodding Ellen towards the back stairs. "And he is attracted to you."

"Not after what has happened in the past!"

"Nonsense! That was not your fault. I'm sure that the marquess realizes that."

"He has probably come to present his accounts."

"Nevertheless, Miss Ellen, you shall not shirk your duties as a hostess. You should have been dressed nicely to begin with. It isn't proper for you to engage in servants' work."

"Oh, very well!" she answered impatiently. "But if he chooses not to wait I shall not be surprised!"

She stumbled hurriedly up the stairs and flew down the hall to her room with Mrs. Everett hard on her heels.

Within forty-five minutes Ellen was bathed and

her hair washed, fanned to a semidryness, and twisted into a soft knot. Clad in a becoming yellow gown she descended the stairs and entered the drawing room. She smiled at Lord Singleton who was gazing out the window and thoughtfully sipping his brandy. "I am so sorry I kept you waiting, my lord," she said. "I hope my butler explained that I was not prepared for visitors."

He turned to her. "Yes, he did. I didn't mind the wait."

"I'm glad." Walking to the sideboard she poured herself a small glass of ratafia. "I see that you have been served."

"Yes. Your butler has taken good care of me."

She sat down, worriedly tongue-tied and devoid of pleasant conversation, waiting for the worst.

"How was your busy day yesterday?" he asked. "Were you successful in your endeavors?"

"Yes, we were. We bottled ever so many peaches. In fact, we just finished them today."

"I hope I didn't interrupt."

"Not at all. I was just setting aside some jars to give to the vicar."

"Shall I assist you in delivering them?"

She gazed at him, noticing as usual how handsome he was. Today he seemed exceptionally fine in his dark-blue coat and white silk breeches, and Ellen was woman enough to derive a certain pleasure from being seen in his company. Patsy Adams and her friend Martha Darvey would be consumed with jealousy at the attention the marquess was showing her. She wanted to go, but could she take the risk?

"It usually does not take a lady so long to accept my invitation," he drawled.

His self-confidence irritated her. "Are you so certain I will accept it?" she asked tartly.

He laughed. "No indeed! You are unlike any lady I have ever met!"

"Now you are mocking me."

"No, I am not. I was making a simple statement. Please, Miss Trevayne, don't fly up into the boughs!"

Ellen glanced at him through lowered lashes. "Very well, my lord. I shall accept your kind offer of assistance."

"Good! My curricle is outside. Have you any objections to riding in it?"

"Your curricle? Oh, what fun!" she cried. "I've never ridden in a curricle! Just wait until I fetch my hat!"

A footman was settling a large basketful of the bottled peaches into the curricle when Ellen dashed onto the front portico. Gallantly the marquess handed her into the stylish conveyance.

"This is wonderful, my lord." Her eyes danced with anticipation as he climbed in and sat down beside her, taking up the reins of the restive horses. There was less space in this vehicle than in his roomy carriage. She became acutely conscious of his hard-muscled leg pressed against hers. "My lord, do you think this is proper? We have no chaperone."

"Is it necessary? In the country, on an afternoon?"

"I . . . I don't know. It probably is."

"If you wish, one of your servants could sit on the perch behind."

She shook her head, taking a deep breath. "It wouldn't be so much fun, would it?"

"No," he replied solemnly.

"Then let us be daring!"

"At your service, ma'am." He sent the team leaping forward.

Jerked off balance Ellen clung to his arm with one hand and to her hat with the other and continued to do so as they swept down the driveway.

"I'm sorry, Miss Trevayne. Did I spring them out too fast?"

"Oh, no! It's very exciting," she answered breathlessly. She looked at him with confusion, suddenly realizing that it was the marquess himself and not the speed that was the most thrilling of all.

His gray eyes briefly met hers and he flashed her a crooked grin. "I'm glad you are enjoying it."

It was an understatement. She was enjoying it far too much for her own good. Reluctantly she relinquished his arm.

"Ellen?"

She started at his use of her first name. "That, my lord," she said primly, "is definitely not proper."

He slowed the horses. "I'm sorry, it just slipped out. From listening to Allesandra speak of you, I suppose. Actually, though, I find it most difficult, if we are to be friends, to continue calling you 'Miss Trevayne.' It is so very stiff and formal. And, please, can't you call me Harry?"

"I could not, my lord," she said, aghast. "What would people think? They would most certainly get the wrong impression."

He shrugged. "We could do it only in private."

"But we scarcely know each other," she said doubtfully. "I, too, tire of formality, but you must admit that there is a place for it."

"Yes, in the halls of society! Cannot neighbors in the country be less formal?"

She sighed. "Very well, my lord . . . Harry. It shall be as you wish," she murmured doubtfully.

"Thank you, Ellen."

They finished the drive to the village in silence, presented the peaches to Reverend and Mrs. Smythe, took tea with them, and began the journey home.

"I have been receiving a great many invitations,"

the marquess told her. "I came to visit today because I need your advice on which to accept."

"I could not presume!"

"Of course you could. Tell me, is there usually this much social activity in the neighborhood?"

"No, it is because of you. All of them wish you to meet their daughters," Ellen blurted. "You are considered a great catch. *I* think it is . . ." She stopped, cheeks flooding with color. "Oh, dear, I shouldn't have said that!"

"Don't apologize! Your candor is delightful. Tell me, what do you think of it?"

"I find it disgusting."

"What? That someone should want to marry me?"

"Oh, no! Anyone would want . . . It's just the way you are looked upon like a prize bull. You are a man, Harry, not an . . . an animal. But then, perhaps you enjoy them fawning over you," she said stiffly.

"I hadn't really thought about it. I suppose it is a compliment."

"I don't think so! They see you only as a wealthy, handsome marquess, not as who you are inside."

"Ellen," he said softly, "my being a marquess has a great deal to do with who I am inside."

"Of course," she acknowledged awkwardly. "I could know nothing of it! Please let us change the subject."

"All right." He nodded agreeably. "Shall we talk of my invitations then? The squire's gathering is next Saturday. I suppose I must attend that. Will you be going?"

"I . . . I haven't decided."

"I would like to escort you there. Will you agree to that?"

"Oh, Harry, I don't know if I want to go. Something dreadful will be bound to happen."

"I would very much like to take you." They had

reached the lane to Bridgeford. Harry turned down it, bringing the horses to a walk. "I enjoy your company, Ellen."

She thought of how perfectly livid Patsy and Mrs. Adams would be if she arrived at their door in the marquess' carriage. They probably hadn't even wanted to invite her, but had done so due to social pressures. They had always taken every opportunity to be cruel to her. Ellen wasn't a vengeful person, but in their case a good set-down would be a pleasure. They deserved every bit of it and more.

"I'll go with you," she declared, "but do not say that you weren't warned!"

Ellen stared at Briarwood Hall with misgiving. She and the marquess had had an unusually quiet drive, making her wonder if he regretted her presence. If he did, she could completely understand, and she wished she could convince him of that. He was too kind a man to suffer such indignities at her hands. And Mrs. Everett was wrong. No man could be attracted to Miss Ellen Trevayne and her myriad of disasters, least of all this handsome, stylish peer. Lord Singleton merely felt sorry for her and was trying to be a good neighbor.

The coachman halted in front of the residence as a footman hastened to open the door. The marquess caught her hand, squeezing it gently and bringing it to his lips. "Good luck, my dear."

A little tremor of delight coursed through her veins. At least for tonight he was her escort, even though propriety would allow him only two dances with her. Every unmarried girl in the neighborhood would be green with envy. Taking his arm, she walked up the steps and into the squire's brightly lit mansion.

It seemed as though all eyes immediately turned on her, some with curiosity, others with pure dislike. Smiling, Ellen proceeded through the receiving line, greeting the florid-faced squire and his haughty wife. Patsy barely acknowledged her, turning instead to the marquess and speaking so softly that he had to lower his dark head very close to her to hear what she was saying. *A trick,* Ellen thought irritably. *Why doesn't he see through it?* She made her way to where Brandon and Allesandra were standing with a group of friends.

Allesandra drew her aside. "I'm very surprised to see you with Harry."

"He was kind in asking me, wasn't he?"

"Yes, but . . . unchaperoned?"

"Dear friend, I am twenty-three years old," Ellen said with a small shrug. "And two servants were present, just as when we came to church."

"That was different, and it was not at night. I have always applauded your independence, but do take care! Harry is . . . very experienced."

"I shall not fall victim to his charms!" Ellen hugged her friend. "Please do not be concerned. He feels sorry for me and is only trying to be a good neighbor."

"I am concerned, Ellen, for your reputation."

"Fiddlesticks!"

"Nevertheless I shall tell Brandon to warn Harry to mind his manners!"

Ellen laughed. "As if he would find any reason to forget them with me! Look at him, Allesandra. He has forgotten me entirely." She nodded towards the marquess, standing completely surrounded by a bevy of females. "You have no cause to worry. We are friends and neighbors and nothing more!"

It was evidently true. When the first dance was called, Brandon claimed his duchess, Harry led out a smug Patsy Adams, and Ellen was left alone on the sidelines with the older married ladies and the dowagers. Every other young unattached girl had a partner.

It was the same on the second dance and the one after that. Ellen knew that it was just as well that she lacked for partners. She considered herself a terrible dancer and had no desire to mortify herself and provide humor for others by attempting it.

On the fourth dance, Brandon forced her to stand up with him. Never before had she danced with the duke and she was surprised to find that she had some measure of success. He must have been such a good dancer that he was easy to follow. More importantly, he didn't make her nervous. She didn't enjoy it, but at least she escaped making a fool of herself.

When the orchestra began a waltz, she found the marquess at her side. "I have been waiting for this, Miss Trevayne."

"I have never waltzed," she protested. "In fact, I dance terribly."

He held out his hand. "I shall show you. It isn't hard at all."

She stood, feeling her cheeks growing very warm. "If you are sure . . ."

"I am." He led her to the floor.

Ellen put one hand on his shoulder and let him clasp her other in his. His arm slid firmly around her waist. "I'm sure there are others who do this better, my lord."

"Perhaps," he said carelessly. "Now all you need to do is relax and follow me." Gracefully he swung her into the movement. "This is nice."

"You think so?"

"You are tall enough that I can look at you and talk with you without contortions."

"Yes, that is true."

"And you waltz delightfully."

"It is because you are such a good dancer," Ellen

replied. "You make me feel as though I had nothing beneath my feet."

"That is how a waltz is supposed to be." He drew her a little closer.

Ellen's senses reeled. His nearness was overwhelming and his touch, almost an embrace, was sending strange shivers through her body. She looked into his handsome gray eyes. "Harry?" she whispered breathlessly.

"Is something wrong?" His pleased expression turned to one of concern.

"No. I . . . I just felt faint for a moment."

"It *is* rather warm in here. Or perhaps you are hungry? It won't be long until the supper dance, which you must save for me, of course."

"Y-yes."

"Are you sure you are all right? Should you sit down?"

"Oh, no! I like to waltz. I'm fine. Truly I am."

The rest of the evening passed in a rainbow-colored glow and soon she found herself sitting beside him as the carriage moved slowly through the darkness, its outside lamps casting a dim, shadowy light into the interior.

"I would have liked to dance the last dance with you," Harry said, "but Allesandra wouldn't hear of it."

"She is right."

"I suppose so, but it isn't fair. You are a most delightful partner."

"Thank you." She swallowed against her continuing breathlessness.

He turned to her. "Ellen, what is the matter? You have been acting strangely. Did something happen tonight?"

"No, no, nothing happened. I . . . I suppose I am overly tired."

"Would you like to rest your head on my shoulder?"

"No!" she cried.

"Good God, I wasn't suggesting . . ."

"I know. Please, Harry, I'm really all right." But something indeed had happened and, because of it, she really wasn't all right at all. Ellen Trevayne had fallen head over heels in love with Harry Singleton. She knew it was hopeless, and she knew she had to do something about it or the rest of her life would be miserable. She remembered what he had said about how important being a marquess was to him and his way of life. Such a nobleman could never love the granddaughter of a businessman, or a clumsy overgrown girl with a pair of bumblesome Saint Bernards. He was far beyond her in position and in sophistication. If she had been younger and prettier and, dear God, graceful, a future with him might have been possible. As it was, nothing could come of her feelings.

Harry tucked her arm into the crook of his elbow. "They are only people, Ellen," he said encouragingly. "And you were enchanting this evening. There were no mishaps."

She forced a laugh. "I didn't step on your toes?"

"Not once!"

"Then I must consider the event to have been successful!" With relief she saw the lights of Bridgeford Grange. "Thank you for escorting me."

"It has been my pleasure."

As she took his hand and alighted from the carriage, she caught her heel on the step and tumbled into his arms. Involuntarily she clasped her hands around his neck.

Harry eased her to the ground, still holding her close against him. "Are you hurt?" he asked worriedly.

Her heart raced as she felt her breast touch his chest. Quickly she dropped her hands to her sides.

''I'm fine.'' She moved away from his embrace and tried to laugh lightly. ''No mishaps?''

He grinned. ''I rather liked that one.''

Ellen looked up at him, warmth flooding her cheeks.

Harry brought her slim hand to his lips, his eyes gazing thoughtfully into hers. ''May I say once more that the evening has been a pleasure?''

The touch of his lips on her hand brought a flush to Ellen's cheeks. Bobbing her head, she said, ''Thank you.'' Hurriedly she sought the refuge of her house.

6

E llen was on the front lawn of Bridgeford instructing her head gardener to thin an overgrowth of Michaelmas daisies when a large entourage passed through the gates, crossed the bridge, and proceeded towards the house. It was a procession such as she had never seen before at Bridgeford Grange, consisting as it did of so many conveyances and servants. There were two roomy traveling carriages, each bearing the crests of their noble owners, followed by two smaller coaches piled high with trunks and baggage. Bringing up the rear was a parade of fine horses led by grooms wearing varied livery. More than one grand household was apparently on the move and had, most likely, lost their way.

Wiping her hands on her apron, she removed it and tossed it onto a stone bench, walking briskly forward to greet the newcomers. There were only two households in the community who would attract such fine visitors, those of the Duke and Duchess of Rackthall and of Lord Singleton. She had heard neither mention a house party.

As she reached them, a handsome, chestnut-haired man stepped from the first carriage and sketched her a graceful bow. ''I do beg pardon, ma'am, I fear we have lost our way. I don't believe that this is the place we seek.''

Smiling, Ellen made a little curtsy. ''This is Bridgeford Grange, sir, and I am Miss Ellen Trevayne, its mistress.''

''Lord Brougham Abingdon.'' He bowed again. ''We were seeking Shadybrook Manor, the residence of the Marquess of Singleton.''

''Then you have just passed it. The Shadybrook land marches with mine. Returning, it will be the next gate on your left.''

''Brough!'' a petulant female voice called from within. ''Is it much further? Susannah and Pamela and I are exhausted!''

Ellen caught sight of the elaborately bonneted young ladies within. ''Perhaps the ladies would care for refreshment,'' she offered politely. ''It would be my pleasure.''

His eyes passed over her as if totaling up her physical attributes. ''Thank you for your invitation, but if Shadybrook is so close by, we could not presume upon your hospitality.''

Flushing slightly, she nodded. ''As you wish.''

''Since we are visiting in the neighborhood, perhaps we shall see you again. Good day, Miss Trevayne.'' He bowed one more and climbed back into the carriage. The coachmen turned the horses and soon the party was trotting down the drive.

Ellen stood and watched them until they had gone through the gate and turned down the road. So the marquess was entertaining guests. It seemed strange that he hadn't mentioned it, but then why should he tell her his every plan? She couldn't help feeling dismayed that there seemed to be so many women in the group. From the glimpse she had gotten, they were very fashionable. With sophisticated London ladies at his disposal, he wouldn't have time for her.

* * *

A short distance from Bridgeford, the elder of the three females in the first carriage demanded, "Who was that girl?"

"She said that her name was Miss Ellen Trevayne and that she was the mistress of that estate. Quite pretty, wasn't she?"

"*You* certainly seemed to think so! Really, Brough, didn't you notice that she was somewhat taller than you? Such a towering girl!" Marie Westhaven pushed back an errant lock of chestnut hair. "Rather old, too. Do you suppose that Harry knows her?"

Her brother chuckled. "I should think so! The two estates border upon each other."

"You found out a surprising amount of information for such a short conversation. No doubt she was wishing to impress you."

"Don't be catty, Marie. It doesn't become you," he said dryly.

"Well, she certainly is not in the first blush of youth like Susannah and Pamela. No doubt she is desperately hanging out for a husband. She must be well into her twenties! A girl like that can become quite wily in her efforts."

He laughed. "Are you seeking to advise me, madam? I assure you I have escaped more traps than you can imagine!"

She smoothed the green skirt of her elegant traveling ensemble. "You are vexatious, Brough. Of course I do not wish to see you wasted on a nobody! Actually I was thinking of Harry."

"He has avoided more ambushes than I have! He will probably escape this one of yours too, Marie." He glanced at the two young ladies, who dimpled prettily. "Why cast Susannah and Pamela at Harry when you have Christopher and Aubrey and me to choose from?"

Pamela giggled. "You are like family, Uncle Brough."

"You see?" Marie wailed. "You are completely out of the running, brother. Dear me, I think that Jonathan married me for the sole purpose of finding husbands for his sister and his niece! Not that it will be difficult, mind you. They are both exceptional young ladies! I am enjoying their company to the fullest."

"You have done well with them," he admitted.

"Why, Brough! A compliment from you? I never thought I'd see the day!" She looked out the window and a new worry assailed her. "Oh, dear, I do hope Harry is at home."

"If he isn't, it will serve you well, arriving unannounced as we have. Really, Marie, this isn't good *ton*."

"Fustian! He'll be glad to see us. He's probably growing bored."

"With that beauty next door?" he teased. "I think not. I don't like your scheme, Marie, and I fail to understand how I became involved in it, except that I mentioned dropping down to visit Bran."

"Which is exactly what you are going to do. Harry is your good friend and he will be happy to play host to us."

"It's taking advantage. Why can't you stay at Bran's? Harry would see the girls there."

"We are too large a party to impose on any one person," she said firmly, knowing that the duke's home could accommodate their number and many more. "Some of us will stay with Harry; others will go to Woodburn."

"Then by rights you and the girls should stay in a house with a hostess."

"Don't interfere. I know what I am doing!"

He frowned. "This is damned embarrassing and I'm sorry I ever let you talk me into it."

"Don't curse in front of the girls, Brough."

The caravan turned into the lane to Shadybrook Manor and wound its way to the house. From the library window where he had been tending to correspondence, Harry had seen them coming and had immediately recognized the carriages. His friends were coming unexpectedly to visit and, from the size of the entourage, they had brought along some extra guests. It didn't matter. Shadybrook was large enough to accommodate them all and, if he knew Brough, he'd be going on to Woodburn. He was more the duke's friend than he was his.

Harry went down the hall to greet them, pausing along the way to ask Mrs. Hopkins to begin preparing rooms. Stepping onto the portico, he was surprised to see Marie Westhaven, Brough's sister, alight. It was odd that she would be traveling with her brother.

"Harry!" Brough called as he handed two young ladies from the coach. "I hope we aren't imposing."

"Not at all! Marie." He kissed her slender hand. "Delightful as usual. And . . ." He glanced at the two girls.

"This is my husband's sister, Susannah Westhaven, and his niece, Pamela Michaels," Marie said. "They are making their home with us."

"It must be a pleasure, Marie, to have two such lovely young ladies to keep you company," he said smoothly, bowing.

Blushing, they both made their curtsies.

"Hello, Harry." His friends Aubrey Standish and Christopher Brerely and Marie's long-suffering husband, Jonathan Westhaven, strode up from the other carriage.

Harry grinned. "Actually, I had considered having a house party."

Brough looked uncomfortable. "We'd have sent word, but . . ."

"Nonsense! You know you're always welcome."

"We won't strain your hospitality. Some of us will

travel on to Woodburn and stay with Bran and Allesandra.''

"As you wish. But come have refreshment first. I'm sure you're in need of it.''

"Indeed!'' Lady Westhaven sighed. "I don't know when I have been so exhausted! I can scarcely bear to move another inch.''

Harry exchanged a look with Brough and from it knew exactly why Marie had come with her brother. She was husband-hunting for her two wards and he was the target. Amusedly offering the lady his arm, he led her inside and into the drawing room. "If you will sit down, Marie, you'll soon be quite the thing again.''

"I fear I haven't regained my strength since my last child, Harry,'' she said as though she were an elderly matron instead of being several years younger than himself.

"Then you must rest. My servants are preparing a comfortable room for you with a view of the gardens. Shadybrook's gardens are considered to be quite beautiful, Marie.''

"You are so kind,'' she said languorously.

Hopkins appeared with brandy for the men, tea and ratafia for the women, and a large tray of cakes and small crustless sandwiches for all.

Sipping his brandy, Brough drew Harry aside. "I'm really very sorry about all of this. I made mention of coming to Kent and nothing would do but that Marie and her entourage would come too.''

"It's perfectly all right. I would expect you to do the same for me.''

"You know I would.'' Brough sighed. "It appears that Marie has refused to budge. If you will agree to house her and Sir Jonathan and the young ladies, Chris and I will go on to Woodburn. Aubrey can stay here to help occupy the females. He's much better at it than poor Jonathan, who will probably closet himself in your library.''

"Whatever you wish, Brough." Harry frowned thoughtfully. "I have another idea as well. Since we are having a house party, dual house parties to be exact, I believe I shall give a ball and I'll put it all in Marie's hands. That should keep her and the young ladies busy."

"An excellent plan! If you don't mind, that is."

"Not at all."

"And Harry, about the young ladies . . ."

"They are regular schoolroom misses, aren't they?"

Brough grinned. "Very close to it. I hope you don't think that I had anything to do with this. It was Marie's idea."

"I understand, Brough. Aubrey and I will be on our toes to avoid permanent entanglement!"

They laughed together.

"I did," said Brough, "meet a very attractive young lady, though terribly tall, when we mistook her estate for yours."

Harry sobered. "Ellen Trevayne."

"Am I treading where I shouldn't?"

"No," the marquess said slowly, feeling a spark of jealousy.

Brough looked closely at his friend. "Well, she's much too tall for me. I only wondered . . ."

"Be careful, Brough," Harry heard himself say. "She is the mistress of mishap." Turning, he strode back to the table on which sat the bottle of brandy.

Mistress of Mishap? Brough thought. He could have sworn she had said she was the mistress of Bridgeford Grange.

A born hostess, Marie Westhaven delighted in Lord Singleton's plan to give a ball. Consulting the Duchess of Rackthall, she drew up a list of guests and with the assistance of Susannah and Pamela invitations were sent out in the short space of two days. She ordered cases of champagne and delicacies to be sent from London and turned her attention to the house, which became a beehive of cleaning and polishing. Being Harry's hostess gave her a great many more benefits than if she had been having the party herself. Most importantly, he was not inclined to economy as Jonathan was and he gave her free rein to spend as much as she desired. With that freedom, the ball was bound to be a success.

Sir Jonathan Westhaven hid from his wife and her frantic activities. As Brough had predicted, he sought the peace and comfort of the marquess' library while Aubrey Standish and Harry engaged in long rides together. With Marie fully occupied, the two girls found themselves with a surfeit of time on their hands, which they spent reading or doing needlework until both were thoroughly bored. Despite Lady Westhaven's grand designs they were less in the company of eligible men than they had been before they had come. Finally Harry took pity on them and invited them riding.

They set out in mid-morning one sunny day and, after a brief jockeying for position, the dark-haired, brown-eyed Susannah Westhaven rode beside Harry while the fair, blue-eyed Pamela accompanied Aubrey.

"Have you a preference for direction?" Harry asked his companion.

"Let us go along the brook, if we may," she said, her rosy lips curving into a smile. "It seems so shady there among the trees."

They did as she suggested, but it was with misgiving that Harry neared the boundary between Shadybrook and Bridgeford. He knew this was one of Ellen's favorite spots for a walk and he found that he wasn't anxious to meet her while escorting Susannah Westhaven. It wasn't as though he had anything to hide. In fact, Ellen had probably already heard all the details about his house guests from the servants' grapevine. Nor did he feel that he owed her any explanations. They'd had some pleasant times together and that was all. He was free to ride with whom he chose and so was she. Perhaps it was because he feared that she would do something disastrous and thus become the laughingstock of his London friends. So it was with a sinking heart that he saw two boisterous Saint Bernards plunging towards them.

"Look at those beasts!" Susannah cried, her fingers clenching onto her reins so tightly that it made the mare she was riding toss her head.

"Oh, those are my neighbor's dogs," Harry explained nonchalantly. "They're nothing to fear."

"They are so huge!"

The dogs milled around them until, their curiosity satisfied, they lumbered away.

"Do you allow them on your property, my lord?" Pamela asked. "I would be afraid to go walking if they were about. Why, they are so big that they could knock down a grown man!"

"I assure you, Miss Michaels, they are harmless and they are gone now, so you needn't worry."

They continued on, reaching a shady clearing where the banks sloped gently and ancient oaks spread their heavy limbs across the stream. "How pretty!" Susannah exclaimed. "It would make a perfect spot for a picnic! Please, my lord, may we dismount and rest a bit?"

"Of course," Harry agreed, wondering how it could be possible for anyone to grow weary from riding a horse for a quiet walk. Sir Jonathan's sister must be very delicate indeed. He motioned to the groom who had been following at a discreet distance and slipped down, tossing his reins to the man.

Susannah extended her arms to be lifted off and managed to brush lightly against Harry's chest as he helped her from the horse. She gazed up at him with rapt velvety-brown eyes before reluctantly facing the brook. "Look there! Isn't that the girl we saw on our way here?"

He turned to see Ellen Trevayne coming around a curve in the stream and paused to admire her long graceful stride. When she thought she was alone it seemed that Ellen Trevayne was not awkward at all. Catching sight of them, she stopped uncertainly.

"Good day, Miss Trevayne." Harry touched his hat and bowed.

She sketched a curtsy. "How do you do, Lord Singleton?"

"Very well, and I see that you are the same. It's a nice day for a walk." He glanced towards his party of riders. "May I introduce my house guests? Miss Susannah Westhaven, Miss Pamela Michaels, and Lord Aubrey Standish. Miss Trevayne."

Aubrey made an elegant bow while the young ladies tendered their greetings. Susannah possessively slipped her arm through Harry's, leaning slightly against him. "My lord, I am truly exhausted. May I sit down on that nice rock over there?"

"Certainly." He escorted her to the edge of the water and seated her.

Susannah cast a languid glance at Ellen. "Do you often walk on Lord Singleton's property, Miss Trevayne?" she asked in a voice that implied that Ellen was a trespasser.

"Quite often, Miss Westhaven." With an uneasy smile, Ellen began to edge past them. "I really must be on my way. My lord, have you seen my dogs?"

"Yes, a few minutes ago. Bounding up the stream."

"Those horrible dogs are yours?" Susannah's pert nose turned upwards with distaste.

"They are not horrible," Ellen responded with a

touch of pique in her voice. "They are nice friendly dogs who . . ." She broke off at the sound of barking and exchanged a quick look of anxiety with Harry. "Oh, dear."

The dogs burst upon the scene, leaping happily towards their mistress. Susannah, frozen fearfully to her rock, screamed as a wet bushy tail slapped her across the face. Pamela clung to Aubrey.

"Down, Taffy!" Ellen cried. "Down, Friendly!"

Harry sprang to Ellen's assistance, grasping one of the animals by the collar and setting him forcefully onto his haunches. "Get down, sir!"

"Friendly! Mind your manners!" Ellen ordered over Susannah's and Pamela's screams. "Oh, do be quiet!" she snapped at the girls. "You're only making them more excited!" Tripping on a stone, she fell onto her bottom, providing a scintillating view of shapely calves and ankles. "Now see what you've done! Friendly, Taffy! Go home! Now! Home!"

The dogs decided to obey. Taffy dashed away towards Bridgeford Grange, while Harry released Friendly to join her. The joyful barking faded.

"My dress is ruined!" Susannah shrieked angrily.

Pamela continued to cling to Aubrey. "I have never been so frightened. I shall never again set foot outside the house!"

Enjoying the sight of Ellen's lovely legs, Harry extended his hand and brought her to her feet. He grinned at her expression of horror. "Quite a scene, madam. Being a participant, I was unfortunately unable to fully appreciate its many arenas of activity. But then, I am seldom a spectator at these events."

A glint of amusement sparkled in Ellen's eyes. "I will, as usual, send a bill."

They both burst into laughter.

"I fail to find the humor in this!" Susannah said coldly. "I have never been so poorly treated!"

"I'm sorry." Harry smiled at his guests. "It's a

standing joke between Miss Trevayne and me."
Suddenly realizing that he still held her hand, he
released it gently. "I must apologize for my ill manners."

Aubrey raised an expressive eyebrow.

Harry caught his friend's speculatory expression.
"Perhaps we should return the ladies to the house.
If you will escort them to the horses, Aubrey, I'll be
right along."

"With pleasure."

He turned back to Ellen as Susannah flounced off
the rock and irritably walked away.

"I do hope Taffy didn't hurt her," she said softly.

"Fustian! Any hurt she received will be all show.
No doubt we shall be listening to this tale of terror
for days to come and it will become more impressive
each time it's told."

"I shall take care to avoid walking here until your
guests have left."

"You shall not! You have always enjoyed coming
here and I shall entertain no notion to the contrary!
I shall also expect to see you at the ball I'm giving."

"Oh, Harry, no. You know as well as I do that . . ."

"If you do not appear, I shall come for you in
person," he threatened.

She sighed. "Very well."

"Then I bid you good day, Ellen, and don't give
this incident another thought. I assure you, I quite
enjoyed it myself."

"Good day, Harry."

He returned to his guests and mounted his horse.
Pamela Michaels had overcome her fear and was
chatting merrily, but Susannah was silent and petulant, remaining so all the way home. He didn't
care. She wasn't his type. She was immature, boring, and predictable. Marie Westhaven would have
to do her matchmaking in another quarter.

* * *

Ellen walked slowly home, thinking back on what had happened. She had probably made two enemies in the young ladies, particularly in Miss Westhaven. At Harry's ball and at any other social gathering they might attend together, they were sure to join the ranks of those who made cutting remarks and wicked innuendoes about her. She was sure to hear the story of today's mishap repeated over and over. But what difference did it make? Harry's reaction was more important.

She had been certain that he would be very angry. She'd had no right to have been where she was, trespassing on his property, and her dogs had caused his guests real distress. But instead he had laughed and reassured her. In the process he had completely ignored Miss Westhaven and had even fobbed her off on his friend. Didn't he see how beautiful the young lady was? Didn't he care? Perhaps being a handsome, wealthy marquess gave him leave to behave however he chose. Probably he had so many beautiful women to choose from that one more or less didn't matter.

Still, Ellen couldn't help but feel a certain pride that he had turned to her. He must indeed value their friendship to have done so. She did wish, though, that he hadn't insisted on her coming to the ball. The neighbors might be accustomed to her little disasters, but she didn't particularly wish to take a chance with Harry's fine London friends. They would think her a complete ninnyhammer.

The unfortunate matter with the dogs wasn't all they had to gossip about either. Blushing, Ellen remembered how her skirt had flung up about her knees when she had fallen. With everything else happening, she had failed to react to that embarrassing moment. Recalling it, she remembered how Harry had taken a long interested look at her legs. No doubt Lord Standish had done the same. The young ladies, too, would have noted how she neglected to scramble to cover her legs. It was horrible. They would think that she thought nothing of exposing herself.

She couldn't go to the ball. She would plead illness or come up with some plausible excuse that would pacify the marquess. No matter what he threatened, he could not possibly force her to attend. If necessary she would lock herself in her bedroom. Rake though he was rumored to be, he would stop short of breaking down her door.

Nor would she allow her servants to push her into going. They seemed bent on throwing her in Harry's path, but they were wasting their time. Nothing would come of it. Even before this incident there had been no hope of his loving her. Now that he and his fine guests had seen her in such shocking disarray, she could never become his marchioness.

Ellen sat down on a log and began to cry. Why couldn't she have been born petite and pretty like Susannah Westhaven? Why must she be so terribly tall? Then she might have had a chance with this wonderful man, despite having a grandfather in business.

Worse still, why had she allowed herself to fall in love with him? She had known it was hopeless. She had tried to avoid him. Bitterly she remembered how it had felt to be waltzing in his arms and suddenly knew, foolish though it might be, that she would attend the ball. If she were very careful, she might not make a faux pas. To dance again with him would be worth the risk. Nothing had happened at the squire's. Surely she could make it through another social event without disaster.

7

The marquess' ball was the foremost subject of conversation in the neighborhood, particularly among the female sector. While the duke and duchess and other wealthy residents had given parties of significance, no one had ever hosted an affair of such magnitude. Delectable tales of the planning flowed through the servants' grapevine and were quickly related to curious matrons and misses. Mainly they were reports of the elaborate refreshments being sent down from London and of the orchestra which was said to be a favorite of the Prince Regent, but there were also details of the gowns Lady Westhaven, Miss Westhaven, and Miss Michaels would wear.

Not to be outdone, the country ladies examined their wardrobes, became dismayed, and ordered new dresses from the few local mantua makers. Swamped with the flood of business, the dressmakers worked far into the night and hired any girl who could sew a straight seam. Though the quality may have suffered, the clientele were generally pleased with their purchases. They would grace the ball in new dresses of what seemed to be the latest style. Only the vicar's wife, who couldn't afford it, the Lady Allesandra, who already had dozens of gowns made by the most fashionable modiste in London,

and Ellen Trevayne, who could afford it but cared
little for modishness, would appear in what they had
at hand.

With the assistance of Mrs. Everett, Ellen reviewed her small stock of ball gowns. None of them
were new, nor were they in the first stare of fashion,
but they had been well cared for and were in good
condition. All were cut in a simple style designed
not to call attention to their wearer's height.

"Try this one, my dear." The housekeeper removed an ice-blue silk with a diaphanous silvery
overskirt. "I do believe that it matches your eyes."

"It was my choice too." Ellen shrugged into the
cool soft fabric. "It has been worn less than the others. I think I know why." She smiled ruefully at her
reflection in the mirror as the housekeeper did up
the long row of buttons. "It is cut too low. I shall
have to tuck lace."

Mrs. Everett frowned slightly. "No, I don't think
it's necessary. Not at . . ."

Ellen laughed. "Not at my age?"

The housekeeper flushed. "You are at the very
nice age, miss, when it isn't necessary to dress like
a girl from the schoolroom."

Ellen looked at her softly rounded bosom. "I don't
know. Doesn't it show a great deal of me?"

"I think Lord Singleton will like it very much."

It was Ellen's turn to blush. "He doesn't look at
me that way, Mrs. Everett," she said firmly.

"Then he should! Now that this is settled, how
will you do your hair? I do wish you had a proper
lady's maid!"

"Oh, no! Remember that odious Miss Salten who
tended Mama? No one liked her. I don't even think
that Mama did! Dora shall do my hair as usual."

Mrs. Everett tipped her head thoughtfully. "Perhaps you would consider making Dora your abigail.

Her talents really are wasted as a downstairs maid. I don't think that she is very happy in her position.''

''She isn't? Has she told you so?'' Ellen asked with concern.

''No, miss, but it isn't difficult to tell. And I did hear from one of the footmen that Dora desired to be a lady's maid and had considered going to London to try to improve her position.''

''Does she have friends or relatives there?''

''I don't think so, miss.''

''Then London would make mice feet of her!''

''Indeed,'' the housekeeper agreed, ''especially since she has no experience in being what she desires.''

''Very well.'' Ellen sighed. ''Please ask Dora if she would like to be my abigail, but be sure to explain to her that I cannot bear being coddled!''

''I'm sure that she will fill the position perfectly.'' Mrs. Everett lifted her shoulders triumphantly. It seemed a small step in transforming her mistress into the lady she knew she could be, but Mrs. Everett knew she had crossed a major obstacle. Dora had an inborn sense of style and would delight in seeing that her lady was always at her best in the event of chance meetings with his lordship. And Miss Ellen was too kind and caring a person to thwart her efforts. Mrs. Everett allowed herself a small smile of satisfaction.

Dora reported to her new position shortly after luncheon. ''Oh, miss, you can't know how happy I am! I've always wanted to be a lady's maid and I'll be a good one, you'll see. I learn quick. You just tell me what you want me to do, but I have a bit of an idea about it already. I remember Miss Salten and . . .''

''Please, Dora, don't be like Miss Salten! I couldn't bear the woman. Why, she acted finer than Mama!''

''No, miss, I could never act like Miss Salten! But I remember how she cared for Lady Trevayne and her clothes. I can do that too. You've always liked the way I do your hair. Let's send to London for fashion magazines. We'll see all the latest styles!''

''It isn't necessary,'' Ellen interrupted. ''We'll be going to London after the harvest. I'll be visiting my grandfather.''

''And I'll go too?'' Dora asked with awe.

''Of course. You are my lady's maid. You will go where I go.''

''Even when you marry the marquess?''

''Dora!'' Ellen cried irritably. ''What is wrong with everyone in this house? I am not going to marry the marquess! In the first place, he hasn't asked me. In the second, he never will! He is too fine, too high in the peerage for me.''

''Then he is a very unfortunate man.''

Ellen couldn't help smiling at her new abigail's loyalty. ''I'm sure he doesn't think so! But please, Dora, you of all people, now that you are the closest to me, must realize and tell the others that Lord Singleton and I are only friends and neighbors. And that is all that will ever come of it,'' she said, nodding emphatically. ''Now that we have concluded that piece of gossip, let us go on to other things. I suppose you should begin by familiarizing yourself with my wardrobe. Why don't you tidy my bureau drawers and my dressing room? You will see what I have, where I keep it, and if anything needs repair.''

Dora bobbed a curtsy. ''Yes, miss.''

Ellen started to leave the room, then hesitated. ''And Dora, I promise you that when we go to London, we'll visit all the famous shops and buy a lot of new things. You'll be too busy to think about whom I might marry.''

''I shall like that,'' the maid said dreamily. ''Still, it is a shame. The marquess is so tall!''

* * *

On the evening of the ball, Ellen experienced her usual nervousness, but she was pleased with her appearance. Dora, taking her duties seriously, had pressed the ball gown to perfection, bathed her mistress in essence of roses, wound flowers into the knot of her hair, and chose a delicate diamond pendant and small drop earrings for her to wear. There was no question of wearing the lace tuck. Ellen could readily see that it would give her the appearance of an overgrown ingenue.

As always, it was difficult making her entrance alone, but when a footman took her wrap, Ellen caught Harry's eye as he stood in the receiving line and smiled at his nod of encouragement. Taking a deep breath, she joined the other guests in greeting their host and the Westhaven contingency.

The line was long and it moved slowly, since every female seemed to take an inordinate amount of time chatting with the marquess. There were two young ladies of eligible age, along with their mama and papa, standing in front of her and whispering and giggling disgustingly. When introduced to him they blushed and simpered, breathlessly murmuring inanities and flashing him coy, doe-eyed glances. Ellen wondered how he could stand it, but Harry greeted them smoothly and charmingly, complimenting them on their prettiness and kissing their hands lingeringly. Her eyebrows knitted ever so slightly. What a practiced flirt he was!

He turned to her. "Miss Trevayne," he said formally, but with a rakish glint in his eyes. "How nice of you to come."

"It seemed to be the thing to do, my lord." She curtsied and extended her hand.

He kissed it and bent his head closer. "Do you disapprove of me, Ellen? I detect a certain irritation."

"I . . . I . . . Whyever should I disapprove? Your

conduct, I am sure, is above reproach and most fitting to the situation.''

''Bravo.'' He retained her hand in his a bit longer than was necessary. ''You will save me the first waltz?''

Her heart doubled its beat. ''I shall.'' Neatly she turned her hand out of his and proceeded on to the formidable Lady Westhaven.

''Oh, yes. You are the dog owner.'' The attractive lady haughtily lifted her aristocratic nose. ''Your animals quite frightened my sister-in-law and my niece.''

''It was most unfortunate,'' Ellen replied. ''I fear they are too boisterous. Er . . . the dogs, that is.''

The marquess chuckled softly.

Cheeks warming, she hurried through the rest of the receiving line, uttering pleasantries and making no more awkward statements.

Ellen sat out the first dance, but on the second accepted the Duke of Rackthall as a partner. ''Brandon, will you never tire of rescuing me from the ranks of the wallflowers?''

''Not at all.'' He made his bow. ''You dance divinely.''

''Fustian! You, sir, have kissed the Blarney if you think so!''

His blue eyes sparkled. ''You look very pretty tonight, Ellen.''

''Thank you.'' She smiled back, enjoying his light flirtation. Allesandra was truly the luckiest of women to have him for a husband. Almost as lucky as Harry's wife would be.

''I should like a waltz with you, but I fear Allesandra would strangle me.''

''And so she should! Besides, I would probably step all over your toes.''

''I think not. I haven't noticed Harry having any

such difficulties. The two of you seemed to dance quite well together."

"Lord Singleton is a master of the art. Like you, Your Grace. I suppose that it is well that I am able to perform tolerably with my only two partners." She smiled at him, and went on, "Also the waltz is an easy dance, unlike this one where one must remember which step comes next. You will have noticed that I am always a trifle behind you?"

"No, I did not." The set came to an end with his bow and her curtsy. "Nor do I believe that you will have only two partners tonight. In fact, here is another now." With a nod he handed her to Lord Aubrey Standish.

Surprised that she had been sought out by that fine gentleman, Ellen's conversation evaporated. He skillfully drew her out, however, and by the end of the set they were chatting comfortably. But despite his pleasantries, she was thoroughly happy when the dance ended and further dismayed when Lord Christopher Brerely approached.

"My lord, may we sit this one out? It is very warm, don't you think?"

"It is indeed." He inclined his head. "Please allow me to bring you refreshment."

"That would be most agreeable." She took a seat by a window, thankful for his brief absence. Casting her eyes over the dancers, she spied Harry with Pamela Michaels. A stab of jealousy throbbed in her breast as he bent his head to the petite blonde's ear and whispered something that made her laugh. She couldn't let her thoughts of him do this to her. It was bad enough that her servants had expectations. If she allowed her own emotions to get the better of her she would be miserable indeed. After the greeting in the reception line he hadn't exchanged one word with her, had probably not even looked at her. Her feelings were against all reason.

Lord Brerely returned with champagne. "Lady Allesandra tells me that you'll be going with her to London."

"Yes."

"You will enjoy Rackthall House. It's very comfortable."

"I'm sure it is, my lord, but I shall be staying with my grandfather. I'm going to London to visit him."

"Indeed. Perhaps I know him?"

Ellen felt a sense of rising panic. Her own revelation had caused this polite man to inquire after her family and now she would have to admit to him that her grandfather was not of his social class. She gritted her teeth. What difference did it make? Most of the people here knew it. If it exposed her to further ridicule it was nothing more than had occurred before. "I doubt you know him, my lord," she said stiffly. "My grandfather, John Frampton, is a banker. He also has wide business interests to occupy his time."

"I see," he remarked with a touch of curiosity.

"Do you? Please excuse me, Lord Brerely. I must have a breath of fresh air." Without waiting for him to rise, she leaped to her feet. Champagne from her glass sloshed onto his leg. Not again! Mortified, she fled from the stifling room and found her way to a side portico.

"To Hades with it all!" She threw the glass onto the stone floor where it shattered into a thousand slivers. She could have avoided that mishap. If she'd simply kept her wits about her, she could have risen politely and walked away.

She glanced around to see if anyone had witnessed her fit of temper. There was no one present, but behind her Ellen heard voices heading her way. Without hesitation she strode down the stairs and into the garden, disappearing behind some tall boxwood. Finding a small stone bench she sat down and let the cool air drift over her.

Damme, she thought. Why should she feel ashamed of her grandfather in front of these people? He was every bit as good as them and probably more intelligent than most. After all, he had started with nothing and made millions. Most of the guests at this affair had their fortunes handed to them. He, not they, should be thought superior. And he would find her an honest, intelligent, hardworking husband like himself whom she could be proud of. There would be no more dreams of tall, dark, handsome noblemen.

Ellen felt tears prickle her eyelids. "But oh, Grandfather . . ." she whispered aloud, "it just isn't fair."

There were two parts to her, at war with one another. On her father's side, she had inherited the birthright to belong to the *ton*. From her mother she had received the money to do it, but not the cache of an old family. If her paternal grandfather had ranked higher in the peerage she might have overcome the taint of trade. As it was, she teetered between the two worlds. She felt like a child grasping for a piece of candy that was always held just out of reach. It hadn't really mattered until she had met the marquess. He had overset everything. How the guests would laugh if they knew that Ellen Trevayne was in love with the Marquess of Singleton!

She had to go home. She would return to the house, order her carriage, and leave immediately. And tomorrow she would begin preparations to leave for London as soon as possible. The harvest could go on just as well without her. No longer would she allow herself to be swayed by the chance of seeing him or feeling his touch.

Single-mindedly she quickly stood, darted

through the garden, and collided with the man she most wished to avoid.

"It was our waltz," the marquess said softly. "I looked everywhere for you." His hands rested lightly on her shoulders. "Are you all right?"

"No. No, I am not. I must go home." Reluctantly she looked up at him. "I don't feel well."

Disappointment flashed in his gray eyes. "I shall take you."

"You mustn't leave your guests," she said hurriedly. "I'll be fine. Please call my carriage."

"What has happened, Ellen?" Gently he lifted her chin and studied her searchingly.

"Please don't do this!"

"What?" He paused, gazing thoughtfully at her, then lowered his lips to hers. When he encountered no resistance, he gathered her into his arms.

Ellen melted into his embrace. Though she had never before been kissed by a man she seemed to know instinctively what to do. Her lips parted, softening sweetly. She slipped her arms around him and savored the sensation of his body against hers. It was wonderful, wonderful to be kissed by a man one loved.

But he couldn't love her. There was no way he could love her in return. He was a handsome, wealthy peer and there was no place for her in his life. She drew back. "How dare you trifle with me!" she said breathlessly.

"Trifle?" He looked stunned. "Ellen!"

Turning on her heel, she ran to the house, threaded her way among the guests, and hurried into the hall. "Hopkins, I wish my carriage!"

"At once, ma'am."

She waited nervously. How could he have done that? How could he have taken such complete advantage of her? Especially when he had been so kind! It was beyond all imagination.

Of course, kisses probably meant nothing to a charming, sophisticated flirt like Harry Singleton. Most likely he handed them out by the dozens. Glancing over her shoulder, she saw him bearing down on her.

"Ellen! What nonsense is this?"

"Your carriage, ma'am." Hopkins saw his employer and, realizing the need for privacy, hastily drew away.

Ellen swept out the door with Lord Singleton hard on her heels.

"Trifle? What do you mean?" he demanded.

"You know very well what I mean. You are very . . . what shall we say? Experienced?" She entered her coach. "Good night, Lord Singleton."

"Dammit, Ellen . . ."

"I thought we were friends!" Clenching her teeth, she pulled down the window shade and leaned back.

Her protective servants, knowing their mistress was overset, sprang the horses to a high rate of speed and left the marquess standing in the dust.

Harry walked softly down the stairs and entered the library. After the guests had left, he had been the last to retire, but despite having consumed a fair portion of champagne, he had been unable to sleep. He couldn't take his mind from Ellen Trevayne.

Was that what he was doing? Trifling with her? It had happened so quickly that he hadn't even thought of it. She had been so beautiful in the moonlight and had seemed so distressed that he had wanted nothing more than to comfort her. It had seemed the natural thing to do.

He uncorked the brandy and drank straight from the bottle. He had known that she was vulnerable. Had he taken advantage of her?

There was one thing certain that he had done. He had made her very, very angry. It was strange. At first, she had welcomed his kiss. He had kissed too many women to be unsure of that. She had wanted his kiss and she had kissed him back.

Taking another deep drink, he remembered how tenderly Ellen's slightly parted lips had molded to his own. It had been a gentle kiss, not designed to incite passion. He had never kissed a woman in quite that way before. And it seemed all the more special because of that. What was happening?

Shaking his head, Harry sat down, this time pouring the brandy into a glass like a civilized gentleman. The memory of that sweet kiss and the soft feel of her in his arms made him want her more than he had ever wanted any woman. It didn't matter whether or not she fit his list of perfect requirements. He didn't care if she or her dogs knocked him into the mud every day. Bran would have to change his notions of Harry's perfectionism. It seemed he was in love with Ellen Trevayne.

8

Harry awoke early, despite his late, restless, enlightening night, and went thoughtfully down to breakfast. Expecting to find none of his guests up at this hour, he was surprised to see Aubrey Standish in the breakfast room, dismally nursing a cup of black coffee. Greeting him, Harry filled his plate at the sideboard and sat down.

"Aubrey, you look like the very devil. Shoot the cat last night?"

"No, but I had my share, of course. You don't look so wonderful yourself." He eyed Harry's plate of food with distaste. "God, man, how can you eat all that this early?"

"Very easily. I'm starving." Harry sank his fork into a thick ham steak.

"I never could abide breakfast until ten or eleven. Nor can I be conversable until then."

"Why, Aubrey, I would never have suspected it! Whatever has become of your congeniality?" Harry teased. "I've never seen you so disgruntled."

His friend shrugged languidly. "It's Marie Westhaven. I can't believe that a sister of Brough can be such a managing old biddy. She didn't used to be that way. I can't stand it any longer. I'm leaving, Harry, if you'll take me to the nearest stage stop."

103

The marquess smiled at the thought of Lord Aubrey Standish embarking on a common mail coach. "You may take my curricle or I'll lend you a phaeton, but tell me, why the haste?"

"The phaeton," Aubrey said morosely. "I couldn't take a man's curricle. Why the haste? Because I'm damn sick and tired of Marie's matrimonial plans for those two girls. You were the quarry, you know, but you've shown a decided lack of enthusiasm. Besides, there are two of them, aren't there? So Marie is attempting to cast her net over me. Pamela isn't so bad, but that Susannah . . . I've never seen such a namby-pamby female."

"Have to marry sometime, Aubrey!"

"That's well for you to say. I believe you've made up your mind, and I like her, Harry, really I do, but I'm not ready to take that step."

Harry nearly choked on the muffin he was eating. "Who are you talking about?"

"Ellen Trevayne, of course. Do you think I'm a fool not to have noticed? I've known you too long for that, my friend!" Aubrey tossed down the coffee as though it were a shot of liquor and returned to the sideboard to refill his cup. "I'm not wrong, am I?"

The marquess stared at him speechlessly.

"It's the way you look at her, Harry. And that protective way you have towards her. Do you deny it?"

"I don't suppose I can," he answered slowly.

"Well, then, congratulations are in order. You'll be the second of us to go. How about that? First Bran, then you. Both of you the biggest womanizers in England! Strange, isn't it?"

"But I haven't asked her yet! Your felicitations, Aubrey, are premature. I scarcely know her, nor she, me. Besides, she may not wish to marry me."

"Ha! What girl wouldn't marry you? Ask her before I leave. I want to see Marie Westhaven's face when she hears the news.''

''Aubrey!''

''If you've made up your mind, you might as well do it. The sooner the better.''

Harry *had* made up his mind . . . almost. What he didn't like was Aubrey's attempt to manipulate, nor the way his friend had seen through him. Was it so obvious to everyone?

''Well?'' Aubrey asked, mischief glinting in his blue eyes. ''When are you going to depart on your mission?''

''As I told you, we scarcely know each other,'' Harry said firmly. ''It will take time.''

His friend groaned, casting his eyes heavenwards. ''For God's sake, Harry, why wait? You should have seen yourself at the stream when those big dogs of hers overwhelmed us! You thought it marvelously amusing. It was obvious that the two of you shared something that the rest of us didn't. And the way she was last night at the ball! She could hardly concentrate on her dancing because she was looking for you.''

''Indeed?''

''Yes! She's in love with you, mark my words. Ask her. She'll accept!''

''Not yet, Aubrey! I must be sure,'' he protested.

''You are wasting time. I believe that you're afraid of marriage, Harry.''

''I? Take a look at yourself, friend! I don't see you rushing to the altar!''

Aubrey laughed. ''Don't skirt the issue.''

''I am not. I am merely proceeding cautiously, for when I marry it will be to the right lady. I do not intend to harbor mistresses or to spend my evenings at White's for want of entertainment.''

''The *perfect* marriage, eh?''

The marquess shoved his plate aside and stood.

"My appetite is gone, and I have things to do. If you are bent on leaving, Aubrey, I shall order the phaeton. If not, I will see you at luncheon."

"Luncheon then. I've changed my mind about leaving so soon. I believe I'll stay for a while . . . to see what happens and to help keep Marie's girls off your back."

"Thank you. I appreciate your assistance with the young ladies. And one other thing too. You won't repeat our conversation to anyone?"

"Never."

Harry nodded.

"Are you going to see her now?"

"At this hour? Really, Aubrey, this is outside of enough! No, I am not going to Bridgeford Grange! I am going to the estate office to go over accounts and I do not expect to be disturbed!"

Lord Standish raised an eyebrow. "But you'll visit Miss Trevayne later?"

"I am not at all sure about that. Perhaps tomorrow."

"Idiot." His friend dismissed him with the wave of a hand.

Harry left the dining room and, requesting Hopkins to bring him coffee, made his way to the office. There he would be certain of being alone unless he was interrupted by the steward. If that happened, at least he would be relieved momentarily of the knotty question which had plagued him all night long.

He sat down at the desk and stared thoughtfully out the window at Shadybrook's manicured lawn. Did he really love Ellen Trevayne? Enough to marry her? The answer to both questions was yes. Aubrey was right. He should hurry right over to Bridgeford and ask her to be his wife.

But he hesitated. She had been peeved at him last night. Perhaps it would be better to give her a day to ease her irritation. He would go tomorrow afternoon. In the meantime he would have a large bouquet of flowers sent. That should pave the way. Satisfied with his plan, he opened the account book and began work.

Ellen awoke wearily from a miserable night's sleep. Seeing the brilliant sun streaming in her bedroom window she knew she had overslept, but what difference did it make? It was a wonder that she had slept at all with the way her mind had been filled by unsettling visions of the handsome dark marquess.

After ringing for Dora she slipped from bed and shrugged into her dressing robe. As soon as she had dressed and breakfasted they would begin packing for London. She must never lay eyes on Harry again. If she did, her resolve would weaken. Hopefully they would be ready to leave for the city by the next morning and she could end this foolishness.

"Good morning, miss," her maid said cheerfully as she entered the room. "I came in earlier but you were sleeping so soundly I didn't have the heart to waken you." She set down her tray and poured her mistress a cup of coffee.

"Dora, can we be packed and ready to leave for London by tomorrow morning?"

"Of course, Miss Ellen, but . . ."

The conversation was disturbed by the sound of horses' hooves in the drive below. Hurrying to the window Ellen saw a large black traveling coach, impressively accompanied by four outriders, draw up to the front of the house. A footman leaped down to open the door and out stepped a sort, portly gentleman. Surveying his surroundings with distaste, he started up the steps.

"Oh, look, Dora!" Ellen cried. "It's Grandfather! What a wonderful surprise!"

Dora, who remembered the overbearing old man

from previous visits, was less enthusiastic. Mr. Frampton hated being in the country and often took out his spite on the servants. "I thought we were to go to him."

"Yes, that was my intention. I must confess that I haven't answered his letters yet. He is probably angry with me."

"Oh," the maid said, full of dread.

"Don't concern yourself with him, Dora. His bark is worse than his bite!" Ellen laughed. "This is famous! He hates the country, you know!"

"Yes, I do."

Unmindful of her unkempt appearance, Ellen dashed from her bedroom and down the stairs to throw herself into his arms. "Grandfather, I can't believe my eyes!"

"Neither can I." He patted her back. "Just out of bed, are you? No matter, you're a pretty sight despite the disarray. Well, missy, what have you to say for yourself!"

Ellen smiled fondly at him. "Coming to check up on me, are you?"

"Someone should!" he said gruffly.

"Hm! You know I am very capable of taking care of myself!"

"Too capable for a female."

"Now, now, we've been over this before." She tucked her arm through his. "Come into the drawing room and tell me the real reason you are here."

"That is the real reason. I am here to check up on you." He looked up threateningly at his granddaughter. "You don't answer my letters, young lady."

"I meant to. The time went by so fast. Will you have coffee with me, Grandfather?"

"I'll have port."

Ellen nodded the order to Gore, who moved quickly to obey her.

Mr. Frampton selected a large wing chair and collapsed into it. "Well, miss, when are you coming to me?"

"After the harvest, I had originally thought, but . . ."

"Well?" he asked belligerently, lighting a cigar.

"So long as you are here, I would be wise to return with you." She wrinkled her nose. "Grandfather, that smells terrible."

"Don't play the saucy drawing-room miss with me! I'm too old! I'll smoke whenever and wherever I please!" He gaped at her as he suddenly realized that she had agreed to accompany him home. "So you're coming with me? Just like that? No fights? No fuss?"

"No, Grandfather." Ellen narrowed her eyes. It wouldn't do to let him know that she had intended to leave the very next day. Conceding so easily would give him the upper hand, a position Mr. Frampton would certainly use to his advantage. He would also be suspicious of her reasons. As it was, his arrival had played him unknowingly into her hands.

"I had arranged to travel with the Duke and Duchess of Rackthall, but since you are here already, it seems foolish to put it off."

"Duke and Duchess! What do people like that know of caring for you? You're right, you'll be better off in your grandpapa's company," he heartily agreed.

"Allesandra and Brandon are my friends. They are coming to London this fall and I intend to visit them on occasion. You will understand that."

"No, I don't. I don't hold much store in the nobs, missy. They're a lazy, high-nosed lot! Either got money that someone else left 'em or they're flat broke." He nodded emphatically. "Give me a good man who's willing to work for his blunt!"

"By that," Ellen said tartly, "I may assume that

Lord Rackthall does not keep his money in your bank, nor invest in any of your schemes."

Her grandfather laughed loudly. "Now that sounds more like my Ellen! I was beginning to think you'd turned into a namby-pamby! All right, I won't stand in the way of your visiting your fine friends! Just don't expect me to participate for I'd mortify you beyond all belief."

She couldn't help laughing. "I shan't expect it!"

"Now that that's all settled," he said with satisfaction, "what about my other suggestion? You need a husband, missy. Lord knows, you need someone to keep you in line. I won't be here forever and I need a good man that I can trust to carry on my financial affairs."

"Does it have to be a man?" Ellen asked cynically. "Why couldn't I learn your business?"

"You?" he sputtered. "A woman?"

"Why not?"

"You'd be laughed out of London! I hope you're not serious, missy, or you'll be sorely disappointed."

She sighed. "What kind of husband are you going to buy for me, Grandfather?"

"For one thing, a man with a good head for business," he began. "And what's this about buying? Anyone would want to marry you."

"No," she murmured, "not anyone."

He frowned. "What? Has some young fool trifled with you?"

Ellen flushed, glad to see Gore arrive at that moment with refreshment and thus interrupt the conversation. "Grandfather, here is your port. I believe I shall go on up and dress. Can't we continue this discussion later?" Without giving him the opportunity to reply she hastened out of the room.

True to his reputation for tenacity, Mr. Frampton picked up the topic of most current concern to him as soon as he and his granddaughter were seated at the dining table for luncheon. Heaping his plate with great slabs of beef, roast potatoes, and peas, he forged into the conversation. Ellen, expecting it, was prepared.

"I won't marry just anyone, Grandfather, because you say he is suitable. At least I must like him."

"I've several men in mind. You'll like them. They're all sons of friends of mine. Like father like son, I always say."

"And he must be reasonably good-looking. And interesting, too."

"You'll have trouble choosing between them!"

"He must, of course, be kind to me."

"Nothing to worry about!" Mr. Frampton ate his meal with appreciation, not noticing that his granddaughter merely picked at hers. "They're all anxious to meet you, and, believe me, missy, there's no buying involved. This marriage will be a merger!"

Ellen's food seemed to stick in her throat. She wondered about the anonymous young men her grandfather had given his approval to. What did they think of this? Did they have others they really loved and couldn't marry, due to circumstances beyond their control? Probably not. Any man chosen by Mr. Frampton would have a shrewd head for business. Love wouldn't play any part in his marital plans.

Her heart ached. How could she marry anyone else when she was so in love with Harry? How could she let anyone else touch her?

"Tell me a bit about the young men, Grandfather."

"A bit about them?" He paused, the fork halfway to his mouth. "They're intelligent, serious men. Hardworking. Not given to fantasy. Any of them would make a good solid husband. No nonsense about them!''

''Do they laugh?''

''Laugh? I suppose they laugh. Doesn't everybody laugh once in a while? What kind of question is that?''

''Are they enjoyable company?''

Mr. Frampton threw back his head and guffawed. ''Good God, missy! Husbands aren't supposed to be enjoyable! They're supposed to be reliable. Who put these ideas into your head? Your fine father, or that duke and duchess?''

''No one!'' she snapped.

''I think there's something bothering you,'' he said more kindly. ''I don't suppose you'd like to talk about it?''

''There is nothing to talk about, except to say that I despise this whole business. I feel like a horse on the auction block!''

''It's not that way at all. In this case you'll do the choosing.''

''Shall I examine their teeth?''

''Missy, you are giving me indigestion! Now, I have tried to give you the the pick of several fine young men. Any one of them would be good enough, but whichever one you choose, God help him, I'm beginning to feel sorry for him!''

She fell silent. She had, after all, agreed with this farce and she supposed she must carry it through.

''Furthermore, I want to leave as soon as possible. Have you ordered your maid to pack your things?''

''I have.''

''Good! May I assume that we will leave in the morning?''

''I shall be ready.'' Ellen stared at the uneaten food on her plate. When next she supped at Bridgeford Grange, she would be a married woman. At least she hoped she would be able to return to the country. A husband that suited her grandfather might hate the country just as much as he did.

She glanced up as Gore entered the room, carrying an enormous bouquet of roses. "Oh, how lovely!"

"From Lord Singleton, miss."

"Is he here?"

"No, Miss Ellen. A footman brought them."

Pain stabbed her breast. She looked at the card. *I fear I overstepped my bounds*, Harry had written. *Please accept my apologies.*

"Who is Lord Singleton?" Mr. Frampton demanded.

"A neighbor, Grandfather," Ellen murmured. "Only a neighbor."

9

Her hasty departure from Bridgeford Grange had been for the best, Ellen told herself as she settled into her grandfather's comfortable house in a newly developed section of London. It had been hard enough to drive past the gates of Shadybrook without leaping from the carriage and refusing to travel another foot. If she had seen the marquess, even to say good-bye, it would have been more than her nerves could bear. There was a chance that she would see him when Allesandra and Brandon came up to the city, but by then surely she would have become accustomed to her new life. Perhaps she would even be betrothed. That would solve everything. Not that she was going to accept the first young man her grandfather sent her way; she would become thoroughly acquainted with anyone she might choose before making a decision that would affect the rest of her life.

Mr. Frampton had pressed her to have a dinner party for his candidates immediately. Ellen had forestalled this, claiming that she needed some time to grow used to her new surroundings and to replenish her wardrobe. Grudgingly he had given way and even agreed that all the bills be sent to him.

So Dora had her shopping experience as a lady's

abigail, many of them in fact. She had encouraged her mistress to buy all the latest fashion journals and then had studied them minutely, poring over every detail that would turn Miss Ellen into a charmer and, incidentally, herself into the best lady's maid in town. Furthermore she had insisted that her charge put herself in the hands of Lady Rackthall's modiste, Cecile, who was beyond a doubt the finest dressmaker in London, and the most expensive.

Ellen didn't mind. In fact she took a savage delight in spending her grandfather's money. This was his idea and he could pay dearly for it. She swept aside such feelings of guilt that she had experienced in going along with it. Her future might be considered an investment for him. To reap the dividends, he must put forth the cash.

As the bills mounted, Mr. Frampton finally exploded. Calling Ellen into his library, he waved them at her. "What is all this? Who is this 'Cecile' and what kind of rig is she running with my money!"

His granddaughter eyed him coolly. "Cecile is the finest dressmaker in England, Grandfather. Would you have me dress as a tradesman's daughter to greet your friends?"

"And what is wrong with that?"

"I daresay their wives and mamas would far outshine me, assuming of course that your friends are well-to-do."

"They're more than that," he grumbled.

"Then I'm sure their ladies dress fashionably."

"I don't pay heed to women's clothes. Where did you hear of this Cecile?"

"From my friend Allesandra, who dresses beautifully."

"Ha! The duchess! I might have known! So I'm to dress you as a duchess, am I?"

"No, Grandfather, it isn't necessary. I shall return the dresses and confess that they are beyond my means.'' Ellen reached for the offending statements. ''Cecile will understand, and I'm sure she will be able to sell them without difficulty.''

He jerked them back. ''I've got as much blunt as that damn duke! Probably more!''

Ellen raised an eyebrow. ''I don't want to appear to be above my class.''

''God in heaven!'' Mr. Frampton shouted. ''Above your class! This family is as good as any! Better than most! I'll not listen to any . . .'' He broke off, eyeing her shrewdly. ''Well, you've caught me neatly, missy, that you have. If you were a man, what partners we would be!''

''As I've said before, why not teach me your business?''

''You tend to your own business, which is marriage and a home and a family. Let me and your husband make the money.'' He smiled suddenly. ''And you keep your pretties. I want to be proud of you.''

''Very well,'' she said gravely.

''You *are* looking better, I suppose.'' He tucked the bills into his top drawer. ''Was that dress you have on made by Mademoiselle Extortionist!?''

''It was made by Cecile.'' Ellen twirled before him, surprising herself when she didn't trip over her own toes. She felt pretty in the new gown, and even graceful. The delicate blue fabric was as soft as a whisper and the style was as simply elegant as the drapery of a Grecian goddess. The Frenchwoman was a true artist in cloth. With the snipping of scissors and the stitching of needles, she had transformed Ellen into a quietly modish young woman.

Mr. Frampton nodded his approval. ''It suits you. You look nice.'' He reached for two stemmed goblets and poured himself a glass of port and for her, one of sherry. ''Now let's have a comfortable coze. I've another topic to discuss.''

She flashed him wary glance. "Why do I receive the impression that it will be something I dislike?"

Her grandfather ignored her question. "I've been thinking . . . It's only fitting that you should have a chaperone. It's not right that a young lady shouldn't."

"Oh, no! I won't agree! I won't have some old termagant peering over my shoulder watching every move I make! I won't do it."

"It is proper, missy."

"For a young lady, yes, but I am not that age anymore. It isn't necessary," she said with finality. "When I am shopping, Dora is a perfectly acceptable companion. Other than that, you will escort me."

"Why do I have such trouble with you?"

"Because you try to treat me like a schoolgirl!" Ellen snapped. "I dislike arguing with you, but I will not allow you to trample me! I have already had my Season in London. Many years ago, I might add! I have lived alone and have managed my estate quite well, as you should know from poring over the books. I do not need a chaperone."

He rubbed his forehead and looked so perplexed that Ellen almost pitied him enough to go along with his plan.

"All right, missy, all right. You win on this as well. But what will you do if your fine friend the duchess asks you to a party? I certainly will not attend!"

"In that event she shall be my chaperone. She is a perfectly respectable married lady."

"Married to that fribble Rackthall!"

Ellen sighed. "Grandfather, why do you bear such enmity to the peerage? If you met Brandon and Allesandra, I think you would like them. They are very nice people."

"They and their kind are lazy do-nothings who

look down their noses at anyone who doesn't have a title.''

''They don't look down their noses at me!''

''Due to your father,'' he said smugly. ''We'll see what they do when you marry.''

''Father had a title and you seemed to like him,'' she persisted.

''I bought him,'' Mr. Frampton said bluntly. ''It was your grandmother's wish that her daughter wed a titled gentleman. Your mama was crazy over him. I was forced to take him, penniless though he was. I suppose he turned out to be satisfactory. After he forgot all those notions about his fine friends!'' He shook his head. ''I want more for you. It worked out well for your mama, but it doesn't happen that way very often. A man should have more money than his wife.''

''Mother and Father were very happy,'' Ellen said thoughtfully, sipping her sherry. ''I was probably their only disappointment. They would rather have had a boy, I'm sure. And they certainly would have preferred a dainty, pretty daughter to me!''

''Don't give me that, girl! They loved you dearly and so do I! That's why I intend to have the best for you!'' Mr. Frampton winked at her. ''Including those expensive clothes. You're all I've got!''

Ellen suddenly felt very sorry for him. He had started with nothing and had made millions. He should have had a son or a grandson to share his love of business. He was solely depending on her to provide him with a grandson-in-law to join his firm. And he had gone so far as to decide upon who would fill the bill. For him, she must look at them all with an open mind. For herself, well . . . for herself, she must try very hard to forget Harry Singleton.

On the day that Ellen left for the city, Harry rode over to Bridgeford Grange to call upon her. Tossing his reins to a footman, he climbed the steps to the door and lifted the butt of his riding crop to tap on it when it was opened immediately by the butler.

"Good day, Gore. Is Miss Trevayne about?"

"She is not at home, my lord," the man said unhappily. "She has gone to London with her grandfather."

"To London! But I thought she wasn't to leave until after the harvest!"

"Her grandfather was very insistent, sir. He can be that." The old servant peered closely at his lordship's face. Something disturbing had happened the other night at Shadybrook. Miss Ellen hadn't been at all the same when she came home. However, he got no clues from the marquess. Aside from a flash of surprise in those cool gray eyes, Lord Singleton's expression had remained carefully blank.

"I see." Harry said quietly.

"May I offer you refreshment, sir?"

"No, thank you. There is no point in staying." He started down the steps and turned. "Gore, what is Miss Trevayne's grandfather's name?"

"Mr. Frampton, sir. Mr. John Frampton."

"Thank you."

The butler watched the tall, handsome marquess gracefully mount his horse and ride away. What a fine figure of a man he was! His lordship obviously cared for Miss Ellen and she, just as obviously, was running away from him. What a terrible mistake she was making!

"Damn," said Gore under his breath, regretfully shutting the door. He hoped that his lordship would prove up to the chase.

Riding slowly up the driveway Harry, too, cursed to himself. Why had Ellen left without even saying good-bye? Even if her grandfather was in a hurry, the least she could have done would have been to send him a note. Perhaps this was her answer. Instead of words, Ellen might be using her actions to show him how little she cared for him.

Harry didn't believe it. The sweet way she had responded to his kiss proved that to be false. Though her manner had been inexperienced, he could sense an underlying current of desire. For a highly intelligent, well-brought-up young lady it could mean only one thing. She was in love with him.

"Damn it all!" he said savagely. He removed a gold timepiece from his waistcoat pocket. If anyone knew the details of Ellen's hasty departure, it would be Allesandra. If he hurried he could go to Woodburn Hall, have a nice chat, maybe learn something, and still get back to his damnable guests before dinner.

Setting the horse into a long canter, he sped through the gates and turned in the direction of the duke's estate. He must handle his inquiry carefully. It was bad enough that Aubrey knew of his *tendre* for Ellen. Brough Abingdon and Chris Brereley were guests of Brandon and Allesandra and would probably be present when he called. If he could help it, he certainly didn't want all of his friends to be aware of his secret.

What he wanted to do was to rush off to London, but he couldn't go away leaving guests in his house. Aubrey would gladly depart, but the Westhavens would probably show no impulse to follow his example. He had to devise some acceptable way to get rid of them. Perhaps he could think of something to say to Brough that would aid his sister's speedy departure. Again, he would have to be very careful or they would all guess the reason why.

He pulled up his lathered, heavily breathing horse two miles from Woodburn and walked the rest of the way, cooling the animal so that he wouldn't appear to have come in great haste. Stopping in front

of the big brick mansion, he dismounted nonchalantly and gave the reins and a coin to the waiting
servant. "Rub him down well."

"Yes, m'lord." The boy led away the big horse,
muttering softly about nobs riding fine horses so
hard that they were ready to collapse.

Harry trotted up the steps and nodded to the butler.

"Good afternoon, my lord. His Grace is in the
drawing room. If you'll come with me?"

The marquess handed him his hat, whip, and
gloves and followed him down the hall and into the
drawing room.

"Lord Singleton," the old retainer announced formally.

"Harry! Good to see you!" Brandon said cheerfully.

"Marie and the others aren't with you?" Brough
asked.

"No, it was a spur-of-the-moment decision. I went
riding and found myself nearby, so . . ."

Brough chuckled. "You were probably trying to
get some peace and quiet. I'm sorry, Harry! I imagine that you and Aubrey are getting weary of being
matrimonial targets, aren't you?"

The marquess shrugged coolly, feeling slightly irritated with his friend. He had just about had his fill
of the Westhavens. Marie was Brough's sister; as
such, she, her husband, and those two girls were
Brough's responsibility. However apologetic the earl
had been, he had dumped them at Shadybrook.
Why couldn't he realize that their welcome was
wearing thin?

Allesandra patted the sofa beside her. "Come sit
with me, Harry, and tell me the news of Shadybrook."

It couldn't have been better. She was the one he
wanted to talk with anyway. The duchess, he be-

lieved, had a small suspicion that there was more than friendship between himself and Ellen.

"I'm afraid that there isn't much news. Things have become rather dull," he said with a pointed glance toward Brough, which the earl chose to ignore. "I did pass by Bridgeford and found that Miss Trevayne has gone to London. That's the only news I have."

"Yes." Allesandra eyed him curiously. "She sent me a note."

"I see. I thought she was going with you," Harry said casually.

"She was. I suppose her grandfather was impatient for her company."

"Anxious to marry her off," the duke added.

"Brandon," Allesandra said quickly, "I believe I would like a glass of ratafia. And you haven't offered Harry anything."

"Damme! My abominable manners! Harry, you'll have brandy?"

"Thank you." He felt as though everyone were staring at him. Did his feelings for Ellen show on his very face? Or had everyone merely guessed?

The duke set down his own glass and moved to serve him. "The old man's planning to arrange a marriage for her. I suppose he thinks he knows what he's doing, but if I know Ellen, she'll give him a merry dance. Still, she should wed someone."

Harry began to feel ill. A marriage of convenience? And evidently Ellen approved or she wouldn't have gone away with her grandfather. He thought of their kiss in the garden. She had accused him of trifling with her. She had no idea how he felt about her. He *had* to rid himself of the Westhavens and hurry to London before Mr. Frampton overturned everything. Ellen didn't think he cared for her. He had to make her realize that he did. And he'd have to do it in a very short time.

"She's too tall for most men," Christopher remarked.

"Yes, and I think . . ." Brough began.

"Who gives a damn what you think?" Harry said shortly. "If you thought, you wouldn't have saddled me with your obnoxious family."

The earl flushed. "I can't believe you said that, Harry. I explained it all to you and you acted as though you understood."

"You're a milksop, Brough." No sooner had the words left his mouth than he realized the horror of the situation. All eyes upon him, he quickly stood and bowed to Allesandra. "I'm sorry my dear. I seem to be creating disorder in your home. I'll leave now."

"No, Harry, it is . . ."

He strode from the room, wishing that he had held his temper and kept his mouth shut. The earl had every right to call him out. If Brough weren't such an even-tempered gentleman he probably would have done so then and there.

"Brandon!" Allesandra cried. "Do something!"

Her husband stood stunned, still holding Harry's glass. "What do you suppose got into him?"

With a mew of aggravation she sprang to her feet and hurried after the marquess.

The butler was worriedly explaining to Harry why his horse wasn't ready and waiting. "I'm sorry, my lord. We had no idea that you would leave this soon."

"Well, be about it as quickly as possible! I'll wait out here." He stepped outside and took a deep breath.

"Harry!" Allesandra caught his arm. "Please don't go off like this."

"Why not? Or shall I stay until he has no choice but to challenge me to a duel?" he asked stiffly.

"We are all your friends and we know something's bothering you."

Harry impatiently tapped his riding crop against his boot. "I can't talk about it."

"Allesandra." Brough came up behind her and motioned her back to the house, then took her place beside the marquess. "I want to apologize," he said quietly. "I had no right to allow Marie to take advantage of our friendship."

The marquess shook his head. "It is I who owe you the apology. I did understand the situation you were placed in. I'm sorry I struck out at you."

"Marie can try a man's nerves. It's understandable."

"That's not it. She hasn't been so bad," Harry muttered.

"Then what is it? Can I help? Can we all help?"

"No." He forced a smile. "I'm just glad that we don't have to square off at each other at ten paces."

Brough grinned. "That isn't my way of solving problems, especially with my friends. Come back in, Harry, and let's have a drink together."

A groom led the marquess' rangy chestnut up to the steps. The earl noticed that the horse bore signs of a hasty rubdown and that he had been ridden hard and fast. Whatever had happened, Harry had come rather hastily to Woodburn.

"I'd better leave, Brough, but let everyone know we've no hard feelings between us."

"Of course, but I wish . . ."

"Good-bye." He swung his long frame into the saddle and turned the horse down the lane.

It was a gloomy company that assembled for dinner in Woodburn's big walnut-paneled dining room. After Harry's abrupt departure, the conversation had turned to other topics but each one privately thought about the marquess and speculated on what was bothering him so. No one was willing to broach the subject, however, and was waiting for someone else to do it.

Finally Christopher broke the ice. "I don't believe I've ever seen Harry with a problem. Other than choosing between two mistresses!" He laughed, then flushed. "I'm sorry, Allesandra. I sometimes forget that you are not a man."

"Thank you, I'm sure," she said in mock pique.

"Really, love," the duke said with a grin, "from this crowd that is a very high compliment indeed."

"I know that!" She looked fondly from one to the other. "I also think I know what is wrong with Harry. And so do you, Brandon."

"I do?"

"Please tell us," Brough begged. "No matter what he said, I still feel guilty about Marie."

"I'm surprised you all haven't noticed. Harry is in love with Ellen."

"With Ellen Trevayne! I can't feature it," Chris said flatly. "Miss Trevayne is so . . . so unlike the kind of lady he would choose."

Allesandra shrugged. "Believe what you wish. I'll believe what I've seen."

"I agree," her husband said quietly. "That's exactly what's wrong with him."

"I get it!" Brough cried. "Miss Trevayne has gone to London and Harry can't go because of his guests."

"Exactly. Brandon, don't you remember telling about Ellen's grandfather's plans to marry her off?" Allesandra went on.

"Good God!" Chris said, struck. "No wonder he became so overset!"

Brough pushed back his plate and rested his elbows on the table. "Well, the first thing we have to do is to get Marie out of there. Then Harry can go up to London, pop the question, and all will be well.''

''We?'' Brandon asked. ''Have you a mouse in your pocket, Brough? Marie is your sister.''

''All right then,'' the earl said with distaste. ''Me. I suppose I will have to regain my manly reputation. I damn well don't want to be thought a milksop!''

''Bring the Westhavens here,'' Allesandra offered. ''Tell Marie that I long for a lengthy visit with her. Make it seem to be an insult if she refuses.''

The duke made a gagging sound. ''Then how are *we* to go to London?''

''If you recall, we weren't going until after the harvest.''

''Oh, no, I won't miss seeing old Harry bite the bullet, Allesandra!''

''Nor shall I!'' Brough and Christopher exclaimed simultaneously.

''We can't go running to London as though it were an exhibition,'' Allesandra said firmly.

The three men grinned.

''We can't! You are behaving like mischievous little boys. Brandon, please!''

''She is right.'' He sighed. ''We'll have to carry on the house party for a few days at least. Then . . .''

''Brandon . . .''

''Very well. We shall let Harry do his courting in peace. But what if he needs our advice?''

''He won't.''

''But . . .''

''Harry is quite capable of handling the situation, I believe.'' She stood up. ''Now I'll leave you to your port. I shall see you in the drawing room for coffee. And gentlemen, no subterfuge!''

10

Mr. Frampton tied his cravat rather haphazardly, horrifying his valet, and shrugged into his black evening coat. Tonight was the first night in his parade of suitable bachelors. He hoped that his granddaughter would dress stunningly.

He had planned to host one large dinner party for all his particular friends and their wives and sons, but Ellen had thwarted his arrangements. She had claimed hotly that it would be like a livestock sale and refused to participate unless he limited his introductions to one eligible at a time. He went along with her, as he had lately found himself doing, and decided to take each family alphabetically, hoping that his recalcitrant granddaughter would be well enough pleased by one of the early candidates so that he could forget this nonsense and get back to his regular routine.

He loved Ellen dearly, but she was beginning to grate on his nerves. The chit was stubborn and hardheaded—rather like himself, he had to admit. It seemed that she deliberately took the opposite view to his every suggestion, idea, or order, and usually she ended up getting her own way. When she didn't confront him directly, she used her feminine wiles so that she got around him before he realized what

127

was happening. He began to believe that he should indeed teach her his business. In the financial world she would be formidable.

It was just too bad that she was a woman. There was a fine brain going to waste in that handsome body. But at least she could become an excellent helpmate to her husband, if he were strong enough to control her.

Mr. Frampton didn't envy the unknown gentleman. Her mixture of quick mind, independence, and femininity, combined with volatility, was enough to give the best of men a brilliant headache. He felt slightly guilty about foisting her off onto the innocent son of one of his associates, but they, like himself, looked upon the match as a business deal. Whichever son she chose would be extremely lucky and he would consider himself honored. The Frampton interests and fortune would more than make up for the difficulty of living with that headstrong girl.

He let himself out into the hall and strode heavily to his granddaughter's door, rapping loudly. "Are you ready, Ellen?"

"Not quite, Grandfather," she called back. "Only a few more minutes."

"I'll be waiting in the salon."

Staring into the mirror, Ellen made a face of distaste. "Dora, I'm not at all looking forward to this."

"But you are so pretty tonight, miss!" The maid formed a final wispy curl and set aside the curling tongs.

"Something terrible will probably happen and Grandfather will be furious."

"Don't even think about it. Nothing has happened in a long time."

"The fates have been saving up for tonight," Ellen predicted direly, then shook herself. "Oh, so what? If it turns him away, I'll have one less to deal with!"

"Now don't say that." Dora applied a touch of coloring to her mistress' cheeks. "He might be The One."

Ellen shook her head. None of them would be The One. Harry would always have that distinction. She might become fond of another, but she would never really love him, not like she adored the marquess.

Her spirits fell. This was the first entertainment in some time when she wouldn't have the thrill of seeing him. What was he doing now? Continuing with his house party, flirting with the fashionable young ladies? Had he forgotten her completely?

Pain constricted her chest. She shouldn't have left until after the harvest. At least she could have seen him once in a while. He might have even kissed her again—although on reflection, she doubted it. Hadn't he apologized for "overstepping his bounds"? The kiss in the garden at the Shadybrook ball had meant nothing to him.

"Oh, miss, I've smeared it."

"I'm sorry; it's my fault." Ellen held her head perfectly still while Dora reapplied the color to her left cheek.

"There now. You're ready."

The heavy fall of the brass door knocker resounded through the house. "They're here!" Ellen cried. "And I am late to greet them." Hastily she stood up. "Are you sure I look all right?"

"Why, you're fit to meet a prince!" Dora said cheerfully. *Or a marquess,* she thought. Whoever the young man was, he wasn't right for Miss Ellen. Only Lord Singleton was good enough for her.

Ellen hurried down the stairs; when she reached the bottom, she saw her grandfather standing in the hall with two men. She nodded pleasantly, walking towards them. Her grandfather turned, hearing the click of her heels on the marble floor.

"Ah, Ellen, I knew you wouldn't be late. Gentlemen, may I present my granddaughter, Miss Ellen Trevayne."

She dipped a slight curtsy while the men bowed.

"My dear, may I introduce you to Mr. Gerald Bradford and Mr. Gerald Bradford II."

She smiled pleasantly. "How do you do, gentlemen?"

"Shall we go to the salon?" Mr. Frampton offered her his arm and led the way.

Ellen took a chair as distant from any others as was socially acceptable. Her grandfather, frowning slightly, waved young Mr. Bradford to the nearest seat beside her and motioned a footman to serve the wine. With a pointed look at Ellen, he drew the elder Mr. Bradford aside.

She lowered her eyes, taking in the appearance of Mr. Gerald Bradford Junior through her lashes. He was not bad-looking, she decided. His brown hair and eyes were rather nice, though he did seem a bit nearsighted. She wondered if it came from poring over mathematical calculations all day long.

He was dressed neatly, but without the perfectly tailored style of Harry and Brandon. His figure, however, might be improved by Weston tailoring. There was no doubt that he could afford it. A wise wife could do much towards enhancing his appearance.

His most unfortunate feature was that he must have been an inch or two shorter than she was. Even the very flat heels on Ellen's shoes didn't make a difference. In her bare feet she would be taller than he.

Gerald Bradford Junior shifted uncomfortably. "I hear you have just come from the country, Miss Trevayne."

"Yes, from my estate, Bridgeford Grange."

"It must be cooler in the country."

"It is, but our weather here in London has not been unpleasant. I believe I can tell that fall is coming. Our nights are becoming much more agreeable."

"Indeed they are." He slowly sipped his drink. "I've never spent any amount of time in the country. Well, none, actually, unless you count travel to Southhampton or Portsmouth. My mother, who is deceased, you know, always wished for a place in the country. Unfortunately, it just wasn't practical. Papa did build her a nice house on the outskirts of London, but I don't suppose you could call that 'country,' could you?"

"I don't suppose so." Wed to Mr. Bradford, she would be quartered in London year-round.

"No. Well, with our business interests, that was the best he could do."

"I'm sure she appreciated the effort." Ellen struggled to think of something else to say. "Tell me, Mr. Bradford, what business are you in?"

"We own a shipping line."

"How interesting! I've always wanted to travel on a ship."

His eyes glowed. "You must allow me to take you to the docks sometime, Miss Trevayne. I'm sure you would be impressed."

"I'm sure I would. It all sounds very interesting. Please tell me more."

Happily, she had hit on a topic that could occupy Mr. Bradford for the entire evening. At dinner the conversation expanded to include the elder Mr. Bradford and Mr. Frampton. Embracing the subject with vigor, the older man told of several of his experiences when he was master of his first ship, the *Bonnie Jean*. The tales were interesting, particularly the one in which Mr. Bradford had been accosted by pirates, but when the time came for the gentlemen to have their cigars and port, Ellen was glad to escape to the drawing room.

When the men rejoined her, Mr. Gerald Bradford Junior made a beeline for her, seating himself quite unself-consciously beside her.

"Did I tell you, Miss Trevayne, that the names of our ships always begin with a 'B'? That is for 'Bradford,' of course. First there was the *Bonnie Jean,* then the *Barbara Ann,* and so on, right down to our newest, the largest ship in English trade, the *Becky Jane.*"

"How fascinating," she murmured. If she married Mr. Bradford she wouldn't even have a ship named for her.

"Indeed." He leaned closer. "May I be so bold to say, Miss Trevayne, that I have never met a lady with your interest in ships?"

"That is strange. Shipping is such an exciting business." She smiled, finishing her coffee.

"Oh, yes, and don't forget, when the *Becky Jane* comes in I shall escort you to the docks to see her! More coffee, Miss Trevayne?"

"No, thank you. I have had enough." Ellen had definitely had enough. She'd had enough coffee, enough of ships, and even though he meant well, she'd had enough of Mr. Bradford for one evening. It was a blessing that it was a weeknight and that the Bradfords needed to rise early in the morning to go to their offices, so they didn't make a late evening of it.

Mr. Bradford Junior lingered beside Ellen at the door. "I have had a lovely time, Miss Trevayne. May I call on you again?"

Mr. Frampton overheard. "I'm sure my granddaughter would enjoy that, young man. She knows so few people in London."

"Then we shall plan some outings," he said enthusiastically.

Ellen smiled noncommittally. "Good evening, Mr. Bradford."

Her grandfather shut the door. "Well, you seem to have impressed that young man!"

"I did nothing but ask him about his ships."

"That's the ticket! A man likes nothing better than to talk about his business!" He chuckled. "Oh, I can see that you'll do capital well! Your papa should have left it up to me years ago. Introduced you to the wrong crowd, he did. Can't expect results that way!"

"No, Grandfather." She was too tired and too bored to contradict him. "Goodnight." She kissed him and started up the stairs, pausing at the landing. "Who is next?"

"On Thursday we'll entertain the Derifield family. They're in wool."

"I see." She continued on to her bedroom. *Dear God,* she thought, *what shall I spend that evening doing? Talking of sheep?*

A black-lacquered carriage drawn by a blooded team of grays and bearing the crest of nobility drew up in front of the Frampton home. The blue-and-gold-liveried footman leaped down, drew out the steps, and opened the door. His lordship stepped out, turned, gathered up an enormous bouquet of flowers from the seat, and strode confidently up the steps.

Watching from within, Gordon, the butler, felt a slight sense of panic. No one like that had ever called at his master's residence. Not since his service with his previous employer had he greeted a member of the peerage. He sprang to the mirror to check his attire. Satisfied, he took a deep breath and opened the door before the brass knocker could fall.

"My lord." He bowed deeply, so low in fact that

he briefly wondered if his elderly bones would raise him again.

"Yes." His lordship looked at the head so far below his. "I have come to see Miss Trevayne. You may tell her that the Marquess of Singleton is calling."

Gordon managed to get himself upright. For a moment he was mesmerized by the splendidly tailored deep-blue coat, the powder-blue waistcoat, the creamy pantaloons, and the perfectly exquisite cravat. He swallowed with difficulty. A marquess! Second only to a duke. Third only to the royal family itself!

"I have come to see Miss Trevayne," he repeated.

The butler stared at the highly polished Hoby boots with their brilliant gold tassels. "She's out!" he squeaked.

"I beg your pardon?" A smile played at the corner of the marquess' lips.

Gordon drew himself up. "Miss Trevayne is out, my lord. She has gone shopping."

"Damme! Isn't that just my luck?"

"Would you care to wait, my lord?"

"No." He sighed. "When a lady goes shopping, a man can wait for hours. Give her these." He thrust the flowers into Gordon's hands and removed a calling card from his card case. "Please inform her that I shall call again."

"Yes, my lord!" Gordon bowed once more, waiting until the marquess had entered his carriage before he shut the door. Turning, he hurried as fast as his legs would carry him down the hall and through the green baize door to the servants' area. There he regaled his audience with every detail of the marquess' clothing and of every syllable he uttered.

Only Miss Trevayne's lady's maid was unsurprised. "I wondered how long it would take him to seek her out."

"What!" he cried.

Dora shrugged. "Lord Singleton has seemed to have a particular interest in Miss Ellen."

"But he is a marquess!"

"So?"

"Miss Ellen is . . . isn't . . ."

"That don't matter. He's a man and she's a woman. That's all that counts."

"A marquess," Gordon repeated wonderingly. "In this house."

"What's to do about that?" The maid looked down her pert nose. "At Bridgeford Grange, members of the peerage are frequent guests. Miss Ellen's best friend is Lady Allesandra Rackthall. When she comes up to town she'll want to see Miss Ellen first thing!"

"A duchess! Do you suppose she'll come here?"

"Why not?" Dora looked at her enthralled audience. "As I said, she and Miss Ellen are the very best of friends."

The knocker sounded again and the butler rushed back to the door, opening it to reveal his mistress herself. "Oh, Miss Ellen, you just missed a caller."

"I did?" She entered briskly, pulling off her gloves, and motioned to the footman behind her who was laden with parcels.

Wordlessly Gordon proffered the flowers and card.

She studied it as if memorizing the inscription. "Oh, dear," she said softly. "He was here just a moment ago?"

"Yes, Miss Ellen."

Ellen cleared her throat. "Please put these in water, Gordon, and . . . and have them brought up to my room."

"Yes, miss."

The butler watched her climb the stairs. Her hand trembled on the railing and her feet seemed uncertain of their destination. What was wrong with his employer's granddaughter? She didn't seem ill. Her eyes were sparkling and her cheeks were a healthy pink. Something else had shaken her. He turned to the young footman.

"Did Miss Ellen suffer any . . . accidents while shopping?"

"No, sir, not that I saw." He grinned irreverently. "She just seemed to have a fine time spending the old man's money."

Gordon frowned. The new lad was good-looking and sometimes seemed a bit too sure of himself. "You didn't try to take liberties with her, did you?"

"Certainly not, sir!" he cried angrily. "What d'you take me for?"

"Oh, go on about your business." The butler departed to the stillroom. He found an appropriate vase and set the flowers in water, his mind continuing to dwell on the lady's distress. He'd known Miss Ellen since she was a little girl. He was all too familiar with her awkwardness, her faux pas, and her calamities. On this visit, however, she'd seemed to be gaining some small measure of self-possession. Clad in her expensive new wardrobe, she'd almost seemed confident at times. What then had overset her today? If she wasn't ill, if she hadn't experienced any difficulties on her shopping expedition, it could only be one thing. It was the marquess. Hadn't Dora intimated that there was something between the two?

Gordon shuddered. No good could come of it. Even if his fine lordship could overlook Miss Ellen's mishaps, perhaps to the point of finding them charmingly endearing, he couldn't ignore Mr. Frampton. Worst of all, that crusty old soul would certainly not disregard him.

Ellen crossed the bedroom floor and sat down breathlessly on the edge of her bed. Harry! Harry was in London and he had come to see her! Her heart raced wildly. She had almost begun to accept her situation. Now he had come to upset it all.

She closed her eyes and gritted her teeth. Somehow she would get through it. Harry was her friend. Even though he had flirted, perhaps trifled, with her, he had apologized. He was her good neighbor. Somehow she would convince herself to think of him as that and nothing more.

There was a scratch at the door. Dora entered, carrying the immense bouquet of flowers. "Look how pretty they are, Miss Ellen," she said, beaming. "Isn't it nice to have his lordship nearby once more?"

"I don't want to talk about it!"

"But . . ."

"I do not wish to discuss Lord Singleton," Ellen said firmly.

"I think he's properly smitten, that I do."

She would have no peace from her abigail, whose mind was set on believing the impossible. Short of a show of outright anger, she would not be able to silence her.

"I'm going riding," she declared. "Please bring out my habit, Dora. I need some fresh air."

"What if Lord Singleton comes back?"

"He has called once; he won't return today." Ellen favored her with a wily smile. "Perhaps I shall see him in the park."

As she had expected, the possibility lent speed to Dora's efforts and soon Ellen was riding through the gates of Hyde Park. Thank heavens that the ruse had worked. If it hadn't, she would still be hearing Dora's speculations on Harry's attitude towards her, while she dressed her at a frustratingly slow rate of speed. She was lucky that the girl didn't know that few gentlemen of fashion were to be found in the park at this hour. With the exception of nursemaids and children, she would have the place to herself.

Ellen set the gelding into an easy trot and turned him towards one of the little-used bridle paths. A brisk gallop was just what she needed. She urged the horse to greater speed, experiencing nearly the same exhilaration as she did while riding in the fields of Bridgeford. Oh, how it cleared the cobwebs from her mind and the aching from her heart! But this was London and distance was limited so she couldn't keep it up for long.

"Miss Trevayne!"

She checked her horse. Had someone called her name?

"Miss Trevayne!" the gentleman's voice repeated.

Ellen pulled up from her less than decorous pace. Cheeks still pink from the exhilaration of it, she turned in her saddle to see who had hailed her.

"Miss Trevayne?" A fair-haired gentleman cantered forward.

Recognition dawned. "Lord Standish," she said politely, remembering him as being one of Harry's houseguests in Kent. He had been kind at the ball, in spite of the fact that he had witnessed the distressing melee at the stream with the dogs.

"How nice to see you, Miss Trevayne," he drawled pleasantly, "and without an escort. Perhaps I may fill that role?"

Her stomach twitched nervously. Merciful heavens! There was no way around it. She couldn't gracefully refuse him. Aubrey Standish had left her no way out. She must take care to act like the most perfect lady.

"I would be honored, my lord," she murmured, "though I have almost finished my ride."

He grinned charmingly. "I too have had my last gallop of the day."

Ellen's rosy cheeks grew even warmer. "So you saw that," she said uncomfortably.

"An enchanting picture."

She decided to be honest. "I fear that most people would not agree with you, my lord. It was rather madcap."

He laughed. "I am not like most people, Miss Trevayne. I greatly admire a lady who rides well. Most don't, or at least they pretend as though they can't."

Ellen looked into his warm blue eyes. "I believe you have given me a compliment. Thank you, my lord."

"Indeed, and I shall render one more. Your appearance, ma'am, is just as enchanting as your equestrian ability. I am quite distracted."

"Fustian!"

"You wound me, Miss Trevayne," he said with a dramatic sigh.

"I am sure that you will rise above it."

"Only with the greatest difficulty."

Ellen giggled.

"There!" he said with satisfaction. "I have succeeded in making you laugh at last. Shall we have another short gallop?"

"As you please."

She let him take the lead and followed behind, happy to feel the wind blowing in her face. He held his horse to match the gelding's slower pace and, as they neared the proximity of Rotten Row, drew in. "Long enough?"

"Yes, thank you. It was lovely, even if it was very improper of me to ride at such a speed."

"Nonsense! I admire your spirit," he said frankly.

She shook her head, laughing. "You know very well, my lord, that daring in a lady is not to be applauded."

"It is a great shame to repress it."

"Perhaps. But that is the way of things."

Even though her ride with Lord Standish had gone along rather well, Ellen was relieved to see the portals of the park. She could scarcely believe that there had been no mishaps, especially since he was a charming, handsome, and eligible man. Many young ladies would give their eyeteeth to ride with him. It was strange that his presence hadn't turned her to jelly.

She smiled radiantly. "You must excuse me now, my lord. Here is the gate and I really must go home."

"I couldn't think of your riding unescorted in the streets," he said, frowning. "I shall accompany you."

"It truly isn't necessary."

"The streets are dangerous, Miss Trevayne. Besides, it shall be my pleasure."

"Very well."

Once again she was surprised to be able to carry on conversation with him without being reduced to nervous spasms. Despite her previous desire to behave like a perfect lady, she found that she just didn't care. If Aubrey Standish liked her, so be it. If he did not, what did it matter? He would not be a part of her future.

She reined in as they reached her grandfather's house. "Here we are, my lord. I thank you for the escort."

He dismounted quickly, tossed his reins to the Frampton groom, and assisted her down. "I've enjoyed it, Miss Trevayne." He gave her his arm as they walked to the door, which was opened to reveal the butler with Mr. Frampton standing behind him.

"Oh, dear," Ellen said under her breath. "He has come home early."

"And where have you been, young lady?" her

grandfather demanded, his eyes not on her but on the gentleman accompaning her.

"Riding," she said mildly. "My lord, may I introduce my grandfather, Mr. Frampton? Grandfather, Viscount Standish."

"A viscount! Will I never be rid of the nobs!" Mr. Frampton turned abruptly and went into the salon, leaving Lord Standish in mid-bow.

Ellen flushed scarlet. "I . . . I do apologize, my lord. He must have had a difficult day," she explained helplessly.

His lordship grinned, exposing his dimples. "I understand completely. Please don't give it another thought, Miss Trevayne." He brought her hand to his lips. "I shall bid you good day. May I call again?"

She nodded worriedly, making a stiff curtsy. He understood completely? Oh, yes, she was sure he did! It probably wouldn't be long before the entire Polite World knew of her grandfather's ill-conduct. But what difference did it make to her? Mr. Frampton was admired within his own circle and that was where she would reside.

11

Harry studied the latest communication from his
man of business. It seemed that several investors wished to buy the piece of Thames riverside
property he owned and were willing to pay a most
generous price. He penned a large "No" in the mar-
gin. Brough moored his yacht there for most of the
year and was always willing to plan a cruise. The
group of friends enjoyed the easy access and had
spent many pleasant hours on the water. Besides, if
the city continued to expand at its current rate, the
land would be worth a great deal more in a very
short time. No, owning the acreage meant more to
him than the money to be gained.

Before he could go on to the next item, the library
door opened.

"Hello, Harry." Grinning, Aubrey showed himself in.

"Aubrey! Just the man to provide me a respite
from business matters!" Harry pushed the papers
aside, rose, and went to the liquor cabinet. "Will
you have a glass of brandy?"

"Have you ever known me to turn it down?" The
viscount drew up a chair opposite the desk.

Harry began to fill the glasses. "I haven't seen

142

you since we returned from the country. Have you been keeping busy?"

"Indeed so. Apparently you've been occupied too. I called late last afternoon and again yesterday evening, but you were out."

"I've been trying to catch up on several items of business that I postponed this summer. Then my aunt got wind that I was in town and insisted that I come to dinner. Believe me, Aubrey, I'd rather have spent the time with you!"

"I'm sure you would have," he said, chuckling, "for I spent part of my afternoon riding with Ellen in the park."

"Ellen?"

"Yes. *Your* Ellen."

Harry stiffened, setting his jaw. A spark of jealousy burned through his abdomen. Aubrey escorting Ellen? The man was supposed to be his best friend. Just what the hell did he think he was doing?

"She is lovely, Harry, and she rides like an angel. Allesandra is a good rider, but I fear that Ellen outshines her on that score."

Harry set the bottle down, picked up the drinks, and turned. "I'm glad that you had an enjoyable ride," he said coolly.

"I certainly did." Aubrey picked an infinitesimal bit of lint from his deep-blue coat. "Have you seen her yet? She must have been shopping since she came to town, for her riding habit was in the very first stare of fashion. Lord, but a tall, slender woman like Ellen is vastly attractive in a habit!"

Harry gritted his teeth. Abruptly he shoved the glass forward, dashing most of its contents into his friend's lap.

"Dammit!" Aubrey cried as the liquor soaked his pantaloons. He fumbled for his handkerchief. "What the hell!"

The marquess gazed woodenly at him as if mesmerized.

"Aren't you going to help me?"

Harry snapped from his daze and extended his handkerchief. "I'm sorry, Aubrey. I'll ring for my valet and . . ."

"Don't bother!" His friend bounded to his feet and stalked past Harry to the cabinet, refilling his glass and drinking deeply. "Dammit, Harry, look at me! What do you suppose that people will think when they see me riding home? Why the hell did you do it?"

"Good God, it was an accident. I don't know why you're making such an issue of it!"

"That's easy for you to say! You weren't the one who was drenched!"

"Well, maybe it served to dampen your ardor a bit!"

"Dampen my ardor?" Aubrey stared at him and then burst out laughing. "Hell's fire and brimstone, Harry, you're jealous!"

"I don't know what you're talking about." The marquess rounded the desk and dropped into his chair.

"You're jealous of me because I rode with Ellen yesterday!"

"I most certainly am not."

"Tell me, old friend, did you try to drown me on purpose?"

"No!"

Grinning, Aubrey returned to his seat. "Let me assure you that my outing was all very innocent. I was trying out a new horse in the park. I came upon Ellen, we rode for a while, then I escorted her home."

"You seem to be on a first-name basis," Harry said as nonchalantly as possible.

"Only to you! I called her 'Miss Trevayne' to her

face. Everything was proper, Harry. I'm your friend!
I wouldn't trespass on your territory!''

The marquess took a long sip of his brandy. ''I
feel like a fool. I act like one too! First I insult Brough,
and now, you. I seem to be setting out to make my
friends despise me. I swear I don't know what is
wrong with me of late!''

Aubrey shook his head. ''The lady has overset
you.''

''Apparently so.''

''Have you called on her?''

''Early yesterday afternoon. She was out, so I
didn't see her, but I left her a bouquet of flowers. I
planned on visiting again later this morning.''

''Was her grandfather there when you called?''
his friend asked curiously.

''If he was, I didn't see him.''

''I did.'' Aubrey feigned a shudder. ''Damme,
Harry, he's a regular old curmudgeon with a vile
attitude towards anyone with a title. What an opin-
ionated old Turk!''

''Ellen's father was a baronet. He must not have
held that view when her parents were wed.''

''Who knows?'' The viscount shrugged. ''He was
in the hall when I brought Ellen home. He made a
comment about wondering if he'd ever be rid of the
nobs and gave me the cut direct. Ellen was mortified. She tried to apologize for him.''

''Hm.''

''That's why I've been so anxious to see you.
You'd best proceed cautiously, Harry, and take
plenty of time to size up that tough old war-horse.
If he has any influence over Ellen, you may have
difficulties.''

''Yes, and if I'm too hesitant, she may decide to
marry one of those Cits that the old man is suppos-
edly pushing at her.'' The marquess sighed.

Aubrey looked at his friend sympathetically. "That's true too. You'll have to ride a fine line."

"So it seems. But for all her mishaps, Ellen has good sense. And she most certainly has a streak of independence unusual in a lady. I trust she won't jump as quickly as Mr. Frampton might wish." Harry retrieved the bottle and replenished both of their glasses.

"Or . . . you might ask her immediately and nip the grandfather at his own game."

"I fear that's a bit too hasty. If you recall, the last time I saw her she was very angry with me. No, I'll proceed cautiously. If I detect any signs of trouble, I'll forge ahead." Harry grinned. "And I'll try to keep her so busy that she hasn't much time to see any of those Cits."

"You know that I'm willing to help in any way that I can."

"Well, I can't live in her pocket. I may have you call on her from time to time."

"Certainly," Aubrey agreed.

"But not too often." The marquess eyed his friend thoughtfully. Aubrey was handsome and he was Ellen's height. With his blond hair and blue eyes and those flirtatious dimples, he could make many a lady's heart beat considerably faster. "I don't want you for competition."

The viscount laughed. "Don't concern yourself with that! I don't intend to marry for a very, very long time!"

"I thought your father was continually pounding you on that subject."

"Now there's another curmudgeon for you! But don't you know how I love thwarting his schemes? No, Harry, you're the sole victim this Season. If you decide to leap into the parson's mousetrap, you'll do it on your own!"

* * *

As Harry mounted the steps of the Frampton mansion, another gentleman was taking his leave. For politeness' sake the marquess touched his hat brim to him, but he felt anything but mannerly. The young man was dressed well enough, though he was not a looking-glass of fashion. He seemed brisk and businesslike as he passed Harry. He was probably one of those Cits that Mr. Frampton planned to wed to Ellen.

The butler, who had remained at the open door, bowed low. "Good morning, my lord."

Harry nodded. "Is Miss Trevayne in?"

"Indeed she is." He took the marquess' hat and gloves and led him to the salon.

Ellen rose from the sofa with a smile of pure delight. "Lord Singleton, how pleasant it is to see you! Gordon, won't you replenish the tea tray?"

Harry bowed and kissed her hand. He experienced a sense of irritation. So she'd taken refreshment with that Cit?

"You've missed a most interesting conversation," she went on. "I know you would have enjoyed it. Mr. Bradford has visited places all over the world. His tales were quite fascinating."

"And quite embellished for maximum effect, I daresay."

She glanced quizzically at him. "I wouldn't know about that," she murmured, sinking once more to the sofa.

Instead of taking the chair opposite, which had probably been occupied by the Bradford fellow, Harry sat down beside her. His eyes drank in her appearance.

Ellen Trevayne was even lovelier than he had remembered. She had a look of polish that hadn't been present in the country. From the top of her shining honey-colored hair to the tips of the soft kid slippers peeking from beneath the hem of her gown, she was perfectly groomed and truly elegant. He wasn't sure he liked the metamorphosis.

"You must tell me the news of the neighborhood, Harry."

He smiled. At lease she hadn't acquired so much town bronze that she refused to call him by his first name.

"There isn't much to tell. My house party broke up soon after you left. Marie and her entourage went to Woodburn for a few days' visit. Aubrey, as you know, came on to London."

"Yes, we had an agreeable ride in the park." Her eyes twinkled merrily. "I'm sure that Allesandra and Brandon—the duke particularly—are enjoying their latest guests."

He burst into laughter. Here at last was the real Ellen, refreshingly outspoken and honest. "Marie is really insufferable, isn't she? And those girls! I wish that Taffy and Friendly had knocked them into the stream!"

"Oh, no!" Ellen's cheeks grew pink. "It was mishap enough as it was! I shall never live it down."

Gordon entered with the tea tray, set it on the low table before them, and backed away, then hovered by the door.

"That will be all," Harry told him.

The butler looked at Ellen, who nodded. "Thank you, Gordon. You needn't fear for my reputation. The marquess and I are old friends."

Friends again! Harry grinned. He was going to prove to her that he was more than just a friend. He reached to take her hand, but she leaned forward to pour the tea.

Damme! He certainly hoped that the Bradford nabob hadn't sat beside her. If so, the Cit would have gotten a tempting view of her soft breasts and the enticing crevice between them. The room seemed to become oppressively warm. Harry took a deep breath.

"I've done something naughty," Ellen said, presenting him with his tea.

"I wish I could," he blurted.

She eyed him inquiringly.

It was his turn to blush. "I mean . . . I . . ."

She bent forward to pick up her own cup and noticed the exposure of her bosom. "Oh, my."

"I wasn't looking there, Ellen, really I wasn't," he babbled, realizing how ridiculous he sounded. "I was referring to something else. I mean . . . Oh, hell! You're a lovely woman. Of course I was looking!"

The pink in her cheeks became fiery red. "I must apologize, Harry."

"For what?"

"Well," she admitted, "I shouldn't have noticed that *you* noticed, thus causing you embarrassment."

He groaned. "For God's sake, let us just forget the incident. Tell me in what manner you have been naughty."

"Oh, *that!*" She laughed, diffusing the tension. "I've sent to Bridgeford for the dogs and one of my horses. Grandfather will be furious, but I am bored, Harry. For most of the day, there is nothing to occupy me. The horse Grandfather provided me is nice enough, but he is no challenge. And I do miss Taffy and Friendly."

"Where will you keep them . . . the dogs, that is?"

"In the mews. There is an empty stall and a large enough area out back to build a temporary run. I've enlisted one of the grooms to assist me with them."

"Be careful," he warned. "Those dogs are used to roaming. Will they receive enough exercise?"

"I think so. They'll have the dog run and they are trained to the leash. I can walk them in the park."

"Somehow I cannot visualize Taffy and Friendly going along on leashes."

"Oh, yes, I trained them to the leash when they were puppies. I am sure that they will remember."

Harry had a horrible vision of what disaster that might entail, but he kept his wariness to himself. Today he had already put his foot in his mouth too many times, first with Aubrey and then with her. He wouldn't risk it again.

"Speaking of the park, Ellen, I would like to ask you to go riding with me. Tomorrow? At five?"

"I would like that very much, but Grandfather is entertaining guests for dinner and I must oversee the arrangements."

"We could ride in the morning, then. Wouldn't that give you sufficient time for preparation?"

"Well . . . all right," she said slowly.

"Excellent! Shall I come by at ten?"

She nodded.

"I shall be looking forward to it." He smiled. "Aubrey tells me that you were quite enchanting yesterday."

Ellen laughed. "Aubrey is kind."

He visited a short while longer and then took his leave. The call had greatly allayed his fear that she was still angry with him over the incident in the garden at Shadybrook. He couldn't believe the faux pas he had made today, however. How could he have gotten caught looking down the bodice of her dress and then, horror of horrors, admitted to it? It was a wonder she hadn't smacked his face and ordered him to leave. Aubrey was right. Ellen had unsettled him beyond anything he had ever experienced. He must take great care in the future or he would truly land himself in the suds!

Ellen wasn't looking forward to the evening with the Derifields. Buoyant from her visit with Harry, she wished she could have stayed in her room and dreamed of him, as fruitless as it might be. But Mr. Frampton had planned this entertainment and she had agreed, even though she had to drag herself downstairs on leaden feet. With any luck at all they would be busy like the Bradfords and make a short night of it. Sizing up her guests, she certainly hoped that would be the case.

Although Mrs. Derifield, with her coarse white hair and her heavy muzzle, had the look of a sheep and the dull, ruminant personality of the species, the talk was not of the animal itself, but of the wool it produced. The Derifields were manufacturers and exporters of fine woolen fabric. Of late they had had their problems with their workmen's reluctance to accept modernization, but their enterprise was much too large to be vastly effected.

Mr. and Mrs. Derifield had two eligible sons, Edward and James. Both, unfortunately, bore a distinct resemblance to their mother. They were Ellen's height, just barely, and while they were not fat, their figures promised stoutness in middle age.

As soon as Ellen inquired about the process of turning fleece to cloth, both took a great interest in instructing her, which did not lessen throughout the long evening. When they finally left, she was ready to swear off woolen garments for the rest of her life. Of the two evenings spent with her grandfather's cohorts, she found the shipping industry, with its tall masts, pirates, and hurricanes, far more preferable a topic of conversation than that of shearing sheep.

"Two in one!" Mr. Frampton said with satisfaction as he closed the door behind them. "Now how did you like those young men?"

"Not as well as Mr. Bradford," she admitted.

"*That* young man is an excellent choice!"

"I haven't chosen yet, Grandfather. I shall see the others."

"It seems we're in for a long haul," he muttered.

"I'll not marry anyone without knowing him. Also, Mr. Bradford is shorter than I am."

"He don't seem to mind it. Sent you a present, didn't he?"

"Yes. A book about ships! I suppose that the Derifields will send me a book about sheep. They think I should turn Bridgeford Grange into a sheep farm."

"I've heard worse ideas, missy."

"Who is next?" she asked in exasperation.

"The Evermans, rival bankers. A good merger that would make! Together we could form a monumental empire of finance! Think of it. And they're tomorrow night, so get yourself to bed, missy. We've a long day ahead."

"You do, perhaps. Except for a ride in the park, I have nothing to do but mope around the house. I am bored."

"Go out and buy yourself some pretties!" he said magnanimously. "I'll stand the toll!"

"I don't want to go shopping. I want to *do* something. At Bridgeford there was always something to do."

Exasperated, he threw up his hands. "I don't understand you, missy! A ride and a dinner party are a sufficient day's entertainment for any woman!"

"Tomorrow is a poor example." She thought of broaching the subject of the dogs, but decided to wait. She had given him food for thought and that was enough for now. She was beginning to realize that it was better to spend several days warming to the subject, rather than confronting him outright. Men! She wondered if Harry was like that.

12

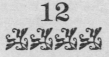

E llen awoke far earlier than was her usual hour of rising since she'd come to London. Lying awake in the gray dawn light, she listened to the street come alive beneath her window with the clop of horses' hooves, the squeak of wagon wheels, and the muffled calls of tradesmen to each other as they made early deliveries to the mansions on the square. A late, late pair of revelers passed by, their lusty young male voices raised in unintelligible song.

The Frampton residence, too, was coming to life. She heard soft footsteps in the hall and the opening and closing of her grandfather's door. There was a scratch at her own door and the chambermaid quietly entered, startled to see her mistress awake.

"Good morning, miss." She bobbed a curtsy and knelt at the hearth to kindle a blaze that would warm the night's damp, leftover chilliness.

"Good morning." Ellen yawned.

The girl sat back on her heels and dusted the stray ash back into the firebox.

Idly watching her, Ellen realized how little she knew of her grandfather's servants. She knew this maid's name and that was all. At Bridgeford she would have known of her hopes and problems, who her family was and their problems as well.

"Are you happy here, Betty?"

Again the maid was astonished, but she dimpled at her mistress' interest. "Oh, yes, miss. This house's a fine place to work in."

"What makes the difference?" Ellen mused aloud. Treatment? Amount of work?

"Miss?"

"What do you like about it here?"

"Oh . . . uh . . . everything, miss." Betty brightened. "I like m'room. There's only two of us to share. In m'first job, there was six."

"Six!" At Bridgeford Grange the few live-ins had their own small rooms.

" 'Tis not uncommon, miss." She edged towards the door.

Ellen saw that she was in a hurry to be about her chores. "Thank you, Betty."

"Yes, Miss Ellen. I'll be sending Dora to you."

"I want her to be sure to finish her breakfast first."

An expression of amazement crossed the maid's face, then she curtsied and took her leave.

Six servants to a room! Ellen shuddered. There would be a complete lack of privacy, space, solitude. Who would have believed that behind the beautiful facades of the great London houses there existed such a paucity of servants' quarters? It pointed out how little she knew of life beyond Bridgeford Grange. That was a failing she could remedy. She had complained about having nothing she could do. Now here indeed was something. She would learn how to run a London house. Many more things must be different about it and after all, she would be required to do so in a short amount of time.

She sighed. So many aspects of her life would soon be changing. Most importantly, she would be caring for a husband. Ellen sank deeper into the feather mattress. Would he share her bed or join her only to . . . to . . . and then return to his own room?

What would it be like to wake up in a man's arms? She could only picture Harry holding her that intimately.

Heat surged through her body as she recalled how he had looked down the bodice of her dress. He must have seen a great deal of her. Oh my, she must never wear that gown again! She wondered how much Mr. Bradford had viewed. Had he, like Harry, been tempted to be "naughty"? Somehow she doubted it. He had been too wrapped up in the telling of his travel adventures.

Truthfully she couldn't visualize Mr. Bradford, or the Derifields either, becoming "naughty" about anything to do with her. They saw her as a sounding board for their stories and as the means of a merger for their businesses. Not Harry. He had looked at her as a man should look at a woman, as someone desirable in her own right. It gave her confidence in her femininity and made her forget her awkwardness. It made her feel beautiful. Couldn't her grandfather come up with an astute young businessman who could do that? If he did, her decision could be quickly made.

Dora's cheerful greeting interrupted her reverie. "Up early this morning, miss?"

"Yes. I'm going riding with Lord Singleton, but not until ten o'clock. I do hope it stays cool enough for me to wear my new velvet habit."

"Yes, miss! It'll drive Lord Singleton to passions!" She plumped up the pillows as Ellen sat up and then set the breakfast tray on her lap.

Ellen laughed. "The marquess is much too sophisticated a gentleman to be driven to paroxysms, Dora. Besides, even if it were possible, I doubt that a riding habit would do so."

"Don't be too sure, miss. He's much attracted to you."

"Yes . . . well . . ." She changed the subject.

While her abigail went about her morning chores, Ellen questioned her thoroughly about her fellow servants. By the time Ellen was dressed for her outing, she had gained a wealth of knowledge about life below stairs in this London residence and in others as well. It was a start. Next she would see the housekeeper and take up the reins as mistress.

The powder-blue habit fitted her perfectly. Ellen felt almost alluring in it, especially with the addition of the jaunty matching hat with its long, curling plume. She smiled at her reflection in the mirror. She certainly looked the part of a stylish peer's companion. Now if there were no mishaps, the day would be hers.

She had already descended to the hall when Harry arrived. She couldn't help tilting her head coquettishly as his eyes raked over her.

"You look most attractive today, Miss Trevayne."

"Thank you, my lord." She took his arm and walked past Gordon and his gawking young footman.

"Since you complained of your horse, I brought you one of my own to ride. Your saddle has already been changed." He grinned. "I believe that I chose well. She matches your habit."

Ellen studied the leggy blue roan, whose mixture of blue-black and gray hairs did indeed complement her apparel. "I never thought of matching my clothing to my horse, or vice versa."

"In London, the ladies consider such things to be quite important."

"Then I shall be in perfect style when my sorrel arrives for I also have a habit of red."

"Indeed. Shall I give you a leg up?"

"Thank you." She slipped her arm across his shoulders and, in doing so, her fingers touched the dark hair at the nape of his neck. An eerie craving stirred in her abdomen. She gazed into his eyes. It lasted only a moment, but it seemed like an eon. Quickly she raised her knee and let him lift her onto the mare. She lowered her eyes, making a science of lacing her reins.

The marquess mounted his own horse. "Are you ready?" he asked gravely.

"Yes."

They rode silently to the park. All conversation seemed to have fled from her mind. Luckily the mare was slightly skittish in the city traffic so she could make a pretense of concentrating on her mount.

Harry led the way down a familiar bridle path. "Do you want to canter or is she still a bit too fresh?"

"I can hold her."

They eased the horses into a canter. Finding the path wide enough for two, Ellen allowed her mount to move up beside Harry's stallion. Her knee touched his and once again she was assailed by the strange yearning. She wanted to hold him and to have him hold her. She wanted him to touch her.

"Do you like the mare?" he called.

"She's perfectly marvelous!"

They entered a copse of trees and rounded a turn. Ahead of them in the path were two horses, an equestrienne and her groom. The young lady was frowning at her sidesaddle which was lying in the dust. The groom had dismounted and was hurrying forward. Ellen and the marquess reined in.

"Lady Christina," Harry greeted her.

"Oh, Lord Singleton, you've caught me in a tumble! That cursed girth broke just as I came round the turn!"

"Are you injured?"

"Only my pride." Her smile encompassed them both. "Now I shall be seen walking home."

"I doubt if it will come to that." Harry dismounted and led his horse forward. His own groom followed suit, taking the reins of the other groom's horse while the man inspected the lady's saddle. "Lady Christina, Miss Ellen Trevayne," Harry said casually.

Ellen exchanged greetings. Despite the fact that it was improper to stare, she couldn't take her eyes off the young woman. Lady Christina was simply magnificent. If ladies truly planned their riding wardrobes around their horses' coats, the girl couldn't have chosen a better effect. Her scarlet habit against the black of her gelding would make a stunning picture. And that wasn't all. She herself was breathtakingly beautiful with hair of a dark, rich auburn and eyes of the purest green. Ellen couldn't help her flash of jealousy. Compared with Lady Christina, she was as plain as a pikestaff.

"We can't fix it here," the groom announced. "I'll change my girth with m'lady's."

"I hate to have you walk," Lady Christina protested.

"I won't, m'lady." He grinned. "I can balance without a girth."

"Hm! I could too if I could sit astride! The day will come when women are not forced to ride in such a dangerous contrivance!"

Harry winked at Ellen. "Lady Christina seems to be quite a revolutionary."

"She's right of course," Ellen heard herself say. "Sidesaddles *can* be dangerous. If she had been riding astride, she might not have fallen."

"Not two of you!" he protested.

"Bravo! I have an ally!" Lady Christina looked at Ellen with new interest. "Thank you, Miss Trevayne. Surely you must agree with us, Lord Singleton. Would you have fallen if your girth had broken?"

"Probably not."

"There now. You see? Admit it!" She placed her

hands on her hips and faced him with mock defiance.

"Very well," he said with a grin, "you ladies have a definite point. But you look so charming the way you are."

Lady Christina fluttered her lashes at him. "I am sure that we could endeavor to look charming while riding astride, couldn't we . . . Ellen? May I call you 'Ellen' since you are my accomplice? And you must call me Tina."

Ellen nodded smilingly, wishing that she were Tina's equal in the ability to flirt. When Harry assisted the girl in mounting, she managed to slip her arm comfortably across his shoulder, chatting at him, before she finally decided to allow him to toss her into the saddle. She was an accomplished minx, but Ellen couldn't help liking her.

Christina took up her reins. "Both of you must come to Grandmama's garden entertainment this afternoon. Lord Singleton, I know you were invited. You must come too, Ellen," she said warmly. "Please do attend! Grandmama's events are usually peopled with a passel of elderly relics. They are *so* boring for me! Won't you promise?"

"I don't know," Ellen said hesitantly.

"*Please!* I know we are going to be the best of friends!"

"I shall try."

"I'll expect you. And you too, my lord." With a saucy wave, she rode away.

"Little flirt," Harry said, mounting his horse. "She needs to have a hairbrush applied strenuously to her bottom."

Ellen giggled.

"She came out last Season, so she is full of confidence. Being a wealthy heiress and the granddaughter of a duke does wonders for her self-regard as well." He chuckled.

"I'm surprised that she hasn't wed. She's so beautiful."

"She has had offers."

Ellen wondered if he had sought Christina's hand. They seemed to be so well-acquainted. But if so, how could she have turned him down?

"You will be attending the event." He made it more of a statement of fact than a question.

Ellen moved her horse into a quiet walk. "I don't really wish to, Harry."

"I think you should. You said yourself that you were bored with London. Tina, as you can see, is never dreary. Come, Ellen. I'll escort you."

She shook her head. "You know my penchant for disaster."

"We'll stay for an hour and no longer. You must allow yourself to experience more than your grandfather's social circle."

"I have!" she snapped. "Don't you recall? I know I told you about it."

"Yes, I remember, and *you* should remember that it was a long time ago," he said patiently. "You have changed."

"Have I?"

"A gathering of a group of antiques is no great challenge," he remonstrated.

"Oh, very well. I shall attend! Now are you happy?"

"Exceedingly so."

"But I shall only remain for an hour," she warned.

"I'll come for you at two."

"If you insist." She shrugged with slight exasperation. "Now, since that engagement must limit our riding time, may we have another gallop?"

"Even though it might be dangerous for a lady in a sidesaddle?"

"Harry, please forget that exchange!"

"As you wish." Grinning wickedly, he touched his horse's sides and sprang forward.

Ellen clung to the marquess' arm as they passed through the imposing home of the Duke and Duchess of Sommerbrook and stepped from the conservatory into the garden. There was a terrible crush of guests, all very polished and refined. The scene brought back memories of her first abominable Season. It seemed as if they were the same people in the identical type of setting, each one of them harboring a cruel propensity to scorn her. She took several deep breaths.

Harry patted her hand. "You see? Nothing but an assembly of musty old antiques. Do not take offense if they peer at you through lorgnettes and quizzing glasses. Without those devices, they probably can't see you."

She giggled. "By the look of them I'm sure you are right!"

Tina rushed up to them. "I'm so glad you came," she bubbled. "How nice you look, Ellen! You must tell me the name of your dressmaker, but first let me introduce you to my grandmama." Taking Ellen's hand, she pulled her into the throng.

Nervous, Ellen glanced back for Harry and was happy to see him right behind her.

Tina worked her way through a small circle of elderly ladies surrounding a tall, stately, white-haired woman. "Grandmama, here is Ellen, the young lady I met in the park today."

Ellen curtsied. "How do you do, Your Grace?"

"Quite well, thank you, and I am delighted to make your acquaintance, my dear." The duchess smiled warmly. "I must also thank you for assisting Christina, and you too, Lord Singleton."

"I believe that the Lady Christina already had the

situation well in hand.'' Harry bowed over her hand, grinning.

She winked at him. ''My granddaughter delights in exhibiting a total lack of helplessness, a trait that most gentlemen do not find endearing. Now tell me, dear boy, how is your mother? When will she arrive in town?''

Ellen studied the duchess as she chatted idly with Harry. The lady was so grand, so attractive for her age, and, miracle of miracles, she was just about as tall as she herself. She wondered if Lady Sommerbrook had ever felt awkward.

Tina drew her apart. ''Grandmama abhors me riding alone with a groom. Perhaps we can go to the park together sometime.''

''I would like that,'' Ellen said shyly.

''Cousin Christina!'' A young man, dressed impeccably in fawn trousers and Spanish-blue superfine coat, bowed to them, his expressive blue eyes raking Ellen from head to toe. ''You must introduce me to this intriguing beauty.''

Tina laughed. ''Ellen, this is my odious cousin, Lord Richard Hawley. Richard, Miss Trevayne.''

''Odious? Tina, my dear, I must protest!'' He turned his full attention to Ellen. ''Miss Trevayne, I am enchanted.'' He took her hand, kissed her fingertips, and held it so long that Ellen was forced to withdraw it gently from his grasp.

''Richard is always enchanted,'' Tina said dryly. ''He is the most accomplished flirt.''

''You wound me, sweet cousin! First you call me odious, then flirtatious! I could retaliate by deeming you outrageous and absurd, but I shall not.''

She cocked her head coquettishly. ''I believe that you just did.''

''Indeed? I am appalled at my ill manners! Perhaps I may redeem my honor.'' He offered both

arms. "Come, ladies, let me escort you to the refreshment table."

Ellen glanced over her shoulder for Harry, but he
was detained by a group of elderly gentlemen. Tina
and Lord Hawley had taken a step through the
crowd. She caught his arm, unwilling to be left
alone.

"I shall be the envy of every gentleman in attendance," he said triumphantly. "I have captured the
two greatest beauties of the afternoon."

"That is a backhanded compliment, cousin."

"But truthful, nonetheless." He procured three
glasses of champagne, then favored Ellen with a
soulful gaze. "Where have you been hiding yourself, my beauty?"

Before she could think of a suitable rejoinder,
Harry materialized at her side and placed her hand
possessively through his arm. "She has been hiding
from knaves like you, Hawley." He smiled, but his
gray eyes were cool.

"Singleton! What brings you here? I should think
you would prefer excitement of a different sort!"
Lord Hawley's words were joking, but his eyes too
had assumed a chilly arrogance.

"Richard," Tina interjected, "you haven't even
spoken to Grandmama! Let us take her a glass of
champagne. She looks to be thoroughly parched!"
Catching his arm, she drew him away.

"What a coxcomb," Harry said.

Ellen raised an eyebrow. "He was only having
fun."

"He is a dedicated, single-minded flirt." He took
her glass of champagne, drained it, and thrust it into
the hands of a passing waiter. "Let us go."

"But Harry, I was truly beginning to enjoy myself, and I was doing rather well. I had actually lost
my nervousness!"

"I just remembered a pressing engagement."

"Oh, then we must take our leave. Let us make our good-byes."

"There is too great a crush." He directed her toward the garden gate. "And I am tired of these insufferable old quizzes."

Ellen sat silently beside him as the carriage crawled through the afternoon traffic. How strangely Harry had behaved! After all, he had been the one who'd insisted on their attending. She shrugged it off. Perhaps he truly did have an important matter that demanded his attention. She smiled to herself. It was more likely that he had a great aversion for the amusing Lord Hawley! But he could have said so, couldn't he?

To her surprise she found she liked young Mr. Paul Everman. He was rather handsome, though not as devastatingly attractive as Harry. He dressed well, had interesting conversation, and, unbelievably, he was taller than she was. She also thought his parents pleasant. Mrs. Everman had been the granddaughter of a baronet and had been raised in his household when her parents died, so her address was excellent. Mr. Everman was tall and dark, like his son, and spoke quietly and intelligently. As the evening progressed Ellen found that she and the young man were getting along quite well together.

"My family has a small estate in Derbyshire," Mr. Everman told her. "Mother inherited it from her grandmother. When I was a boy, she and I spent the summers there. Papa, of course, could spare no more than a few days away from London, but we enjoyed it nonetheless."

"Do you still go there?" Ellen asked with interest.

"I wish I could find the time," he said wistfully.

"How unfortunate."

"Yes, isn't it? I fear I'm tied to London as thoroughly as Papa is."

"One must give up a great deal to remain successful in the world of business," she murmured kindly. At least Mrs. Everman had managed to escape to the country. If she decided upon Paul Everman, she could probably do that too. And he wasn't averse to rural life. Given the nearness of Bridgeford Grange, he might be able to spare more than just a few days to spend with her there.

When her grandfather closed the door and turned to her questioningly, Ellen smiled. "I like him."

Mr. Frampton released a deep breath.

"He can talk about things other than his business interests. And he is rather handsome, isn't he?"

He returned her smile. "Then if Paul Everman is your choice, must we continue through the alphabet?"

"How many more are there?"

"There are three young men."

"To be fair, I really should meet them too."

He laughed, satisfied that she would be able to make a selection. "All right, missy. We shall give everyone a chance! But I am well pleased. The young man has an excellent head on his shoulders and should go far. I believe that he will handle the Frampton interests with aplomb."

"Grandfather! You must not speak of anyone overseeing them but you."

"Do you see me getting any younger?" he asked gruffly. "No, we must look ahead." He winked. "But I'm probably good for fifteen or more years!"

Ellen climbed the stairs, cheerfully thinking of Paul Everman. Perhaps becoming his wife would be the nearest thing possible to marrying Harry. Paul, too, was tall and dark. His eyes were brown instead of gray and he wasn't as handsome as Lord Singleton, but one couldn't have everything! Furthermore he was kind . . . and he was appropriate for her.

My, but the day had gone well! She'd had a pleasurable ride in the park, made a new friend, and attended a *ton* entertainment without faux pas or mishap. She had met Paul Everman. And even before all of that, she had found a way to dispel some of her boredom by her decision to explore the ramifications of managing a London household. She felt a growing confidence in herself. How full life could be, even in the city! She looked forward to the next day.

13

Ellen began her morning by meeting with the Frampton housekeeper. A garrulous woman, Mrs. Benny was soon chatting away on the trials and tribulations of keeping house in the city. Ellen found that much of it was mere common sense.

All food, of course, must be purchased, preferably as early in the day as possible so that it would be at its freshest and not picked over by the numerous shoppers. What it lacked in quality was made up in variety. As a major port, London imported foodstuffs from all over the world. In addition, there were the specialty shops such as Gunter's or Grange's, who prepared the finest of confections and desserts. In Mrs. Benny's opinion, the city outranked the country overall in cuisine.

Before Mrs. Benny could begin her discourse on the cleanliness of the home, Ellen heard a chorus of riotous barking through the open window. There could only be one thing to disturb the peace of the quiet square. Taffy and Friendly had arrived from the country! She still hadn't taken the opportunity to tell her grandfather of the new guests—but it was too late now. She ran into the hall past a baffled Gordon and threw open the front door.

The scene that met her eyes might have daunted

the majority of London residents. A two-carriage entourage had stopped before the Frampton residence.
Big dogs jumped from the second vehicle, whirling
and leaping and swatting their heavy tails, wrapping their tenders in their leashes. Horses shied, demanding the attention of every coachman and groom
not designated as a dog handler. In the midst of it
all stood a laughing Lady Allesandra Rackthall and
her smiling husband, who was at the moment rolling his eyes heavenward.

"Allesandra! Brandon!" Ellen cried.

At the sound of her voice, Taffy and Friendly
dashed towards her, dragging two Rackthall servants after them. They knocked her down to the
steps and nuzzled her, lapping her face with their
huge tongues. Ellen hugged them.

"Oh, it's good to see you!" She struggled to her
feet. "Let us get you to the mews where you'll have
a nice welcome-to-London meal and we'll play later.
Allesandra, Brandon, please go inside with Gordon.
You look in need of refreshment! I'll be there in a
jiffy."

Ellen took the leashes and motioned to the groom
who was leading her Bridgeford Grange horse. With
the dogs boiling around her legs, she hurried down
the alley beside the house to the stable. After secur-
ing the Saint Bernards in their makeshift kennel, she
checked her sorrel's condition and stroked his neck.

"I'm glad you're here too, Autumn." She smiled
at the rather dismayed Frampton servants, who were
exchanging whispers with their Rackthall counter-
parts. "Please make them comfortable. I'll be back
later. And thank you!" She rushed back to the house
and hurried to the drawing room.

"I am so happy to see you!" She embraced the
duchess and extended her hand to the duke, surprised when he gave her a brotherly hug and a kiss

on the forehead instead. "But what are *you* doing with the animals?"

"When you mentioned in your letter that you had sent for them, Brandon thought that we should oversee their transport."

"It was not one of my better ideas," the duke drawled.

"But have you just arrived? You must be exhausted!"

"We reached London late last night, so we kept the animals in our mews."

"Another mistake," said Brandon.

"Did they do damage?"

"Not really." The duchess giggled. "This morning one of the footmen felt sorry for the dogs, penned as they were in a stall and crying their hearts out for attention. He brought them into the kitchen for a bowl of milk and . . . well . . . they escaped into the dining room."

"Oh, dear," Ellen moaned.

"They ate my breakfast," Brandon said. "They stood on their hind legs and cleaned the buffet."

Allesandra laughed. "He didn't need it anyway," she said affectionately. "He is gaining weight."

"I am not!" The duke looked down at his flat stomach. "Perhaps you are thinking of yourself, madam!"

"I think you are both perfectly wonderful," Ellen proclaimed and smiled teasingly. "You know that I always stand good for damages. And here is succor for your empty stomach, Your Grace," she added as Gordon entered with a heavily laden tea tray. "But after your ghastly experiences, you might prefer brandy."

"It could preserve my sanity."

Gordon moved to procure the drink before Ellen could even open her mouth.

"Thank you," Brandon acknowledged. "When

one is beset with such ladies as these, he deserves all the help he can get!"

The butler flushed with pleasure at such a grand nobleman taking personal notice of him. He majestically bowed his way out of the room. Once in the hall, he scurried to the kitchen with his marvelous report.

Ellen poured tea for herself and Allesandra and filled a plate of delicate pastries for the duke. It was good to have them here in London. Tina might be a promising new friend, but the duchess was an old one, dependable and true, to whom she could open her heart.

"Tell me what you have been doing," the duchess said. "Have you seen Harry?"

"Oh, yes, and Lord Standish too. Lord Singleton has been so kind. He has called and taken me riding and to an afternoon event at the Duchess of Sommerbrook's. I've been busy, what with those activities, shopping, and Grandfather's dinner parties."

"Have you enjoyed your grandfather's friends?"

Ellen laughed. "If you had asked me that before last night, I would have had definite reservations!"

"What happened last night?"

"I met a very nice man, Mr. Paul Everman. I think you would like him."

Allesandra exchanged glances with her husband. "Surely you haven't decided yet, Ellen?"

"No. I shall get to know him much better first," she said reflectively. "But if all goes as well as it did last evening, he could be my choice. If he'll have me!" She had noticed the curious way that her friend had looked at the duke. "Is something wrong?"

"Not at all," the duchess said smoothly. "But you must leave yourself open to any possibilities."

"That's correct," the duke agreed. "You shouldn't rush into anything. What about Harry?"

"Harry?"

"We thought there might be a *tendre* there," Allesandra murmured.

"No." Ellen smiled wistfully. "Lord Singleton and I are very good friends, but in other ways . . . we wouldn't suit."

"Why not?" the duke asked bluntly.

"Brandon," Allesandra said repressively. "It is none of our affair."

"But I would have thought . . ."

"Oh, dear, we must be on our way!" The duchess finished her tea and rose. "Ellen, it has been splendid to see you again. Shall we shop together tomorrow afternoon?"

"I would love it."

"Then I shall come by after luncheon."

Something *was* wrong. Perhaps Allesandra was overset because Brandon inquired too personally into her relationship with Harry. But no, the visit had really turned awkward when she had mentioned Paul Everman. It was no matter for speculation now, however; she would probe the duchess more deeply when they had their outing tomorrow.

She accompanied her friends to the door. "Good day, and thank you again for bringing my animals."

"We were pleased to assist." Allesandra kissed her cheek, took the duke's arm, and they were gone.

Smiling prettily, Ellen poured tea for her new admirers: Mr. Bradford, the two Mr. Derifields, and, best of all, Mr. Everman. The four had arrived much at the same time, and though they were acquainted with each other, they were not particularly happy to share her company among them. It was a novel experience for Ellen. She had never before had a group of gentlemen vying for her attention. It was rather pleasant.

They had brought her gifts. Mr. Bradford, who

seemed determined that she become well-educated on the subject of ships, had brought her another book of sea stories. The Derifields presented her with a small, exquisite porcelain sheep. Paul Everman gave her a large bouquet of full-blown pink roses, which she placed in water and set on the piano.

Though she was flattered and uplifted by the young men's interest, Ellen found conversation difficult. Each wished to talk of subjects of his own preference, cutting the others out. It was almost impossible for her to find a general topic which excluded no one. After a discussion of the weather was exhausted, she found herself turning from Mr. Everman on her right, to Mr. Bradford on her left, to the Derifields who had drawn up chairs straight across from her. Mr. Everman fared the best. Being in the banking industry he had a broad knowledge of the other businesses and was able to comment intelligently on them. Ellen found herself warming even further to him.

She served the tea without mishap and invited the gentlemen to partake of the small sandwiches and cakes. "After a day at your desks, I'm sure you are quite famished."

They agreed. "I did get a slight change of scene," Mr. Bradford told her. "The *Becky Jane* came in, so I spent part of my time on the docks."

"Next summer I may be a passenger on one of your ships," Mr. Everman remarked. "We've business interests in the West Indies. Neither my father nor I have been there in two years. Our agent seems to be handling it well enough, but we like to put in an appearance every so often."

"It must be fascinating to travel the world," Ellen mused, thinking that if she married him, she might be able to accompany him. "I've never been farther than London or Brighton. What is it like? Tell me about the West Indies."

"The islands are beautiful, Miss Trevayne. Very warm, with lush tropical plants . . . They're like nothing you've ever seen before."

"Full of overlarge insects." James Derifield grinned.

"Really!" Ellen laughed. "Well, I'm not afraid of that! What kind of business do you have there, Mr. Everman?"

"We deal in sugar."

"Which our ships deliver to England," Mr. Bradford said with satisfaction. "When you make your trip, Everman, be sure to travel on the *Becky Jane*. You'll sleep as comfortably as if you were in your own bed."

Mr. Everman inclined his head. "I shall remember that."

"You have all had such wonderful experiences." Hearing a knock, Ellen glanced towards the door.

Gordon opened it with a flourish. "The Marquess of Singleton!"

She caught her breath as Harry entered. Clad in a mint-green coat and creamy silk waistcoat and inexpressibles, his cravat tied to perfection and graced with an emerald stickpin, he was every inch the aristocrat. The other men, even Mr. Everman who was clothed quite neatly, were totally eclipsed by his quiet elegance. With flawless poise he strode across the room and bowed before her, taking her hand.

"Miss Trevayne." Deftly he turned her palm upwards and kissed it lingeringly.

The gesture was not wasted on her other guests, who had stood at his entrance. Mr. Everman frowned slightly. The Derifields exchanged quick glances with Mr. Bradford.

Ellen's skin tingled where his lips had caressed it. Drawing back her hand, she looked into his amused gray eyes. "How do you do, my lord?" she asked almost breathlessly. "May I introduce these gentlemen? Mr. Paul Everman, Mr. Gerald Bradford, Mr. James Derifield, and Mr. Edward Derifield.''

''Gentlemen.'' Harry nodded. ''Do be seated. I don't wish to interrupt.'' Skillfully he slid in beside Ellen, taking Mr. Bradford's seat.

Gerald Bradford, looking momentarily disconcerted, drew up another chair.

''For you.'' The marquess placed a large box of bonbons in her lap. ''I think you'll like them.''

''Thank you very much.'' She glanced uncomfortably towards poor Mr. Bradford, who now found himself on the outskirts of the group. That had not been nice of Harry, and his gesture had placed him improperly close to her. She tried to edge aside. ''Will you have a cup of tea, my lord?''

''Thank you.''

She managed to pour, her nervousness at his presence shown only by a slight tremble of the teapot lid. Remembering that Harry disliked sugar or cream, she handed it to him without question, further piquing the interest of the others. ''We were discussing the West Indies, my lord. Mr. Everman has business interests there and Mr. Bradford's ships travel the area frequently.''

''Indeed.''

''Have you traveled extensively, my lord?'' Mr. Bradford asked.

''Only on the Continent. I find that I prefer England, particularly my estate in Kent.'' He smiled at Ellen. ''I heard that Allesandra and Brandon had come to town.''

''Yes, they came to see me this morning. They brought the dogs.''

''I'm sure that Bran enjoyed *that* trip.'' He grinned knowingly. ''Did they have any news of the neighborhood?''

''We didn't talk of it. Allesandra and I will be going shopping. I'll hear all of it then.'' She swept her eyes over each of her admirers to involve them in the conversation. "Lord Singleton and I are neighbors," she explained. "His land marches with mine."

"Then you must have known each other for quite a while," Edward Derifield observed casually.

"No, we met only recently upon my inheritance of the estate," Harry said. "But it seems as if we've known each other well for a very long time."

"It must be pleasant to have everything given to you without having to lift a finger," Mr. Bradford replied, his bland expression belying the set-down of his words.

The marquess narrowed his eyes. "Yes, it is. Unfortunately, however, one also inherits the responsibilities of the position. Don't you find that to be true?"

"I?" He laughed. "I am a working man, my lord."

"Come, Mr. Bradford! I doubt that a man of your age could have built up a vast shipping line in so short a time."

Ellen looked longingly towards the door, wishing she could leap to her feet, run from the room, and leave the gentlemen to their sparring.

"That is true, my lord. My father did found the company. But I assure you, I spend a great deal of time in my office, as do the other gentlemen present. We've had nothing handed to us on a silver platter."

"Absolutely correct!" agreed James Derifield. "Also, our parents required us to learn the business from top to bottom. We are able to perform the lowest task as well or better than the laborer whose work it is."

"How admirable," Harry said disinterestedly, his fine nose lifting almost imperceptibly. "If you ever suffer business reversals, you will have some means of employment to fall back on."

The tension in the room was becoming unbearable, with the four Londoners uniting against the marquess. Ellen was sure that Harry could hold his own against the mismatched odds, but he would end up delivering merciless, arrogant set-downs. If only there was some way to ease the situation before one of them lost his temper. She caught Harry's eye, silently begging him to be pleasant. If he ceased pitching his barbs, the others might respond in kind.

"I must apologize for bringing up a certain matter at this time, Miss Trevayne," he began. "I have received a communication from my steward at Shadybrook. There is an urgent matter concerning our estates which we need to discuss immediately."

"Oh, dear."

"It is nothing to distress you. I'm sorry, gentlemen, but Miss Trevayne and I must settle this question in private."

"Lord Singleton!" Mr. Bradford burst out. "Do you think to *dismiss* us?"

"Perhaps, sir," Mr. Everman advised, "if it is a matter of business, it would be more proper to pursue it with Mr. Frampton."

"How little you know of Miss Trevayne," Harry said with dripping pity. "She is a most independent lady!"

The banker frowned.

"Please, gentlemen." She had to stop it now. Her nerves could stand no more. Ellen rose, forcing them all to follow suit. "Naturally I am concerned about my property."

They began their departure, Ellen smiling her good-byes at the salon door. Mr. Bradford lagged behind. "Miss Trevayne, I would like to escort you to the docks tomorrow for a view of the *Becky Jean*."

"She's going riding with me," Harry interrupted, and shut the door between them.

"Oh, I am, am I?" She reached for the doorknob.

He caught her arm and swung her around to face him, resting his hands lightly on her shoulders. "You are."

"No, sir, I am not. I am going shopping with Allesandra. Harry, what has gotten into you? You were rude!"

"Was I?"

"Yes, you were! I am absolutely mortified!"

"I'm sorry," he said without the tiniest tinge of regret in his voice. "Would you rather go to the docks? I'll catch up to Mr. Bradford and tell him so."

"Please do not. I don't wish to go there."

"Then I have saved you from unpleasantness."

"No, you haven't. How dare you chase away my suitors!"

"They aren't good enough for you, Ellen," he said flatly.

"They are very nice gentlemen!"

"I daresay, but not for you."

She became acutely conscious of his hands still resting on her shoulders. "What estate matters do you wish to discuss with me?" she asked, escaping to the settee.

He glanced around the room, noting the roses on the piano. "From one of your admirers?"

"Yes. Now about the estate," she said hurriedly. "What matters . . ."

The marquess grinned. "There are none."

"You made it up? Oh, you are arrogant!"

"I wished to be alone with you."

Ellen's heart pounded as he sat down beside her and took her hand. It was impossible to be angry with him when he smiled so charmingly. She could never gain the upper hand with such a practiced flirt.

Warmth rose in her cheeks. Her hand felt as though it was on fire. She withdrew it and folded it with the other on her lap.

She must refuse to allow him to affect her this way. It only made it harder to accept the fact that there could be no future for her that included the handsome marquess. She must avoid seeing him. No, she must stop it altogether. Only then could she concentrate on selecting a suitable husband.

"Harry," she said softly, "I realize that you do not care for my gentlemen callers. Indeed, you have little in common with them. Perhaps you think that they are not good enough for me, but I must differ from you on that."

"Ellen . . ."

She lifted a hand. "Allow me to continue. You have been such a dear, kind friend, but you must understand. I shall . . . I shall probably wed one of those gentlemen. I must ask you not to call on me again. I . . . I . . . Perhaps you and he can become friends sometime in the future. I hope so." She rose quickly and hurried across the carpet. "After all, we are neighbors!"

"Ellen!"

"No!" She dashed out of the salon, slammed the door behind her, and rushed up the stairs to her room. Throwing herself on her bed, she burst into tears. She had done it. She had broken all ties with him. Now she could look ahead to the future. She would be a wife and mother and the mistress of a fine London residence. She would forget about Harry and her outlandish dreams. She would forgo meeting the other young men and would agree to marry Paul Everman. The man she chose to be her husband just didn't seem to matter anymore.

"Harry! Aren't you getting out?"

The marquess snapped from his trance to see Aubrey peering into the carriage. Behind him rose the stately facade of White's with its famous bow window, filled as usual with curious spectators staring out and making snide remarks. Somehow he had gotten from the Frampton parlor to his coach to Bond Street without even taking note of the event.

"What's the matter?"

This time he wouldn't tell Aubrey of his personal crisis. Someday the truth might come out. In fact it probably would. But right now it simply hurt too much to put it into words. Harry Singleton, scorned by a woman. Damme! That had never before happened to him! And who had done it? The only woman he had ever really loved.

"Harry! Are you ill, man?"

He forced a smile. "Just a bit peaked, perhaps."

"Come in and have a drink with me. You'll soon feel more the thing."

"No, I believe I'll go home. Mayfair!" he called to the coachman.

"Wait, Harry, I'll . . ."

The horses drew away, leaving Aubrey standing perplexed on the curb.

Harry hoped that his friend wouldn't decide to follow him. What he needed most was to be by himself. Alone, he could sort out the turn of events and come to a conclusion on what should be done, if indeed there was anything to do. It wasn't as if it had been a quarrel. Ellen hadn't been angry. She had seemed sad, as though she were determined to do something very distasteful, something she didn't want to do. With that in mind, he must face the realization that he might have lost her.

Closing his eyes, he leaned his head against the velvet squabs. If that were so, he must accept it and resume his search for the "perfect" mate. It should be easy—for if he couldn't have Ellen, he just didn't care who he wed.

14

Ellen sat morosely in the window seat, an unread book in her lap and a soggy handkerchief in her hand. She didn't bother to turn her head when she heard her bedroom door open and close. Dora had already made herself perfectly obnoxious with her whining and cajoling and her attempts to force her mistress to "perk up" and seek a change of scenery.

"I won't go down! I don't care if the king himself is calling," Ellen muttered vehemently.

"Would you reconsider if the caller were a duchess? No, don't answer that. I refused to take my chances so I have come up to you."

"Allesandra!" she exclaimed, turning. Seeing her friend caused the tears to flow once more. "I am sorry! I am just so overset today!"

The duchess laid down her reticule and picked up a handkerchief from the ready stack of freshly laundered ones. "My dear, what can be so awful?" She joined Ellen in the window seat and gathered her into her arms.

"It is nothing!"

"Nothing? You have been weeping more than just a little and you look as though you didn't sleep at all last night."

180

"I didn't." She sniffled.

"May I assume that you have had no breakfast?"

"Nor supper either." Ellen wiped her eyes and blew her nose, then returned her head to Allesandra's comforting shoulder. "I sent Grandfather word that I had a headache. It isn't a lie. My head is bursting!"

"Of course, my dear. Might I send for a tray? Coffee and toast might help considerably." She smiled. "You know I won't leave until you're feeling better."

Ellen nodded numbly.

"Good!" Hugging her, the duchess rose, went to the door, and conversed quietly with Dora who was anxiously waiting in the hall.

"Oh, my, I just remembered our shopping trip!" Ellen moved to the sofa, curling up and drawing a lap robe over her legs. "I am sorry, Allesandra! I won't be able to go."

"No matter. We can go shopping anytime." She seated herself. "Now tell me. Blue devils like this can only indicate a man as the cause."

"*Men,*" Ellen corrected. "A great passel of men."

"Your grandfather's friends?"

"In part. I must choose and I . . . I will." She shook her head. "Yesterday I mentioned one of them to you. I think that I will tell Grandfather that Mr. Everman is my choice. It will end this . . . torment. Allesandra, you cannot know what this is like!"

"You shouldn't be so hasty, Ellen."

"Oh, but I must. Then there will be no further question!"

"I cannot agree," the duchess said quietly.

"But your own marriage was one of convenience. You didn't know Brandon. Your family chose for you, just as my grandfather is doing for me. It turned out wonderfully. You are perfect for each other!"

"We were very fortunate."

"Perhaps I shall be fortunate too." Ellen

shrugged. "With my luck, however, I shall hope only for reasonable happiness. Mr. Everman is kind. I believe that he will be a caring husband."

"Do you love him?"

"No, not yet. I couldn't love him when . . ." She hesitated.

At that moment Dora entered with the breakfast tray. Ellen's heart soared with relief. What foolishness! She had just been on the brink of admitting to Allesandra that she was in love with Harry. Her friend would think her daft.

Dora poured coffee for both of the ladies and pushed the toast towards Ellen. "Please, miss."

"Very well. I shall eat it. You see, Dora? Her Grace has already cheered me. You needn't fuss over me any further."

With a satisfied nod, the abigail curtsied and withdrew.

"Dora is a bully," Ellen remarked.

"She seems quite capable."

"Oh, she is, but she has such a smothering way about her!"

"She cares for you."

Ellen smiled guiltily. "I know it."

Allesandra sipped her coffee, eyeing her friend casually. "Before Dora came in, you were mentioning something about not being able to love Mr. Everman, when . . ."

"I was?"

"Yes."

Ellen shook her head. "I cannot remember."

"I was under the impression that you were going to admit to being in love with someone else."

"Oh? I cannot imagine who that would be."

The duchess took a deep breath. "I thought it might be Harry Singleton."

Ellen's cup rattled in its saucer.

Allesandra raised a dark eyebrow, her green eyes sparkling knowingly. "I believe I have my answer."

Ellen quickly set aside her coffee. "Please, Allesandra, you must mention it to no one, not even to Brandon! Especially not to Brandon, for he might tell . . . It is the height of foolishness for me to be so besotted! If word of it spread, I could not leave this room for the rest of my life. Promise me, please!"

"But Ellen, what if Harry returns the sentiment?" the duchess said.

"He couldn't! I know him well enough to know that! Even without my penchant for mishap, I could never, ever be the kind of wife he would choose."

"I don't know about that."

"I do! Once," Ellen said, blushing, "I told him how awful it seemed that he was sought for wealth and title and not for who he was inside. Do you know what he answered? He said, 'Being a marquess has a great deal to do with who I am inside.' Don't you realize? He would never choose me to be his marchioness!"

Her friend merely shook her head. "Seeing you yesterday wearing your stylish new gown and conducting yourself most comfortably, I thought you had gained greatly in confidence."

"Yes, I have! I have assumed the role of mistress of this house so that I can learn to manage a London residence and to make a gentleman happy. Grandfather is very particular as to his well-being, but I have faith in myself that I can meet the challenge." Ellen continued, ticking off her victories on her fingers. "Since I have been in London, I have participated in several social events without mishap. I have even made a new friend. And furthermore, I am certain that I can be the kind of wife that Mr. Everman requires. I know I'll be a good mother . . . and hostess too. Grandfather's friends, you see, pose little threat. They are not nearly so intimidating as the *ton*."

"Hm." Allesandra took a pastry from the tray and nibbled it thoughtfully.

Ellen studied her carefully. She did so wish to have her friend's approval. Failing that, at least she wanted her to know that she had the inner strength to make her own decision, without the influence of others.

"I know my own mind, Allesandra, and I realize what's best for me. Despite my ridiculous feelings for Lord Singleton, I had the confidence to thank him for all his kindness and to ask him not to come here anymore."

"You did *what!*" Allesandra cried.

"Our meetings were too unsettling for my peace of mind." Lips trembling, Ellen gritted her teeth and set her mouth in a firm line.

"Obviously." There was an unusual touch of sarcasm in the duchess' voice.

"Allesandra, please try to understand. I am gaining confidence. Don't you see?"

"No, I do not. It seems to me that you are simply running away again. In a different manner this time, of course, but running just the same."

"Allesandra!"

Her friend went on relentlessly. "You are running from the *ton* and you are running from your feelings for Harry."

"I am not! I have faced up to a very difficult decision."

"By hiding in your room and weeping?"

Ellen stiffened. "I shall no longer do that. You will see."

"Excellent, but I would really prefer to see you facing your problems. Postpone your decision for a while. Come with me to social functions. Look Harry in the eye. You think that managing this house for your grandfather is a challenge? Take up *my* challenge!"

"I . . . I suppose I could do that," Ellen said bravely.

"Can you?" There was doubt in the duchess' green eyes.

"Yes, I can!" Ellen snapped. "I just don't care about anything anymore!"

Allesandra bit back a smile. "Brandon and I will call for you this evening. His mother is hostessing a small soiree. Be ready at eight."

"Not tonight! My eyes . . ."

The duchess rose. "If you will spend the afternoon dozing with a cool cloth on your face, the night's ravages will disappear. Besides, I thought you didn't care about anything anymore."

"Oh, very well!"

"Until then." Allesandra waved mischievously and left the room.

"Damme!" Ellen cried aloud. "How did I allow her to talk me into this!"

The Marquess of Singleton had passed a dismal night. He had consumed a great amount of brandy and fallen asleep on the sofa in the library. Sometime in the wee hours, his valet had gotten him into bed, where he had proceeded to sleep till noon. Now miserably awake, his head bursting, he proceeded to the dining room. The scent of food twisted his stomach, but he had to begin to recover his senses. As it was, he couldn't even think straight.

How ravishing Ellen had been yesterday and how beautifully her eyes had sparkled when he entered the room! A deep, insatiable longing spread throughout his body. It was all well and good to tell himself that he would marry someone else. It wouldn't work. He had to have Ellen for his wife. Life without her wouldn't be worth the living. But

what was he to do? She didn't want to see him
again.

Harry's butler entered. His nose high, Hollins
glanced at the untouched buffet. ''My lord, is something wrong with the food?''

''No, I haven't gotten round to it yet.''

''Shall I fix you a plate?''

''Later. For now, I wish only this cup of coffee.''

''Very well, sir, but if you delay your luncheon I
must inform you that there are two visitors awaiting. Your man of business and another . . . person.''

''I wonder what Carter wants,'' Harry mused,
''and whom he has brought with him.''

''I wouldn't know, my lord. Perhaps it concerns
one of your investments or . . .''

''I am aware that you don't know, Hollins. I was
merely making idle speculation. It didn't call for an
answer.''

''I apologize, sir, if I have been offensive.''

''Good God, man, you were not offensive! You
are the most *inoffensive*, man I have ever met. This
house is exactly like you. It is predictable, boring,
and unexciting,'' Harry said with frustration.

''My lord!''

''Doesn't anything ever go wrong here? Create
some diversions, Hollins. Let's have some excitement!''

The butler stared wide-eyed at his master.

''You think I've lost my wits, don't you?'' Harry
grinned, regaining his sense of humor. ''Perhaps
you are right. I shall see my callers in here. They
can share my luncheon.''

''My lord, they are men from . . . from the city!''

''Good.'' The marquess smirked. ''Perhaps they
will eat with their hands, lick their plates, and spill
wine all over the tablecloth!''

''Sir!''

"Go on, Hollins. Bring them in."

He refilled his wineglass. Good heavens, what a snob his butler was! It was certainly true that a servant could be more devastatingly discriminating than his master or mistress!

"Mr. Lawrence Carter, Mr. John Frampton," Hollins announced.

Harry started at the name of Ellen's grandfather. Swiftly he reached for his coffee and turned the cup neatly onto its side. The dark brew stained the pristine damask tablecloth.

"Pardon me, gentlemen. It seems I've had an accident." He wiped his fingers on his serviette and stood to shake hands.

Mr. Frampton chuckled. "You should meet my granddaughter, m'lord. At one time she was forever doing things like that!"

"I'm certain I would find her most charming. Won't you share my luncheon?"

"Thank you, my lord," Mr. Carter said politely. "We do apologize for appearing at an inappropriate time. I must assure you that we were prepared to wait."

"Nonsense." He sat down. "I was alone and bored. I'm glad of your company."

His butler had sopped up the coffee, covered the stain with a clean cloth, and placed a fresh serviette at Harry's plate. Setting places for the two other gentlemen, he poured their drinks and stood waiting in stiff disapproval.

"That will be all, Hollins. We'll serve ourselves."

"If it pleases your lordship." He left with a sharp snap of the door.

Harry glimpsed Mr. Frampton's raised eyebrow. "Hollins is a bit tetchy today. We had a small disagreement. Let us help ourselves to the buffet."

"Sometimes one's servants become a bit too high in the instep," Ellen's grandfather commented.

"When they begin to think that they are superior to their master, it's time to fire 'em."

"You have a point, sir."

"Yes, I do. I treat my servants fairly and I expect the same from them. They know that and I'm seldom disappointed. No doubt you're troubled by old retainers. Sit 'em down and tell 'em what you want in no uncertain terms. It'll work. Take my word for it, lad."

Mr. Carter shuddered at the familiarity, but Harry merely grinned. He actually found himself liking Mr. Frampton. The man was refreshingly direct and to the point.

They adjourned to the buffet. Harry and Mr. Carter helped themselves to moderate servings, but Mr. Frampton heaped his plate high. "I like my meals. I suppose that food's my failing."

Harry wondered how the man could consume such a mammoth portion. He did. In fact, he went back for more.

When the meal was finished, the marquess led them to the library. Like Mr. Frampton, he too came directly to the point. "I assume that you've come here to discuss a matter of business."

"Yes, my lord," Mr. Carter began apologetically. "You see . . ."

Mr. Frampton interrupted. "There are times that I prefer to deal directly with the man himself and not his man of business. This is one of these times. Lord Singleton, I am here concerning some land that you own."

Harry glanced at Mr. Carter. "The Thames property?"

He nodded.

"That's the piece," Mr. Frampton agreed. "I'm not sure that you realize, my lord, how important this could be to the development of London."

"And to the investors as well," Harry said flatly.

Ellen's grandfather registered surprise. His eyes

narrowed shrewdly, and then he smiled. "I'll admit that I had intended to emphasize the philanthropy of the sale. I can see that I was wrong. You *do* know business, don't you?"

The marquess hoped that his eyes looked just as calculating as Mr. Frampton's. "Let us merely say that I am not unaware," he said coolly.

"My partners and I are prepared to raise the price one thousand pounds."

"Still I am not interested."

"Fifteen."

"It will be worth far more than that within a very short time."

Mr. Frampton shook his head and raised an eyebrow. "My lord, I don't know why you choose to leave your business to him. You seem quite capable of managing it yourself. Two thousand."

"I have far-ranging investments, in which I am not nearly so interested as I am in this one. And the answer is no. Frankly, sir, I doubt that you will offer enough money to persuade me at this time."

Ellen's grandfather sighed. "Would you be interested in a share?"

Harry thought quickly. "Perhaps." He reflected upon what Mr. Frampton would think if he told him he'd give him the deed in exchange for his granddaughter's hand. The old man might consider it. But that wouldn't work. Ellen must want him herself. Stringing the codger along, however, might give him entree to the Frampton house once more.

"The other investors would have to be agreeable, of course," said Mr. Frampton.

"Certainly. I would wish to meet them as well." Harry wondered if Mr. Bradford was among the group. That fellow must have an interest in developments on the riverfront.

"I shall arrange it." Mr. Frampton rose to take his leave.

"All right." Harry shook his hand. "If possible, I would prefer a more private setting than an office. If one is to enter into business with others, he should meet them informally, such as we have done today."

"That's reasonable," Mr. Frampton agreed. "I'll stand as host. I'll set my granddaughter to arranging a dinner party."

"I shall be pleased to accept." Harry grinned and accompanied the men to the front door. "I'll look forward to hearing from you, Mr. Frampton."

What a piece of good fortune! He could scarcely believe how all of this had played into his hands. He would see Ellen again, for she would certainly act as hostess for her grandfather. He would have one more chance at least. And this time he would not fail.

"I'm pleased to see that you're up and about again," Mr. Frampton said as Ellen entered the drawing room. "And you're dressed up pretty as can be."

"I'm going out," she said shortly, "and you probably won't approve. I am attending a soiree with the duke and duchess."

"Those two! Don't expect me to greet them!"

"I won't. I shall leave as soon as I see them arrive." She peered out the window.

"You will be surprised to hear that I had lunch with one of the swells today. A right fine fellow he was too! Had a good head for business."

"You lunched with a peer?" she asked curiously.

"Lord Singleton it was."

Her mouth dropped open. "Why . . ."

"We may participate in a joint enterprise together, along with the Bradfords and the Evermans. Lord Singleton owns the property."

"I can't imagine . . ."

"I'll ask you, missy, to plan a dinner party for the group. We'll hope to seal the bargain then."

"Me?"

"Now don't distress yourself. He's a down-to-earth lad, not all high and mighty."

"Grandfather, Lord Singleton is my neighbor in the country."

"Indeed? Come to think of it, I do seem to remember your mentioning him. Good! I can count on you to make him welcome."

She heard hoofbeats in front of the house and saw that the Rackthall carriage had arrived. "We shall discuss this at another time, Grandfather. I must leave."

"All right," he agreed genially. "You won't be late, will you?"

"I am not sure."

"No matter. Have a good time! I'll probably still be up when you come home. I've some business matters to attend to."

"Don't stay up on my account."

"I won't." He helped her into her deep-brown Hungarian cape. "Nevertheless I want to set the date of our party as soon as possible, while Lord Singleton is in the mood."

"Very well, Grandfather." She entered the hall just as Gordon was opening the door to Lord Rackthall. "Hello, Brandon, I am ready."

"Why so grim, Ellen? Surely my mother's parties do not have so unfavorable a reputation as that!" He extended his arm.

"No, it is Grandfather. He has just tossed a dilemma my way."

"Nothing you can't cope with, I hope."

"No." She fixed a cheerful expression on her face and slipped her arm through his. "I shall cope with it all right. I *must!*"

15

The dowager Duchess of Rackthall's London home was not nearly so large as the Frampton residence, but Ellen liked its quiet coziness. The lady had recently decorated in the Adam style with pale pastel walls crowned with plaster reliefs, white mantels inset with Wedgwood medallions, and brilliant crystal chandeliers. The furniture fitted the light, airy architecture with its graceful lines and classical chintz upholstery. Soft, delicate Persian carpets covered the floors.

Brandon's mother herself seemed suited to such an interior. She was slender and dainty, her fluffy white hair framing her fine-boned face and merry blue eyes. She kissed her son and daughter-in-law and took Ellen's hand.

"How delighted I am to become acquainted with you! I have heard so much about you."

"I hope what you've heard has been pleasant." Ellen smiled. "I too have heard much of you, and I must say that I envy Allesandra her mother-in-law."

"That is kind of you, my dear. I assure you that all I have been told of you has been most pleasant. Allesandra must bring you around for a chat." With a final pat on Ellen's hand, she turned to greet her next guests.

"She is charming," Ellen told her friends. "You are so fortunate to have her for a mama."

They passed through the crowd into a pale-yellow salon where the crush of people was not so heavy. As Brandon fetched champagne for the ladies, Ellen scanned the unfamiliar faces. No doubt all of them were perfect diamonds of the *ton*, for the dowager was probably very exclusive in the guest list for her small home. Strangely enough she found herself unintimidated. These highborn aristocrats could like her or not as they pleased. Their opinion made not the slightest difference to her future.

Allesandra began to make introductions to Lord This and Lady That until the ebb and flow of the company forced her to give up.

"I'm just as relieved," Ellen said. "I'll never remember them all anyway."

"It *is* a terrible crush," the duchess agreed. "Mama Rackthall is a brilliant success."

"I doubt she could ever be anything else."

"Very true. Her fêtes are always well-attended. I admire her skill as a hostess. And her refreshments are superb. I believe that some guests come only for the food!"

"Then let us have some of it before it's all gone," the duke suggested.

"Oh, Ellen!"

She turned in the direction of the musical voice and saw Tina gliding through the mob, Lord Hawley following in her wake.

"Oh, here is a new friend of mine," she said. "You two go ahead. I'll join you later."

Allesandra looked uncertain. "Are you sure that you wish us to leave you?"

Ellen favored her with a wink. "I told you I had gained new confidence. Shan't I prove it?"

"Very well." Laughing, the duchess took her husband's arm and proceeded towards the dining room.

Ellen turned to greet her friend. She did feel self-assured and it was a heady experience. This was easier than her first foray at Tina's grandmother's. She didn't feel either guarded or threatened. Of course the glass of champagne she'd already consumed hadn't hurt matters either.

"I'm so happy to see you again!" Tina gave her a hug.

"So am I." Lord Hawley bowed. "You look extremely lovely tonight, Miss Trevayne. I vow, you quite take my breath away!"

She glanced down at her celadon gown trimmed in gold. It was pretty, but hardly outstanding enough to inspire such ardor. Nor was she.

She raised an eyebrow. "Such a compliment, Lord Hawley! However untrue it may be."

"My dear lady, do you dare to question the word of a man overcome by beauty?"

"But does it not take breath to speak?" Ellen asked innocently. "You, sir, do not seem to be lacking in that capacity."

He laughed. "Touché, my sweet!"

Tina rolled her eyes. "What a flirt! Two flirts in fact, for I do think you are just as guilty as he is, Ellen. Look, there is a vacant sofa. Let us sit down for a chat while my shameless cousin fetches us a glass of refreshment."

"I am at your beck and call." Lord Hawley escorted them to the settee. "Save my place from the gentlemen who will soon begin to rally round."

"Oh, go on," his cousin ordered.

With a polished bow, he left them to thread his way through the assemblage.

"Wasn't that the Duke and Duchess of Rackthall I saw you with?" Tina asked.

"Yes, they are my dear friends and neighbors."

"Their marriage was the talk of the *ton*. He was quite a sophisticated rake, you know."

"He is no longer."

"I can see why. She's lovely!" Tina said enviously.

"Her beauty is not only skin-deep either," Ellen murmured affectionately.

"She must have had her hands full taming him. And speaking of elegant rakes, where is Lord Singleton tonight?"

"I wouldn't know."

"He didn't accompany you here?" Tina questioned curiously.

"No."

"Have you had a tiff?"

"My goodness, Tina, Lord Singleton and I are merely friends."

"Do you swear it?"

"Of course I swear it!" Ellen forced a laugh. "He . . . he is like a brother to me."

"Well then, if you are positive . . . I find him perfectly marvelous. Not so much as his friend Lord Aubrey Standish, but *that* gentleman will not even give me a glance! It is quite unsettling. Have you met Lord Standish? Do you not agree that he is outstandingly handsome too?"

"Both are very charming gentlemen."

Ellen was glad that a group of young people drifted up at that moment to chat with her friend and make her acquaintance. Others, mostly gentlemen, joined them. When Lord Hawley made his return he was forced to force his way through quite a cluster of admirers.

"Move yourself, Kinsley," he said irritably to the lanky Irish lord who was standing at Ellen's elbow. "I'm trying to balance these beverages."

"Make your own room, my lord." He deftly removed a glass of champagne from Lord Hawley's hands and presented it to Ellen.

She smiled at Tina's cousin and gave her unique

little shrug. It was too bad that poor Lord Hawley had been ousted from his place of honor, but it was rather exciting to find her company so valued. At first she had thought that she would be ignored, sitting next to such a magnificent beauty as Lady Christina, but she soon discovered that wasn't true. When introductions had been made she received just as many compliments and witty praise as her friend. The young men of the *ton* liked her and avidly demonstrated their appreciation.

Ellen sipped her champagne and chatted with one, then another as each admirer tried to claim her attention. This was enormously entertaining and quite flattering too. Of course her captivated audience was very youthful when compared to Brandon and Harry and their friends. They lacked the suave charm and rakish magnetism of the more experienced gentlemen, but in time they too would be smooth, dashing men-about-town.

At one point she saw the Rackthalls return to the room. Allesandra's face registered stunned surprise when she saw Ellen and her group of admirers. She quickly whispered something to the duke.

Grinning, Brandon moved languidly through the press surrounding the two young ladies, which parted rapidly at his progress. He bent over Ellen and gave her another glass of champagne.

"Your lady chaperone was worried about your well-being. I can see that her concern was misplaced," he whispered.

"Isn't it amazing?" she breathed. "I'm having a splendid time!"

"Enjoy yourself. I'll collect you when we're ready to leave. In the meantime, do signal me if you are in need of rescue."

Ellen laughed.

He kissed her hand and Tina's as well, reducing that young lady to speechless blushing.

The other gentlemen, who had stepped out of the duke's way, vied again for position and renewed their conversation. They were joined by others. Lord Rackthall's interest in the two young ladies had ignited the interest of those bachelors who had previously preferred not to face the crush around them.

Ellen began to grow weary of it all. The throng of people made the room terribly hot and stuffy. Her smile felt as if it had been pasted on so tightly that it made her mouth hurt. She wondered if Tina was also fatigued. As she scanned the room for Brandon and his promised rescue, she saw the entrance of two new arrivals.

Overwhelmingly handsome in their faultless attire, Harry and Lord Aubrey Standish paused idly in the doorway, their cool eyes surveying the company. Ellen's heart lurched to her throat. She should have guessed that Harry might appear, but she had so effectively put him out of her mind when she left her grandfather's house that she hadn't really thought about it. Now that he had come, she realized that she wasn't at all prepared for it.

A ripple flowed through the female guests as the two perennial prize catches were sighted. Ellen hoped against hope that they would be occupied by their own onslaught and fail to see her. She sank down further in the cushions and quickly turned her attention to Lords Kinsley and Hawley.

"You didn't tell me that Ellen would be here," Aubrey said softly without turning his head.

Harry was surprised that he hadn't seen her. "I didn't know it."

"I still wonder if the two of you didn't have a spat. You're going to have to tell me eventually, you know."

"Where is she?"

"I doubt you can see her now. She's surrounded by men."

"What!"

"Oh, just a brood of unlicked cubs. No competition, I should think, although there's Hawley and Sir Gilbert Exingham. They're not exactly ingenues."

"Dammit."

Harry finally caught sight of Ellen sitting on a sofa beside Lady Christina. She looked positively luscious in the diaphanous silk gown that so accentuated her exquisite figure. Her face animated, she said something evidently amusing to the dark young lord at her elbow, who laughed and bent close to whisper in her ear.

"Dammit," Harry said again.

"Shall we join them?" Aubrey inquired.

"What? Associate ourselves with that flock of spring roosters? You may do as you wish, but I would not stoop to such dishonor."

"Good God, Harry! Aren't you going to . . ."

"Lord Singleton, Lord Standish! How pleasant to see you again!"

Harry repressed an obscenity and turned to greet Lady Sally Jersey, who was bearing down on them with two young ladies in tow. He and Aubrey bowed smilingly.

"Lady Jersey," Harry drawled, taking her hand and lazily sweeping his gray eyes over her. "Enchanting as always."

"Such a practiced flirt," she admonished. "But I do love it! No one, dear Harry, has quite your style. And you . . ." She extended her other hand to Aubrey. "I am reminded that you have the sort of eyelashes a woman would kill for!"

Aubrey deepened his dimples as the young ladies tittered.

"May I present Miss Marion Grimsley and Miss

Serena Hamilton?'' Lady Jersey drew the chits forward. ''They are distant relatives of mine.''

The gentlemen bowed.

Straight from the schoolroom, Harry surmised. He could practically smell the barley water. If he had to wed a child like this he would prefer that his vile cousin George inherited. He glanced over the girls' curly heads and saw Ellen rising. Now where was she going? He saw Lord Hawley present his arm to her. Damme! He started forward.

''Ouch!'' shrieked Miss Marion Grimsley as the marquess planted his foot squarely on top of her soft slipper.

Harry froze, looking downward.

''Get off!'' cried the young lady.

He leaped backwards, releasing the young lady's tender foot from its rude, and painful, trap.

''My word!'' Sally Jersey exclaimed as she watched Marion grasp her toe in her hand and painfully dance on one foot. ''Stop that unseemly conduct at once, Marion!''

''It's broken!'' she wailed. ''I know it is! He stepped full on it and ground it into the rug!''

Harry felt his cheeks turning rapidly from cool to warm to a flaming inferno as every eye, quizzing glass, and lorgnette turned in his direction. ''I must apologize, Miss Grimsley,'' he stammered. ''Here, let me assist you to a chair.''

The young lady moaned, leaning on his arm. ''I shall not be able to dance at my own ball.''

''Perhaps it is not so bad as that,'' he soothed, glancing in vain for an empty chair. ''Get up,'' he said abruptly to an elderly dowager.

''Well, I never!'' She shook her fan at him. ''If your mama were aware of your behavior . . .''

''Please, Lady Moorhouse! I am in desperate straits.''

She lifted her portly body, along with her needle-like nose. "I shall never forget this affront!"

Miss Grimsley collapsed onto the seat and dropped her shoe. Harry knelt down on one knee to examine the injured member.

"Get away from there!" Sally Jersey squealed, plunging down beside him and stuffing the slipper back onto the swiftly swelling foot. "This is disgraceful! Stop your puling, Marion."

"But it hurts!"

The marquess got back to his feet. Ellen was gone, but Aubrey remained, biting the inner flesh of both cheeks to keep from laughing. A murmur of merriment was spreading among the guests as well.

"Let's get out of here," Harry snapped, and turned on his heel, leaving the house as quickly as he could.

Aubrey joined him on the curb. "By all that's holy, Harry, I . . ." He burst into laughter. "I don't believe I've ever seen you make such an ass of yourself!"

"It's all *her* fault!"

"Jersey?" asked Aubrey.

"Ellen, you dullard!" the marquess shouted.

"Oh, yes. I see! Ellen happens to be in the same room so you pounce onto Miss Grimsley's foot and nail her to the floor. It makes the best of sense, Harry."

"You don't understand anything at all, do you?"

Aubrey shook his head. "I am having a bit of trouble following your logic."

"Ellen got up and took Hawley's arm!"

"So?"

"Just go to hell, Aubrey!" Forgetting his carriage, he stalked off down the street.

"Don't forget old Moorhouse!" the viscount called tautingly after him. "Just wait until she circulates her tale of the bumbling marquess!"

Harry didn't want to think of Lady Moorhouse. He didn't want to think of anyone who might have witnessed that perfectly mortifying scene. Ellen! This was all her fault. Gad, the woman was a regular witch. Even when she was utterly poised and monstrously attractive, she had the uncanny ability to create mishap for others. With scenes like this, he wondered why he so desperately wanted to marry the vixen.

Riding home in the luxurious Rackthall coach, Ellen was more than satisfied with the way that the evening had gone. She had impressed Brandon and Allesandra with her newfound confidence and had attracted a great many beaux. She knew that no lasting *tendre* would form between herself and her splendid admirers, especially when they learned of her family background, but it was amusing just the same.

She hadn't even spoken with Harry or Lord Standish. When she and Lord Hawley had strolled to the dining room, there had been some sort of scuffle surrounding the two gentlemen. After that she hadn't seen either of them again. It was just as well. She must prepare herself more thoroughly before she faced the marquess again or her feelings for him might show on her face.

Brandon chuckled. "Did you see Harry step on that schoolgirl's foot?"

"I saw the aftermath," Allesandra replied. "Poor Harry. He was absolutely mortified. Did you see it, Ellen?"

"I noticed a young lady in the throes of hysterics."

"Harry caused it."

"Fustian! It was an accident. I have certainly stepped on enough toes, male *and* female, and it has never brought on such a riotous scene!'' she said hotly. ''The girl's behavior was disgraceful.''

The duke roared with laughter. ''Harry certainly has a valiant defender in you, Ellen! Unfortunately it won't do much good. This incident will be the talk of the *ton*. I've often wondered if the elegant marquess would ever make—pardon my pun—a misstep!''

His wife glared at him. ''I thought he was your friend.''

''Oh, he is, of course. Allesandra, allow me some pleasure in it. I suffered my share of gossip.''

''And deserved every word of it,'' she murmured under her breath. Before he could begin a rebuttal, she quickly changed the subject. ''Ellen, you were splendid tonight! I'll admit that you did astonish me with your town bronze.''

Ellen smiled, but her thoughts remained with Harry. It wasn't fair that the *ton* would take him to task over a silly chit's frenzy. She could imagine how he must feel. She had certainly experienced the same mortification herself at the hands of the vicious cats. For a refined, cultured gentleman like Harry, it must be devastating.

Brandon added his approval to Allesandra's. ''Yes, you've attached a string of lovelorn gentlemen to your credit tonight! All of the ladies will wish to know your secret.''

Ellen shook her head. ''It wasn't any secret. I just didn't care whether they liked me or not.''

The carriage drew up in front of the Frampton residence. ''We shall do this again,'' Allesandra announced. ''There is a ball a week from Saturday. I'd like you to accompany us. In fact, I shall insist.''

''So shall I,'' the duke agreed, ''as long as you save me a waltz.''

''Very well,'' Ellen assented. ''I shall not hear the last of it unless I do.'' A ball would not be as easy as this had been. She would have to dance. But what did it matter? She could practice the steps beforehand and gain some confidence.

Gordon let her into the house and removed her cape. "Mr. Frampton is in the library waiting for you, miss." He lowered his voice. "He's found out about the dogs."

"Oh, no," she groaned. "Why didn't I tell him previously? Well, I suppose I must face his wrath."

"He isn't very pleased, Miss Ellen."

"Thank you, Gordon." With slow, measured footsteps she went down the hall and entered the library.

"There you are at last!" Her grandfather threw down his pen. "Before we approach the real business of this evening, we have another matter to discuss."

"Taffy and Friendly."

He cleared his throat with a noise of disapproval. "While I was occupied with a serious concern, I was interrupted by what sounded like a ferocious dogfight in the alley. It was so loud, Ellen, that I heard it through closed windows. Lo and behold, I soon discovered that I harbored two giant beasts in a makeshift pen! They'd treed the stable cat and had brought the neighborhood out of bed with their barking."

"I'm sorry, Grandfather." Ellen collapsed wearily into a chair. "I should have told you, but there didn't seem to be the proper opportunity."

"Wrong! You should have *asked* me for permission before you sent for those great mongrels!"

"They are not mongrels! They are purebred Saint Bernards."

"Saints, are they!" he shouted. "Then I would like to see a sinner!"

"Please, Grandfather," she said soothingly, "I shall see that they do not bother you again. I'll admit that I've neglected them. Tomorrow morning I shall take them to the park, where they can run off their excess spirit.''

"See that you do that, Ellen! I won't have the neighborhood up at arms!"

"No, sir."

"If you do not succeed, you will have to send them home."

"Yes, sir," she said tiredly.

"Hm . . . Well, that was easy! Now about our dinner party . . ."

Ellen yawned. "Can't we discuss it tomorrow? I am exhausted."

"No! I'm going to have my secretary get the invitations out tomorrow. This is all you need to know. The two Bradfords, the two Evermans, and Lord Singleton will be the only guests invited. The dinner will be held on Tuesday. I want the finest spread you can muster.'' Satisfied, he leaned back on his chair's rear legs and folded his hands over his stomach. "Any questions?"

"For a *formal* dinner, it is usually proper to invite a balance of male and female guests."

"This is a business dinner."

"Oh, then you will not expect me to attend?" she asked with relief.

"You will act as hostess." With a great creak he brought the chair down to its proper position. "I want you to be especially kind to Lord Singleton. Flirt with him a bit!"

"What!" she cried, astounded.

"A little feminine encouragement has brought many a bargain to a satisfactory conclusion."

"I shall do no such thing!" She leaped angrily to her feet. "I will not allow you to use me in that kind of manner! The next thing I know you'll be asking me to behave like a doxy!"

Mr. Frampton frowned. "You don't know how a

doxy acts, and you shouldn't even know that such a person exists."

"Well, I do, and I won't conduct myself like one for any business deal!"

"Ellen! I'm only asking you to be sweet and . . . and . . . becoming."

"You're asking me to cast out lures!"

"Sit down!" he bellowed.

She did not obey. Instead she began to pace the library. "What are the Bradfords to think of me? What about the Evermans! You wish me to marry one of them. What will be their impression if they see me dallying with Harry?"

"First names? Good, good." He chuckled. "Look at it this way, missy. I only wish you to be a kind and proper hostess, merely singling out the marquess in such a feminine way as to make him feel drawn to our company. In return, I promise I'll never say another word about your dogs and I won't press you into making up your mind about any of the young men."

She halted, eyeing him shrewdly. "Nor do I wish to hear any more snide remarks about my friends the duke and duchess."

He sighed. "Agreed."

She extended her hand to grasp his. "Then we have a covenant. Perhaps it should be in writing."

"It won't be necessary. I'll abide by it!" He shook his head. "Ellen, Ellen, 'tis a pity you can't be in business. You're the craftiest wench I've ever seen."

"Thank you, Grandfather. Coming from you, that's a high compliment indeed. Now may I go to bed?"

He waved assent.

She kissed him and sought her room. Despite her fatigue, she didn't go to sleep at once; her mind was bursting with thoughts of the marquess. He must have had a miserable evening. She hoped he could take the inevitable gossip in stride.

And he would be coming here. At her grandfather's invitation! She must be "sweet" to him? How easy that would be if she allowed her true feelings to surface. But she wouldn't do that. The jolt she'd experienced when she saw him this evening had proven how much she must protect herself. She would be pleasant and that would be that.

She rolled over and closed her eyes. That man! Would she ever cease thinking of him without longing?

16

It was a beautiful morning, cool and crisp with a touch of fall in the air. The sun had burnt away the remnants of an early fog and now shone brightly in the deep-blue sky. It was perfect weather for the dogs' first outing in the park.

"Do you still wish to accompany me, Dora?" Ellen asked as the maid helped her into her modish, new russet spencer.

"Oh, yes, miss. It'll be like walking in the country, won't it?"

"It's as much like that as can be possible in the midst of London." She fastened the gold frogs. "Do you miss Bridgeford Grange?"

"Not much," the abigail admitted. "The city is so much more exciting."

"I suppose so." Ellen didn't want to spoil the girl's enthusiasm by voicing her own sentiments.

"I'm ready, miss," Dora prompted.

"Then we'll go." She picked up her gloves and sailed out of her bedroom.

At the stable she was surprised to see her grandfather's coach standing ready and the dogs within. When they saw her, they barked joyously and leaped from seat to seat, pawing at the windows. If he were to learn of this development, Mr. Frampton would be furious.

"What's going on here?" she demanded. "I planned to walk them, not to take them for a ride."

"Well, Miss Ellen . . ." Matthew scratched his head in consternation. "It's a bit far distance to the park and the dogs, well . . . they're right strong on the leash. We thought it'd be best if they rode to the park, at least till they get used to the city."

Ellen nodded. "I suppose that idea has merit. Let us be on our way then."

After a doubtful glance at the mammoth animals inside the compartment, Dora chose to ride on the box with the coachman. Ellen climbed inside, where the dogs immediately knocked her to the seat. Taffy jumped up beside her while Friendly put his paws in her lap and licked her cheek.

"What a welcome!" She patted them both at the same time and scratched their ears, settling them somewhat.

It wasn't long before she saw the wisdom in transporting the Saint Bernards to the park. They leaped and barked at people on the streets and set up near-pandemonium whenever they sighted another canine. When the coach drew to a halt well within the gates, Ellen's pretty walking ensemble was thoroughly rumpled and her hat was askew. Nevertheless, she fastened the leashes on the dogs' collars and prepared to get out. An outing was just what they needed to curb their exuberance. Given the agreement she'd made with her grandfather, she couldn't risk a repeat performance of the past night.

Matthew assisted her down and called the dogs after her. They plunged to the ground and milled around her, wrapping her in their leashes. Dora stared with horror at the scene while the groom hastened to help his mistress.

"Get down, Dora. I may need your assistance too," Ellen gasped. "Taffy! Friendly! Sit!"

They decided to obey, plopping down on their haunches and watching their mistress with open mouths and lolling tongues. Ellen quickly untangled herself. Her abigail, ever conscious of her young lady's appearance, straightened her hat.

"You see?" Ellen triumphantly told the servants. "They do remember their manners!"

"Shall I walk with you, miss?" Matthew asked uneasily.

"I'm sure there is no need. I taught them to go on leashes when they were puppies. They are very intelligent dogs. They'll soon remember those lessons."

"But . . ."

"We shall be all right. Coachman? Pull the horses over there in the shade and enjoy your time in the fresh air. We'll return shortly."

"Yes, miss."

She moved forward with the dogs walking nicely. In the strange environment, they were content to range around their mistress, sniffing the exotic new odors and looking about with curiosity. When they passed two nursemaids with their charges, they exhibited only mild interest and pressed on to better things.

"You see?" Ellen asked her abigail. "They do recall!"

"They're afraid," Dora ventured. "They're not sure of where they are."

"Fiddlesticks! They are remembering their manners."

As they progressed, the lady's maid's remark proved to be accurate. The two Saint Bernards became friskier, pulling at their leashes and attempting to bound into greater speed. It was all Ellen could do to hold them.

"Help me, Dora."

"Oh, miss, this was a great mistake!" Dora cried, adding her own weight and muscle to the leashes.

"Nonsense! They simply need exercise."

The dogs tugged the women to a trot.

"Miss! Please make them sit! I can't keep up!"

"Then *you* need the exercise too!" Ellen gave a mighty jerk, but the animals failed to heed her. They increased their pace, lurching to a lumbering gallop.

"Oh, miss, I can't hold on!" Dora shrieked. She let go her grasp and fell, rolling on the ground for several turns before she was able to stop herself. "Miss Ellen!"

Ellen twisted the leashes around her wrists and grimly held on. She was running as fast as she could now, shouting to the dogs and attempting to yank them to a standstill. It was like trying to stop a runaway team of horses. Her feet left the ground and she fell hard on her stomach. Ignoring the extra weight, the dogs sped on, pulling her bodily across the grass like a human sledge.

"Taffy! Friendly!" Another voice joined hers.

The Saint Bernards abruptly changed direction, dragged her a few more yards, and stopped, leaping and barking ecstatically.

"Down!"

Ellen drew herself upright to a sitting position, loosed the leashes, and rubbed her burning wrists. She miserably looked up at the Marquess of Singleton. Despite her resolve to avoid him, she was desperately glad to see him now. "Thank you, Harry!"

"Are you all right?"

"Most generally so." She gazed beyond him at Lord Aubrey Standish, who was sitting on his horse and holding Harry's while biting his lips desperately to keep from snickering. "It's all right, my lord." She shrugged. "You may laugh. I'm sure it was vastly amusing."

Lord Standish roared with laughter, unable to stop even when Harry cast him a hard stare. "You should have seen it, Miss Trevayne! You were flying along like a sleigh on ice and Harry was running across the lawn like . . ."

"Aubrey, will you take my horse home?" the marquess interrupted loudly, glancing around to see if anyone had seen them. "I'm going to help Miss Trevayne with these animals."

Even Ellen, despite her leather-burned wrists, was forced to giggle. "It must have been quite a spectacle."

"It was indeed," Aubrey replied with a grin. "I can't say that I've ever witnessed anything like it!"

"Good day, Aubrey!" Harry cried. "I have had enough of your misplaced mirth for this week!"

"Oh, be sporting for once!" Still chuckling to himself, Harry's friend turned the horses and rode off.

Harry helped Ellen to her feet. "Are you certain that you are not injured?"

"My wrists are sore, and I imagine I'll discover a few more aches and pains, but yes, I think I shall live through it."

Dora limped up to her mistress. "Miss Ellen, are you hurt? I'm so sorry, but I just couldn't hold on any longer!"

"It's all right, Dora. I'm fine; are you?"

The abigail rubbed her thigh. "I'll do."

"Then let's be getting back." Harry picked up the leashes of the eagerly waiting dogs and started forward, Ellen at his side and Dora trailing a discreet distance behind. Set in motion the dogs began to lunge again and it was all he, with his masculine strength, could do to hold them back.

Ellen sighed. "They are so frisky."

"That's an understatement."

"Well, it shouldn't be very far. We brought them here by coach."

"Thank God. I was wondering how you managed to get them through the streets." He gave a mighty heave and threw the animals back on their haunches.

"Please don't hurt them, Harry."

"I? Hurt them? They're jerking my arms from the sockets! Ellen, you have *got* to teach these dogs some manners. In the country, it didn't matter as much. They could run away as they pleased. If you want to walk them here, however . . ." He shook his head. "I just don't know how you're going to do it."

"But they have to have exercise!" Her face fell. "I suppose they'd be better off at home, but I missed them so! And Taffy is going to have puppies and I want to be there and . . ."

"Let me think on it."

"Thank you!" She squeezed his arm. "You are the best friend that I could ever have."

"Best friend," he murmured. "I thought you didn't wish me ever again to call on you."

"Oh, *that!* Well . . . Perhaps I had best explain. You see, I thought . . ."

"Lord Singleton, is that you?" an elderly lady cried from a passing carriage. "Harry, do come over here!"

"Damme!"

"Who is that?" Ellen asked.

"Lady Carlson, one of my mother's friends. Wouldn't you just know it!"

"Oh, Harry!" the high-pitched voice called as the vehicle drew to a halt.

"I'll hold the dogs," Ellen offered, reaching for the leashes.

"No, you won't! We'd have another debacle. Come along with me."

"But I look a fright!" She knew her hair was

mussed and, looking down, she saw with horror that the front of her dress was streaked with grass stains.

"No matter. She's already seen us." He jerked the dogs towards the carriage.

"Harry Singleton, I didn't know you were dog fancier! I am glad to see it, for I too am a great admirer of the canine species. What a fine pair they are!" Lady Carlson lifted her lorgnette to peer at Ellen. "And who is this once-fashionable young lady?"

Ellen flushed deeply.

"Miss Ellen Trevayne, my lady." He smiled encouragingly at Ellen. "Lady Carlson, a longtime family friend."

Ellen made her curtsy.

"Miss Trevayne was an unfortunate victim of the dogs' exuberance. They knocked her down," the marquess explained.

"What a pity!" the lady cried sympathetically. "I hope you were not injured, my dear."

"No, ma'am."

"I am glad of it. They are very large dogs, are they not? But then, gentlemen seem to prefer animals of great size. Tell me, Harry, when will your dear mama be arriving in town?"

"I expect her anyday, ma'am."

"Excellent! No one plays whist as well as Eleanor." She directed her attention once more to Taffy and Friendly. "You really should teach them obedience, Harry. I shall be happy to advise you. Just look at my little Muffin, so content to sit beside me on the seat!" Reaching forward, she threw open the carriage door.

"No, my lady!" Ellen cried, but it was too late.

The Saint Bernards saw the tiny lapdog. Before Harry could react, they tore the leashes from his hands. With a brief jostling for position and a chorus of wild barking, they leaped into the vehicle.

Lady Carlson screamed and Muffin squealed. She frantically picked him up and held him to her breast. While Taffy pawed the little dog from her hands, Friendly lapped at the countess' cheek. Screeching the most unladylike invectives, she batted at his big face. Her little Muffin fell to the floor and rolled out on the ground, taking to his heels with Ellen after him.

Catching him easily, she gathered him up and turned back to the fray. Harry and Lady Carlson's groom had leaped into the carriage and were trying to catch the frenzied Saint Bernards. The horses had become excited and the coachman had his hands full keeping them under control.

Ellen groaned as Taffy pushed the marquess into the countess' lap. The lady's bonnet flew off and fell under the wheels. The agitated team moved the vehicle back and forth across it.

"Oh, my," Ellen whispered.

The groom got a strong hold on Taffy's collar and jumped to the ground, pulling her after him. Harry caught Friendly's haunches and heaved him out, plummeting after him. The buttons flew from the marquess' fine willow-green coat.

"Down, God dammit!" he shouted, grasping the leashes.

The dogs sat, staring up at him expectantly.

Stroking and soothing the frightened Muffin, Ellen moved forward and deposited the roughed-up ball of fur on the seat beside his mistress.

"Bless you, my dear," Lady Carlson said, weeping, "you have saved my little darling. And you!" She turned like a viper on Harry. "I have never witnessed such a display in all my born days! Such conduct! From a peer of the realm! Just wait until your mother hears of this!"

"Madam," Harry said wearily, "you must accept my apology."

"I shall accept nothing from you! I have never been so sorely used!"

Harry's face flamed scarlet. "Madam, I—"

"I can explain," Ellen said hastily.

"No, my dear." The countess reached out to pat her cheek. "I am only sorry that you had to be a party to such a disgusting exhibition, but I am glad that you were here to save my Muffin's life. My best advice to you is to stay as far away as possible from that young man." She reverted her attention to Harry. "And to think that I once considered you to be a fine young gentleman! Coachman! Drive on!"

The carriage lurched into a hasty departure.

"Her hat!" Ellen spied the crumpled bonnet and started to reach for it, but stopped, noting its flattened condition. "Perhaps it's best if this isn't brought to her attention."

Harry kicked it savagely. "Welcome to the *ton*, Ellen—of which I am no longer a member!"

The dogs, seeing the marquess' antic, snatched up the headgear and tore it into fragments.

"It can't be as bad as all that," Ellen said comfortingly. "Explanations can be made."

"You don't explain to the *ton*! The news of this escapade will be all over London by evening. Coupled with last night's incident, I'll be the biggest laughingstock the town has ever seen!"

"I'm sorry," she said woefully. "But really, Harry, you must learn to take these things in stride."

For a moment he looked as if he might strangle her, but luckily his hands were full of leashes. Instead, he clamped his teeth together and set off towards the Frampton carriage with Ellen and Dora half-trotting to keep up.

Ellen sat uncomfortably in the Frampton coach as the coachman drove from the park. The dogs at least had calmed themselves and were stretched out on the seat, yawning and preparing to nap. She glanced at her silent, bedraggled companion and was glad that she had ordered her driver to drop Harry at his house in Mayfair before taking her and the dogs home.

The poor marquess looked terrible, worse even than when she had splashed him with mud or caused him to fall into the stream at Shadybrook. His coat hung open, the buttons gone and only frayed thread remaining where they had been attached. His cravat was disheveled, its once-elaborate knot dangling loosely to one side. His boots were scuffed and his breeches bore the dusty paw print of a Saint Bernard. From the expression on his face, he must be feeling as ravaged as he appeared.

Ellen began to silently weep. How could he ever have sought her friendship when she repeatedly treated him so abominably? Surely he must hate her now.

"My dear?"

"You must despise me!" she sobbed aloud. "I have precipitated so much grief for you!"

"Ellen, my dear." He produced a handkerchief so snowy-white that it seemed incongruous to the setting.

"Once again I have destroyed your appearance. I have ruined your clothes! I have caused you embarrassment of the worst sort."

"Hush now." He gathered her into his arms. "It isn't that bad."

"I shall understand if you never wish to see me again! I will suffer your cut direct! No one could want a friend like me!"

"You are wrong," Harry said softly. "I want you very much."

"You do?" She sniffled, wishing that propriety would allow her to snuggle more closely against him, but even with Dora sitting up on the box with the coachman, it was impossible.

His breath ruffled her hair. "I want you more than you would ever realize."

"Oh, Harry, you are so *patient* with me!" She wiped her eyes and lifted her head. "I promise I shall do better."

"You are a darling just the way you are."

Mesmerized, Ellen saw his mouth moving closer to hers. He was going to kiss her! Her stomach turned a crazy somersault. This time she would not accuse him of trifling and she would not worry about protecting her vulnerable heart. She would simply . . . enjoy it . . . just this once. She closed her eyes, her lips parting slightly of their own accord.

The carriage drew to an abrupt halt. Ellen quickly straightened as the marquess withdrew his arms from around her. She avoided meeting his gaze.

"Here we are, m'lord." Matthew opened the door.

"Thank you." Harry nodded sharply to him and turned again to Ellen. "You are all right?"

"Yes," she breathed.

"I'll call on you. In the meantime, do not take out the dogs alone." He kissed her hand and was gone.

The coach moved on. Ellen looked back, but only caught a glimpse of him striding towards a magnificent brick mansion. She dropped her head back onto the squabs. Dear God, how could she forget him when there were moments such as this? She must tell herself over and over that this was nothing but a flirtation, such as she had relished with the gentlemen last night. Harry was a charming man-about-town and was used to such pastimes. She must force herself to keep matters in their proper perspective.

"What in heaven's name has happened to you?"

"Mama!" Surprised, Harry turned towards the

open salon door and saw Lady Singleton sitting in her customary chair beside the crackling fire. "Where have you come from?"

"Don't be a ninny, my son. I've come from York-shire, of course." She tilted her head and looked at him appraisingly. "But where *I* came from is of no consequence. Where have *you* been?"

"It's a long story, Mama." He entered the room and closed the door. "I'm sure you'll hear many versions of it, along with certain other tales."

"You look as though you've been in a dogfight or a gin-house brawl, but knowing you, I realize that both are beneath your dignity."

"Think again, ma'am." He bent to kiss her cheek. "You might say it was a dogfight."

"Gracious!" she cried. "Do I detect a bit of scandal?"

"Probably so," he said morosely, walking to the sideboard to pour himself a large glass of brandy.

"Do tell!" Her eyes twinkled mischievously. "I cannot imagine how you could become involved in such an adventure!"

"Well, I have a friend, a Miss Ellen Trevayne."

"A young lady?" The dowager marchioness observed him with heightened speculation. "Continue!"

Harry provided her a brief summary of his acquaintance with Ellen and of the calamity in the park. "I'm sure you'll hear it once more from Lady Carlson."

Lady Singleton laughed until the tears flowed down her cheeks. "Ha-ha! Poor Penelope and that prissy, obnoxious Muffin!"

"I don't think it's that funny," Harry protested.

"Oh, my dear boy! It's beyond funny. It's the most hilarious event I have heard of in years! Did you say that you sat in Pen's lap?"

He stiffened his shoulders. "You may laugh. *Your* reputation is not at stake!"

"I am sorry, I cannot help it!" She dabbed at her eyes with a delicate lace handkerchief.

"Nearly everything I do lately seems to be tinged with the ridiculous!"

"Surely not."

"It's true. I'm making myself into a laughing-stock!"

"It shall pass." Lady Singleton gasped for breath and waved her hand at him. "Please fetch me a glass of sherry."

He dutifully obeyed, his mind still full of his degradations. "Mama, just look at me! I can scarcely believe . . ."

"Tell me about Miss Trevayne."

"Haven't I done so already?"

"No. You haven't told me that you are in love with her."

"Mama!"

"You are, aren't you? A man, especially a man like you, Harry, would not suffer such abuse and keep coming back for more unless . . ." Her body shook with pent-up laughter. "Unless he was in love with her!"

"So what if I am?" he said defensively, walking towards the door. "I am not at all sure that she returns the sentiment. She thinks of me as a friend."

"Have you told her differently?"

He ignored her question. "I am going to change my clothes, Mama. I shall converse with you later. You may be interested in further tales of my mortification."

"I am indeed!" Lady Singleton cackled as the door closed behind him. "Perhaps I may see a grandchild yet," she mused cheerfully.

17

His mother might find his mortification vastly amusing, especially when he'd added a recital of the events in Kent. To Harry, everything that had happened was a complete disgrace. For years he had been a cool, sophisticated aristocrat, a ladies' man, a pink of the *ton*. Now he had humiliated himself. Why couldn't she realize the emotional turmoil he was experiencing? All she could talk of were grandchildren! In desperation, he got up the nerve to go to his club for luncheon.

As he entered the quiet, dark-paneled retreat, surreptitious smirks and snickers told him that the word of his downfall had spread. Chin high, his lips pressed together in a fine line, he strolled aloofly to the dining room. As luck would have it, Aubrey, Brandon, Brough, and Chris were seated at a table with their heads together. He had to join them. It would be enormously peculiar if he didn't.

"I can guess what, or should I say whom, you are discussing," he said coldly, drawing up a chair.

The four couldn't conceal their guilt.

"Harry," Brandon began, "in the eyes of the *ton*, you don't seem as ridiculous as you might think. Consensus of opinion blames Miss Grimsley for being an hysterical goose. Sally Jersey will not enjoy

having the girl's piece of foolish behavior to overcome."

"I am so relieved," the marquess said impas-
sively. "Although she will probably blame me for
providing the opportunity for Miss Grimsley to shine
so dimly."

"Do you really care?" Aubrey asked.

"Of course I care! I don't wish to reap Lady Jersey's enmity."

"She can't afford it, Harry. You're too great a
catch."

The others agreed. Harry had to admit that they
might have a point. If Sally Jersey was attempting
to assist the firing off of her young relative, she
would make all haste to hush the gossip.

Brandon continued. "As for the dogs, well . . ."
All four bit their lips in an meager attempt to hide
their grins. "It seems that Ellen has come off the
winner there. She has become little . . . little . . ."
The duke burst into laughter and the others followed suit. "Little Muffin's champion!" he finished,
wiping his eyes.

Harry smiled faintly. "How it pleases me to be the
source of such amusement to you all."

The waiter appeared at his elbow, obviously trying hard to keep his expression dispassionate. For
an employee of White's to exhibit other than a
sternly sober countenance proved just how amused
everyone was.

"You too?" the marquess said to the man se-
verely. "Never mind answering. Just bring me a
beefsteak and whatever you have to go with it."

"You may as well laugh, Harry. What else can
one do?" Aubrey said cheerfully.

"I'm sorry to disappoint you. I just don't feel like
laughing at present. Neither would you, you bunch
of—"

"Come now, Harry, you laughed enough at me back in my wenching days."

"You asked for it, Bran. You had a penchant for choosing ladybirds who created the worst scenes."

The duke shrugged. "No matter, you still laughed."

"All right, so I did! But I have yet to find humor in this situation. I shall endeavor to ignore it."

Harry's steak arrived. He set into it, his stiff shoulders daring anyone to mention Saint Bernards or schoolgirls. He knew that his friends were trying to ease the situation, but he wasn't in any mood to view it all as anything but a total downfall. Perhaps someday he would look back and laugh. But for a suave, prideful nobleman, that day was a long way away.

Ellen had thought that Harry might call. He had said that he would. But as the afternoon lengthened, the possibility grew faint. Despite a twinge of disappointment, she realized that his absence was in her own best interest. Once again she had permitted herself to be swayed by the handsome marquess. Dear Lord, she'd almost allowed him to kiss her! In the future she must be strictly on her guard to avoid his advances. At least her grandfather's dinner party would afford no opportunity for intimacy.

Her day did turn out to be busy with other callers. Her gentlemen friends from the city arrived with gifts: a book of pirate tales from Mr. Bradford, bonbons from the Derifields, and a lovely hand-painted fan from Mr. Everman. Tonnish beaux she had met at the dowager Lady Rackthall's called, bringing flowers enough to fill the entrance hall and drawing room. She learned from them that the news of the Saint Bernards had spread.

Her heart went out to Harry, who was fully implicated in the gossip. Even though she admitted ownership of the now-famous dogs, it made little difference in the tongue-wagging. Everyone derived too much enjoyment from laughing at the marquess.

When the last of her callers left, she sank down wearily on the sofa. Then and there she quickly made up her mind to return Taffy and Friendly to the country. They would truly be happier there and they would further endanger no one's reputation. She had just begun to relax from her exhausting day when the butler entered the drawing room.

"Lord Singleton," Gordon intoned.

Ellen hurriedly arranged herself in a ladylike sitting position, but not before Harry could have seen a brief view of her ankles. Oh, what did it matter, she thought resignedly. He had witnessed that and even more in the past.

"You have had quite a busy day," he said. "I've come by several times today only to find any number of horses, carriages, and curricles out in front. I'm glad to find you finally alone. You look tired, Ellen."

"I am."

"You should not be at-home to callers you are not interested in. But then, perhaps you are interested in them all."

"I don't wish to be rude to them." Her gaze met his dark one. "Harry, are you angry with me? If so, please deliver your set-down and get it over with."

"I? Angry? Why, Ellen, I adore being mauled by Saint Bernards and ridiculed by the *ton.*"

"I am sending the dogs home," she announced uncomfortably. "They do not belong in London and it was a mistake to think that they did."

"Won't you miss them?"

"Yes, but . . . It's the best for all concerned."

"Crying craven?"

"I am being practical. I couldn't live with myself if they were to cause another such event."

"As you wish. I doubt that you yourself would ever be able to control them in the park. For that matter, I doubt if even *I* could."

"I think you did an admirable job!" she protested. "It was the fault of that Lady Carlson. The woman was very foolish in exposing her ridiculous little dog to Taffy and Friendly. She claimed to have such knowledge of canine behavior! She should have known better!"

Harry shrugged.

"And as for that silly goose at Lady Rackthall's," Ellen went on heatedly. "Such a display over nothing!"

He couldn't keep from grinning. "I see you're willing to stand champion for me."

"Of course I am! You have been dreadfully misused and I certainly know what it feels like! All those cats with their sharp teeth and claws . . . I hate the *ton* and I hate London!"

"You shouldn't feel that way. My dear, you have been a success."

"Perhaps I have. Honestly I don't care!" Unable to remain seated, she rose and went to the sideboard, pouring a glass of brandy for him. "Just because I am not at present a victim of their viciousness does not mean that I cannot be angry for someone who is!"

He joined her, taking his glass from her white-knuckled hand and setting it aside. "Let's just leave it, Ellen. You're becoming overset."

"No, I am not!" Her lips quivered. Tears moistened her eyes. "I don't like your being the butt of their scandal. You are so wonderful . . ."

Harry lifted her chin and gazed into her tear-filled eyes. "Do you truly think so?"

Her cheeks burned. "Yes . . ." She looked away from his intense gaze. She wanted to turn her head, but his light touch held her as securely as if he had used force. His mouth descended on hers, brushing her lips with feathery tenderness.

"Thank you," he murmured.

Her heart thumped against her ribs. She hazarded a glance at him, mesmerized as his head lowered once more. He kissed her again, this time with greater intensity. An extraordinary warmth suffused Ellen's body. She felt herself drawn against him, his arms circling her waist, his fingers caressing the small of her back. A bell of warning chimed in her brain. She stiffened, pulling away.

"Harry, we mustn't."

"Why not?" His voice was husky, almost unintelligible.

"Because . . . because we must not."

"My sweet . . ."

"Please!" She whirled away and went to the window. "It is growing late. I must dress for dinner. Grandfather likes to have his meal as soon as he comes home."

"Do you wish me to leave?" he asked softly.

"It is growing late," she repeated.

"Then I shall bid you good day, Ellen."

"Good day . . . Harry." She heard the door close behind him and rapidly sought the nearest chair, half-falling into it and pressing her palms against her flaming cheeks. The kiss . . . dear God, the kiss! How much she had wished it to continue; how avidly she had wanted to slip her own arms around him and hold him close. She must be stronger! She could not allow this to happen ever, ever again.

On the following evening, her thoughts still unsettled, Ellen stood beside her grandfather in the drawing room and greeted their guests. Remembering the time when her city callers and Harry had tossed their barbs at one another, she speculated upon how the younger gentlemen would conduct themselves towards the marquess. More than that, she wondered how *he* would behave with *them*.

Mr. Bradford and Mr. Everman, schooled in the art of business transaction, would likely be straightforward and congenial. They and their fathers wanted the property Harry possessed; therefore, they would do nothing to threaten the proposed arrangement.

Harry, on the other hand, probably didn't care whether or not he became a part of this joint affair. He didn't need the money. Like most members of the wealthy nobility, he would have many investments, which he entrusted others to manage. He had a personal interest in the prosperity of his estates, but Ellen doubted that his attention could be captured by a matter such as this. In fact she was surprised that he had participated in the venture this far, instead of merely turning over the negotiation to his man of business. He must have a hidden motive. Perhaps he intended to score revenge on the city gentlemen for the set-downs he had suffered at their hands, when they had met on that awkward afternoon in the Frampton drawing room.

"Ah, Lord Singleton! Good evening to you," Mr. Frampton said jovially.

"Good evening, sir." Harry shook his hand.

"I believe you are acquainted with my granddaughter."

"How do you do, Miss Trevayne." He bowed over her hand, his lips brushing her fingertips.

"My lord." She made a pretty curtsy.

How handsome he looked in his pearl-gray evening attire! Beyond a doubt he cast the others in the shade. She hoped that her sleek bishop's-blue gown of gossamer silk matched his stylish elegance.

Mr. Frampton made introductions. The three younger men exchanged the expected pleasantries as though they had not met prior to this night. Ellen, however, couldn't help noticing a certain degree of calculation in their eyes.

The company seated themselves as Gordon served hors d'oeuvres. Ellen was careful to choose a chair within a neutral distance of them all. Despite her grandfather's admonition to her to be particularly friendly to Harry, she refused to compromise herself. The marquess might enjoy the deference, but he would probably have an instant awareness of what was afoot and be afforded considerable amusement at her expense. Nor did she wish to slight Mr. Everman, who in all probability was her future husband.

Conversation was general and desultory. Topics were confined to subjects that would be familiar to each member of the diverse group. The main purpose of the evening would be discussed after dinner, over port, when Ellen had left the room. No man present would lower himself to talk of business in the presence of a woman. Heaven help her, she might have an opinion of her own!

Ellen grew bored. She longed for the witty, lightning-sharp repartee to be found in such drawing rooms as Allesandra's. In small talk like that, a lady could at least show some intelligence by her neatly turned phrase. She was relieved when Gordon announced the meal.

The dinner was a credit to her abilities as a hostess. From the delicate turtle soup through the succulent roast sirloin to the rich darioles topped with toasted coconut, the meal was prepared so well as to please the most jaded, fastidious appetite. The service was quick, efficient, and orderly. No food arrived at the table either warmer or colder than it was intended. Ellen knew that she owed the most of her success to the excellent kitchen staff and to Gordon and his finely trained footman, but she was proud nonetheless. Most surprisingly she hadn't even thought of mishap. She had been too busy even to think about it.

"Excellent, my dear," Harry said approvingly after he finished his last bite of the delectable cream-cheese tart. "Had I known that you set such a fine table I would have made it my practice to visit Bridgeford at mealtimes."

She glowed. A compliment from the marquess, who had sat down to the finest dinners of the *ton*, was truly gratifying. "I'm pleased that you enjoyed it, my lord," she said with a smile. "One of Grandfather's most definite requirements is a fine cook."

"Even the best of cooks must be directed by a splendid hostess. Very commendable, Miss Trevayne."

His felicitations were followed by those of the other diners. Responding politely, Ellen rose to take her leave. "Please enjoy your port, gentlemen, and afterwards join me for coffee in the drawing room."

"Thank you, missy, we shall." Mr. Frampton nodded, obviously anxious to commence the business at hand.

Ellen went first to her bedroom to refresh her coiffure, returning to the drawing room half an hour later. Sitting down on the sofa before the low tea table, she imagined that it would be at least a half hour more before the guests rejoined her, but as the time dragged on she began to question whether they would come at all. For a tonnish aristocrat like Harry it was still early in the evening, but Mr. Frampton, the Bradfords, and the Evermans did not usually keep late hours.

So this was the manner of business dinners? The gentlemen's ladies must be terribly bored if this was the way they entertained themselves. Looking ahead to a lifetime of entertainment such as this, Ellen had doubts as to whether she wanted to marry at all. What fun was there in arranging a fine meal and then sitting alone or with other women just as for-bearing as she must try to be? Luckily the men joined her just as she was on the edge of committing the unpardonable sin of dozing off.

"Rubbish," Harry said to her under his breath, taking quick advantage to sit down beside her.

Ellen almost laughed, realizing that he was just as weary of the evening as she. "Truly, my lord," she whispered, "I did wonder at your great interest in the world of commerce."

"At the moment I'm much more interested in the coffee," he admitted as Gordon set the tray before his mistress. "I hope it's strong."

"So do I." She served him the first cup. "Did you come to an agreement?"

"Ellen!" he hissed. "Would you inquire into a man's business?"

She lifted her chin airily. "I have been known to do so. Just ask Grandfather!"

"I'm sure I would have derived a great deal more enjoyment from dealing with you."

"And greater challenge too." She served the rest of the gentlemen their coffee, making small talk with never a drip or the rattle of china.

When all had been served, Harry caught Ellen's attention again and said, "I believe you mentioned a challenge?" The other guests had drawn away slightly and begun their own conversations; Ellen was glad to have Harry to herself.

"In five minutes flat, I could own your house in Mayfair," she teased.

"That might not be a bad idea. My servants would probably prefer answering to a mistress. In all hon-esty, however, I must warn you that it does stand in need of redecorating. But as to the Thames prop-erty . . ." He shook his head. "Now *that* is a prime piece of land!"

"A vacant acre!"

"Not far from the heart of the London docks. Beyond the area of easy flooding."

She left off her playfulness and lowered her voice even further. "It's worth a fortune now, and will be worth even more in years to come."

"Exactly so." He grinned. "I don't *have* to sell it, Ellen, nor do I need any income from it. Brough has built a small wharf and keeps his yacht there most of the year. We've derived a great amount of enjoyment from it."

"Then don't let them have it," she advised, feeling like a traitor.

Humor glinted in his eyes. "And block the advancement of the city's growth?"

"Fiddlesticks! London is big enough already. For now, at least." She hazarded a glance at Mr. Frampton, who appeared vastly pleased to see her easy conversation with the marquess. She felt even more guilty. "You must do, of course, what you think is best."

"What would you do?"

"Goodness, Harry! Do not tease me so. How could you ever think my opinion worthy of consideration?"

He sighed eloquently. "Another mindless female?"

"I most certainly am not!" she countered.

"I didn't think so. Actually, Ellen, I would prefer dealing with you. You do not mince words. I dislike including your grandfather in this statement, but I have just spent the last two hours with the greatest clique of cutthroat robbers it has ever been my dubious pleasure to encounter."

"Then tell them all to go to Hades!"

"I did." He smiled. "Politely of course."

As the hour had grown very late for those who would go to work the next day, the Bradfords and the Evermans left and, shortly after that, Harry took his leave.

Instead of bidding Ellen good night in the hall, Mr. Frampton took her arm and led her back to the salon. He carefully closed the door, sat down with her, and poured them both another cup of coffee.

"You seemed to chat quite happily with the marquess."

"We are old friends."

"I'm sorry to say that I didn't fare as well with him. He turned down our offer, Ellen."

She bit her lower lip. "Perhaps you should seek other property."

"We have already bought property on each side of his. His land is the heart of the whole plan. We didn't estimate him to be so difficult."

"I am surprised. At you, not at Lord Singleton." Ellen couldn't keep from voicing the set-down that was so readily on her lips. "It was a very poor decision on the part of your company."

"It was not!" he cried. "It was a calculated risk. The man is an aristocrat! Naturally we thought him to be a profligate philanderer!"

"So you thought wrong. That is the price of having a prejudiced attitude."

"All right!" He threw his hands in the air. "I'll take back whatever I've said in the past! Do you want me to grovel on the ground?"

She smiled. "No."

"He's shrewd, Ellen. Damme, but he's shrewd! He saw through every scheme we pitched at him!"

She shrugged. "*I* would be ashamed to admit to such unfair practices."

"It's done every day!"

"Then I am glad that Lord Singleton confounded you," she said smugly.

"Whose side are you on? I've seen you in action

and you yourself are not beyond tricks and deceptions to get your way!''

"But I do not cheat and that is the difference. Whose side am I on? I am always on the side of honesty. If the lot of you had been aboveboard, you would probably have had your damn piece of property!''

He bristled. "Watch your tongue, missy.''

"If you can say 'damn' to me, I can say it to you!''

He shook his head. "Every time. *Every time*, you come back at me! You twist my words and you use them against me.''

Ellen stood up and moved behind him to rub his tense shoulder muscles. "Perhaps I am more like you than either of us would ever believe.''

"Perhaps.'' He returned to the events of the evening. "In truth I can't help admiring Singleton. He's certainly not what I expected. Too bad he's a swell. Now *he'd* have made me quite a grandson-in-law!''

18

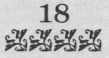

Harry set the finishing touches to his sumptu-ously magnificent cravat and stepped back to admire himself in the cheval mirror. For his first appearance in society following the devastating "dog incident," he cut a figure as elegantly polished as he always did. If looks did not deceive, he would recapture his image as the ideal pink of the *ton*. Furthermore, he would dispense the famous Singleton charm and delight all the ladies, young and old, sending them off into spasms of enraptured delight. By the end of the evening, everyone would forget that the Marquess of Singleton had stepped on a young lady's toes and sat in a countess' lap.

He would also take care to dance with little Miss Grimsley and would ask his friends to do so too. Her behavior had not escaped censure either. A bit of attention from several prime catches would go far in redeeming her reputation.

But most importantly, Bran had told him that Ellen would be attending the ball. Harry planned to sweep her off her feet as well. He was growing tired of playing her games of "old friendship" and "good neighbors." Tonight and in the days following he would move swiftly upon her and capture her heart. The last kiss they'd shared had proved once more that she was not indifferent to him. Even the memory of that sweet embrace gave him a shortness of breath and a heightening of desire that was fast becoming too potent to be disregarded. He would win her and he would do it soon.

"I am anxious to meet Miss Trevayne," the dowager Lady Singleton announced when he joined her in the hall. "I remember her father. A splendid gentleman! Unfortunately he wed a lady who was not of his social rank—although if I recall correctly, she had been educated in the finest ladies' seminary. One can't have everything, I suppose. If you have chosen Miss Trevayne I am sure that she is perfectly agreeable."

In spite of his determination to win Ellen, Harry was cautious enough not to rush his fences. "Remember, Mama, I have not made my offer yet. She might refuse me."

"Fustian! Who would be foolish enough to do such a thing? If you have made up your mind, then that is the way it shall be. Grandchildren! With her mother deceased, I shall be their only grandmama!" Lady Singleton gloated. "Why are you waiting? Why do you not press your suit? There is nothing to be gained by hesitation! A proper wedding takes time to plan. Time, Harry, before you can go about your business."

"Mama!" he protested. "You are too outrageous!"

She laughed. "I shall not bandy words. The providing of heirs is your responsibility as the head of the family. Take it from me. Your father, handsome as he was, was a slowtop, at least where it concerned me. As a result, you have no brothers or sisters."

His eyes danced. "I assure you, Mama, that if Ellen marries me and we do not have more than one child, it shall not be from want of trying."

"Naughty boy!" She tapped his arm with her fan. "Now let us be on our way. As I have told you, I am most anxious to meet my future daughter-in-law."

"Just remember that I haven't proposed to her yet," Harry repeated. "Don't precede me by acting as if the matter is settled."

"Far be it from me to do anything that might endanger the outcome!" She slipped her arm through his. "Just don't drag your heels."

"I promise you that I shall do so no longer."

He escorted her to the coach and listened to her speculations concerning grandchildren all the way to the ball. As preoccupied as she was with the subject, he prayed she wouldn't tip his hand. The dowager Lady Singleton painted a picture of a daughter-in-law who would be in an interesting condition for nine months out of every year. If Ellen thought that would be her lot in life, she'd probably take to her heels and run.

For better or worse, his mother did not have long to wait for her introduction. The Rackthalls and Ellen were in the vestibule removing their wraps when they arrived. Ellen rendered a deep, graceful curtsy to the dowager.

"How pretty you are!" the marchioness said warmly, surveying her with a practiced eye. "What a fine figure you have!"

Harry held his breath. The type of feminine form his mother noticed was not the same as he beheld. Instead of enticing curves, she would be looking at bone structure about the hips. He hoped she would not forget herself and describe in detail her obstetrical evaluation.

"My son has told me so much of you. You must call on me soon. Do you play whist?"

"Not well, ma'am," Ellen admitted ruefully.

"I shall teach you. Every lady should be adept at indoor amusements for those times when—"

"Excuse me, Mama," the marquess interrupted. "One of your friends is beckoning to you."

"Fustian!" She pressed Ellen's hand. "We shall chat later, Miss Trevayne."

Harry guided his mother towards a group of her friends, any one of whom would have hailed the marchioness if they had seen her. He dropped back momentarily to speak with Ellen. "The first waltz and the supper dance?"

Her eyes sparkled like aquamarines in the candlelight. "I shall be happy to save them for you, my lord."

"Until then." He kissed her fingertips and followed the dowager.

The evening plodded along. He danced a few sets with simpering young ladies and spent the rest of the time visiting with friends and watching Ellen. She certainly had no lack of admirers. She had a partner for every dance and occupied the minutes in between surrounded by a group of gentlemen who hung on her every word and made mooncalf eyes at her. It was aggravating, especially since she seemed to be enjoying it to the fullest. Couldn't she see through that lot of smooth-tongued coxcombs? When the hell was their waltz? To pass the time, he decided to seek out Miss Grimsley and perform his duty dance with her.

Ellen *was* enjoying herself. She felt particularly attractive tonight in her shimmering mulberry satin ball gown with its delicate overskirt of creamy net. Allesandra had complimented her on it, and as everyone knew, the duchess herself was in the very first stare of fashion.

Once again she had garnered the attentions of a great many young blades of the *ton*. As the evening progressed she knew she would eventually grow weary of their glib flirtations. But for now, it was pleasant to be the focus of their adulation.

Dancing a boulanger with Lord Hawley, she noticed that Harry was partnering Miss Grimsley. That was kind of him after what had happened at the dowager Lady Rackthall's, but the young lady did not appear to be pleased. Her face was twisted into a rather petulant expression. Apparently she was a rather silly, sour-tempered little goose. Any girl with a modicum of wits about her would have felt honored to be chosen to dance with the handsome marquess. Ellen caught Harry's eye and smiled consolingly.

"It has been a pleasure as usual, Miss Trevayne." Lord Hawley bowed and escorted her to Allesandra's side. "My heart, however, is all to pieces because you did not save the supper dance for me."

"I am certain that it will not prove fatal, my lord. I have heard that such ailments are cured most rapidly at the sight of a pretty face."

"But my dear," he protested, "you are the only lovely lady I wish to look upon. Alas! I shall have to admire you from afar."

Their banter was interrupted by a strident, hysterical voice. Ellen, Allesandra, and Lord Hawley, along with all the other occupants of the room, turned quickly towards the direction of the conflict. At the edge of the dance floor, Miss Marion Grimsley stamped her foot and glared at Lord Singleton.

"You have stepped on my toes until I am totally lame!" she cried. "Now you have spilled champagne all over me! My gown is ruined! I shall have to go home!"

All eyes rested on the hapless marquess. Even the orchestra, which had just struck up a waltz, was distracted to the point of coming to a whining halt in mid-beat. Only the thoroughly practiced waiters continued their movement through the crowd, balancing their massive silver trays of glasses.

A flush slowly crept up Harry's neck and suffused his face with scarlet. He proffered his handkerchief to the incensed miss, but she batted it away. He set his jaw.

"Singleton again." Lord Hawley smirked. "And if I do not miss my guess, it's the same young lady whom he trampled in the past."

"Poor Harry," Allesandra murmured, casting a glance at Ellen. "His mind is plainly elsewhere."

A low ripple of laughter spread through the room.

"It isn't fair!" Ellen said hotly. "It was an accident!"

Lord Hawley chuckled. "Come now, my dear. The marquess seems to have gone beyond that. I fear he has become a regular bumblesome fool."

"He has not! He is a perfectly wonderful gentleman who is merely having a run of bad luck!"

"Such a tender heart you have." He languidly removed his quizzing glass to better view Harry's humiliation.

Ellen's temper flared. From the corner of her eye she saw a waiter approaching with his laden tray. She lifted her chin in a silent beckon. The servant nodded in return and made his way towards her. He paused slightly behind her.

"Thank you." Removing a glass of champagne, she prayed that her timing was good and the angle was right. Turning swiftly she cracked her arm hard into the silver rim.

The tray and its contents flew high. Champagne splashed over everyone in the vicinity, including Ellen herself, before the glasses splintered on the floor. People leaped sideways. Ladies screamed. The *ton*'s attention quickly left Harry and centered on her.

"Oh, dear." She gazed wide-eyed at the chaos. "How awkward of me!"

Lord Hawley dropped his quizzing glass and stared at her in horrified disbelief.

She affected a trembling throughout her body. "I am most overset!" She collapsed against Allesandra and in doing so, chucked the remaining contents of her glass into Lord Hawley's face.

The duchess reeled into her husband, regained her balance, and slipped her arm around Ellen's waist. "You did all of that on purpose," she hissed, her eyes dancing, "and you shall never make me believe otherwise!"

Ellen turned her head and favored her friend with a hasty wink.

The duke began to laugh.

Lord Hawley angrily wiped his eyes. "Damme!" he cried. "You threw that at me! What is the matter with you?"

"For all your pretty words," Ellen snapped, "you also have a vicious side to you, Lord Hawley, which I dislike intensely. Perhaps that is the manner by which you cover your own shortcomings."

"I? Shortcomings? At least I am not a Cit's—"

Harry hastily crossed the room. "Another word, sir, and you'll meet me at sunrise."

The huffy peer gaped at the formidable Lord Singleton, muttered to himself, and moved away, his feet crunching on the shards of shattered crystal.

"Come, Ellen." Harry clasped her arm and firmly drew her from the scene of the disaster.

"Where are we going?"

"Home."

"No doubt that is the best idea," she said cheerfully. "My repute is probably in a shambles."

"Along with mine."

"Oh, I shouldn't think that yours has suffered so greatly. I am sure that when people look back on this evening they will recall the appalling mishap of

the Cit's granddaughter and forget all about Miss
Grimsley's little scene.''

''Is that what you think?'' Harry retrieved her
cloak from the footman at the door and settled it
over her shoulders, then slipped into his greatcoat,
gloves, and hat. He tucked her hand into the crook
of his elbow and escorted her outside.

The coolness of the evening was a welcome relief
from the stuffy warmth of the ballroom. Ellen drew
a deep breath of the night air. She was glad to be
leaving.

Harry helped her into the carriage, gave the direction to his coachman, and climbed in beside her. The
coach drew away from the tangle of waiting horses
and vehicles. From within the brightly lit mansion,
Ellen heard the muffled strains of the orchestra strik-
ing up once more.

''You are drenched with champagne. You must be
cold.'' The marquess solicitously spread a robe over
her wet knees.

''Truly I am fine now. I am just so very happy
that you rescued me from my latest mishap. You
cannot imagine how perfectly mortified I was!''

He leaned back against the squabs. ''You didn't
look mortified, Ellen.''

She shot him a quick, surreptitious glance, but he
was looking out the window. With his head turned
it was impossible to fathom his expression in the
darkness. What was he thinking?

''I must be gaining in poise,'' she remarked, ''if I
am able to commit such a calamity without falling to
pieces.''

''Indeed,'' he replied. ''And when I saw you wink
at Allesandra, I wondered if you hadn't done the
whole thing on purpose.''

''Fustian, Harry! Why should I purposefully set
myself up as the laughingstock of the *ton*?''

He turned to her. ''I don't know. Perhaps you'd

best tell me, for it simply doesn't make any sense. You've become a very desirable young lady. I scarcely see you but what you're surrounded by a gaggle of moonstruck men."

"Grandfather has introduced me to many—"

"I'm not referring to your grandfather's Cit friends. I am speaking of peers in their own right and sons of peers. Ellen, don't you know? You've become an outstanding success!"

Ellen laughed lightly. "Oh, they are probably hanging out for my fortune!"

"Indeed? Lord Hawley is one of the wealthiest young men in England."

"Lord Hawley? Yes . . . well, I doubt that I shall see him nearby me again. I drowned him most thoroughly."

"Why, Ellen?"

It was her turn to look out the window. She bit her lip. Why was the carriage moving so slowly? The streets were nearly vacant and yet they toiled along as tediously as a butcher's dray. Lord, she could walk home faster than this!

"Why?" he repeated.

She gave her characteristic little shrug. "I wish I knew." She sighed dramatically. "You of all people are acquainted with my penchant for mishap. Let us talk of something else."

"I'd rather you told me why you knocked over that tray."

The carriage passed through the gates of Hyde Park. "Where are we going?" she demanded. "This is not the way home."

"I know. I wanted plenty of time to talk with you."

"I am cold."

Harry opened his greatcoat and enveloped her within, drawing her close. "Is this better?"

"Y-yes." Her senses lurched at the touch of his

body against hers. She inhaled deeply of his warm masculine scent of spicy Imperial water. Looking up, she gazed at his strong jawbone and finely chiseled patrician nose.

"Tell me about it."

"Oh, Harry." Tears prickled her eyelids. Conquered by his embrace she dropped her head against his chest. His heartbeat amazed her. In contrast to the calm persistence in his voice, it was racing.

"Ellen?" Harry brushed his lips against her silky hair.

"Very well," she whispered. "You are correct. I did it on purpose."

"Why?"

"Because . . ." She felt his breath stirring her hair. "That silly girl's behavior was outside of enough!"

"Perhaps, but I *am* guilty of dancing on her toes and spilling champagne all over her."

"Mere bad luck! She should consider herself fortunate that you took notice of her at all."

"Did I? I cannot even remember her appearance. I was too well occupied with looking at you."

"Well, no wonder you treated her in such a manner," Ellen chided him. "You weren't paying attention to what you were doing. Why were you looking at me? Was I doing something ridiculous?"

"I was looking at you, my dear, because you were the most beautiful lady in the room."

"I?" Ellen gasped. "Fiddlesticks!"

He gently lifted her chin with his fingers and regarded her soberly. "I am not trifling, now or ever. You are the most beautiful, desirable, adorable woman it has ever been my privilege to know."

Their eyes locked together. A tear slid from Ellen's eye and trickled down her cheek. Still lightly holding her chin with one hand, he dabbed it away with the thumb of his other.

"My love, will you marry me?"

"Harry! You cannot feel . . ."

"I have loved you for a very long time."

This time the trembling in her body was no mere pretense. "You . . . you have?"

He nodded. "Won't you say yes and make me the happiest man in England?"

"But I caused you to be covered with mud on more than one occasion! I nearly drowned you in the stream! And then there was the incident in the park . . . Harry, you have suffered so much ruination at my hands!"

He grinned. "You knocked me off my pedestal and brought me out of the doldrums. I needed that. I was becoming abominably stuffy."

"No, you have always been perfectly marvelous." Shyly she reached up to touch his cheek. "I, too, have been in love with you for the longest time."

"Then you will marry me?"

"Oh, yes!" She threw her arms around his neck. "But are you sure? Think of my propensity for mishap!"

His answer was a kiss, deep and soul-satisfying. Ellen melted into his arms, parting her lips and kissing him back until they were forced to pause for breath.

"Your wife," she murmured dreamily, then looked at him with alarm. "I shall have to be your marchioness as well!"

"You will be charming in either role."

"Your mama may have other opinions. She is so very grand!"

"Don't worry about Mama," he said firmly. "I can assure you that she will be delighted. In fact, she is already!"

"And Grandfather!"

"I shouldn't think him to be a problem. I'll take you in exchange for the Thames property."

"Harry! I will not be traded like a parcel of land!"

"It's been done before."

"Well, it won't be done now!" she cried hotly. "I shall handle him."

"No, you won't. I will. And I shall do it tonight if he is still awake when we return."

"He means well, but he can be so stubborn and obnoxious."

"We'll see." He tapped the carriage roof to signal the coachman. "I have some thoughts in mind."

"What are they?"

He drew her close and silenced her questions with a kiss.

"Mr. Frampton, may I speak with you in your library?" Harry exchanged a smile with Ellen and received her trembling nod of encouragement.

The older man stared at the couple who stood before him holding hands. "Why do I assume that this matter has absolutely nothing to do with that Thames property?"

"Grandfather!" Ellen said, blushing.

"I'm not blind, missy! I can see that you've made your choice." He heaved a great sigh. "And I suppose that you, m'lord, have popped the question. Good neighbors, bah! There's been more brewing than I've been made aware of. Let's not waste breath. You have my blessing."

She stared at him speechlessly. "That was easy."

"Hm! Singleton's the only man I've met who might stand a chance of controlling you." Mr. Frampton threw up his hands. "M'boy, you've got your work cut out for you. And there'll be no deliberations in my library. Your man of business and I will handle the details of the settlement. If I went into the library with you, I'd probably end up on the street without a penny to my name!"

Harry grinned. "I couldn't be quite that cruel!"

"I wish you'd join me in my business, but I suppose that's not reasonable. I'll just have to wait for my second grandson. Nobs in the family! Here I go again!'' He shook Harry's hand. ''If I turn up my toes before my time, at least you're smart enough and tough enough not to let anyone pull the wool over your eyes. Not like that fribble Trevayne!''

''My father was a fine gentleman,'' Ellen sputtered.

Mr. Frampton hugged her soundly, halting her protest. ''Now, missy, you turn your mind to your own husband and to giving me grandchildren!''

''In that, my mother will concur,'' Harry agreed.

''Oh, no!'' Ellen cried. ''Your mama! We've left her stranded at the ball!''

''I should fetch her, though someone will surely take her home. Come with me, Ellen? She'll be delighted to hear the news.''

''May I, Grandfather? It probably isn't proper, but then . . .'' She smiled happily. ''I fear that nothing has been proper about this evening!''

''You're betrothed,'' Mr. Frampton said with a chuckle. ''I suppose you can't be compromised any further. Well, I'm happy for you both, but I did hate losing that Thames acreage.''

''Oh, that, sir,'' Harry said slowly. ''I've decided I'm willing to part with that after all. I am going to give it to my wife as a wedding present.''

''What! Why, I'll . . . I'll have to deal with her!''

''Exactly so.''

''Dammit, Singleton! She's worse than you!'' he cried, then began to laugh. ''You've confounded me again, haven't you? Well, at least the property's still in the family!''

Ellen and Harry hurried from the house. Gordon, closing the door behind them, scrambled rapidly towards the back stairs. Surely someone he might tell was still awake!

In the carriage, Ellen returned her head to Harry's shoulder. "You are truly giving me the land?"

"Yes."

"To do with as I please?"

"Just as you please, love." He kissed the top of her head. "What do you intend?"

"I shall be fair to Brough, of course." She giggled. "And I shall make the merriest time ever for Grandfather!"

The kisses on the journey to the ball still warm on his lips, Harry seated his mother in the carriage and took his place beside Ellen. "We have something to tell you."

"Grandchildren," Lady Singleton breathed in delight. "I had nearly given up hope."

"Please, Mama, not yet!"

"I shall be in attendance when they are born and they must visit me several times a year."

"Mama, you are proceding too quickly," Harry muttered.

"So I am!" She laughed girlishly and leaned forward to take Ellen's hands. "Welcome to the family, my dear. I assure you that I am most ecstatic!"

"Thank you, ma'am," Ellen said happily. "I shall try very hard to be a good wife."

"And mother," the dowager added pointedly.

"That too." Ellen glanced shyly at Harry.

"Well, now it is settled! Come to me tomorrow, my dear, *dear* future daughter-in-law, and we shall begin making plans for the wedding. Merciful heavens! We must make haste!" She clasped her hands together in excitement. "We haven't a moment to lose, you know!"

EPILOGUE

"**G**et off of me," the marquess demanded. "Get off of me, you great lummox!"

Ellen, her head pillowed on his shoulder and her arm thrown across his bare chest, came drowsily awake.

"Get off of me, you mammoth beast!"

"Harry, I *am* sorry," she mumbled.

"Not you, darling." He hugged her. "This brute of a dog! He's jumped into bed with us and he's got me pinned."

"Oh, dear." She sat up, and in the moonlight Harry got a tantalizing view of his wife's beautiful body. "Come, Friendly, you shouldn't do that to Harry." She tugged at the Saint Bernard's collar.

"Ellen, you've got to be firm with those animals or they are going to continue to take advantage of you."

The big dog compromised by flopping down between them and licking his lordship's face.

"Dammit, Ellen!"

"I'm sorry!" She fumbled for her dressing gown. "I'm trying!"

He got out of bed and shrugged into his robe. "I'm going to take these two dogs to the stable where they belong."

247

"Oh, Harry, it is so unseasonably cold and they are not used to it yet! Their coats aren't heavy enough. It will make them ill."

He pulled Friendly off the bed. "Say good night to your mistress."

"Harry!"

"*All right*, Ellen! Shall I wake the landlord and rent them a room?"

"That is a good idea." She brightened, snuggling under the covers. "See that he lays a fire."

"They will be warm enough."

"Harry . . ."

"I'll see to it," he muttered. He leashed the dogs and took them out. In the hall he changed his mind and climbed the stairs to the upper floor, knocking loudly on his valet's door.

"My lord!" The sleepy servant surveyed the scene before him. "Oh, no, sir! I have ridden with those dogs all day. They have tried to sit on my lap, they have licked my face . . ."

"Daniel, there is extra payment—large payment—for dog handling."

"Indeed?"

"Indeed!" The marquess thrust the leashes into his valet's hand and departed.

"That was awfully quick," Ellen said suspiciously.

"I took them to Daniel's room." Shivering, he joined her under the covers and drew her close.

"Does he like dogs?"

"Daniel loves dogs more than anyone I know."

"Then we may depend upon him."

"Yes, we may."

"Good." She gently combed her fingers through his hair. "Harry?"

"Yes, love?"

"I am very much awake. I thought . . ."

"Yes?" He teasingly kissed the tip of her nose.

"Well," Ellen murmured, flushing, "I thought if you too were quite awake, we might . . . do what we have been doing?"

"With pleasure, Lady Singleton." He brought his mouth to hers and savored her welcoming response. Interference by dogs, Harry decided, was not such a bad thing after all.

Avon Regency Romance

Kasey Michaels

THE CHAOTIC MISS CRISPINO
76300-1/$3.99 US/$4.99 Can

THE DUBIOUS MISS DALRYMPLE
89908-6/$2.95 US/$3.50 Can

THE HAUNTED MISS HAMPSHIRE
76301-X/$3.99 US/$4.99 Can

Loretta Chase

THE ENGLISH WITCH
70660-1/$2.95 US/$3.50 Can

ISABELLA   70597-4/$2.95 US/$3.95 Can

KNAVES' WAGER   71363-2/$3.95 US/$4.95 Can

THE SANDALWOOD PRINCESS
71455-8/$3.99 US/$4.99 Can

THE VISCOUNT VAGABOND
70836-1/$2.95 US/$3.50 Can

Jo Beverley

THE STANFORTH SECRETS
71438-8/$3.99 US/$4.99 Can

THE STOLEN BRIDE   71439-6/$3.99 US/$4.99 Can

Buy these books at your local bookstore or use this coupon for ordering:
....

Mail to: Avon Books, Dept BP, Box 767, Rte 2, Dresden, TN 38225   B
Please send me the book(s) I have checked above.
☐ My check or money order—no cash or CODs please—for $_____ is enclosed
(please add $1.50 to cover postage and handling for each book ordered—Canadian
residents add 7% GST).
☐ Charge my VISA/MC Acct#_____ Exp Date _____
Phone No_____Minimum credit card order is $6.00 (please add postage
and handling charge of $2.00 plus 50 cents per title after the first two books to a maximum
of six dollars—Canadian residents add 7% GST). For faster service, call 1-800-762-0779.
Residents of Tennessee, please call 1-800-633-1607. Prices and numbers are subject to
change without notice. Please allow six to eight weeks for delivery.

Name_____

Address_____

City_____ State/Zip _____

REG 0592